Frank Merriwell's
Endurance

or, A Square Shooter

BURT L. STANDISH

Author of the celebrated "Merriwell"
stories, which are the favorite reading of
over half a million up-to-date (1904)
American boys.

BOOKS FOR ATHLETICS

LONDON
IBOO PRESS HOUSE
86-90 PAUL STREET

Frank Merriwell's
Endurance
or, A Square Shooter

BURT L. STANDISH
Author of the famous Merriwell Stories.

BOOKS FOR ATHLETICS

Layout & Cover © Copyright 2020 iBooPress, London

Published by
iBoo Press House

3rd Floor
86-90 Paul Street
London, EC2A4NE UK

t: +44 20 3695 0809
info@iboo.com II iBoo.com

ISBNs
978-1-64181-947-3 (h)
978-1-64181-948-0 (p)

Printed in the United States

Frank Merriwell's
Endurance

or, A Square Shooter

BURT L. STANDISH

Author of the celebrated "Merriwell"
stories, which are the favorite reading of
over half a million up-to-date (1904)
American boys.

BOOKS FOR ATHLETICS

MERRIWELL SERIES
Stories of Frank and Dick Merriwell
Fascinating Stories of Athletics

A half million enthusiastic followers of the Merriwell brothers will attest the unfailing interest and wholesomeness of these adventures of two lads of high ideals, who play fair with themselves, as well as with the rest of the world.

These stories are rich in fun and thrills in all branches of sports and athletics. They are extremely high in moral tone, and cannot fail to be of immense benefit to every boy who reads them.

They have the splendid quality of firing a boy's ambition to become a good athlete, in order that he may develop into a strong, vigorous, right-thinking man.

Contents

FRANK MERRIWELL'S ENDURANCE.

CHAPTER I

L'ESTRANGE.a

On the way East with his athletic team Frank Merriwell accepted the invitation made by Hugh Morton to stop off at Omaha and visit the Midwestern Athletic Association.

Morton, a young man of twenty-five, was president of the Midwestern. He and Merriwell, the former Yale athlete, had met and become acquainted by chance in Los Angeles some weeks before, and there seemed to exist between them a sort of fellow feeling that caused them to take unusual interest in each other.

Merry and his friends were invited by Morton to witness the finals in a series of athletic events which were being conducted by the club. These contests consisted mainly of boxing and wrestling, although fencing, which was held in high esteem by the association, was one of the features.

In explanation of the rather surprising fact that fencing was thus highly regarded by an athletic association of the middle West, it is necessary to state that a very active member of the club was M. François L'Estrange, the famous French fencer and duelist, whose final encounter in his own country had resulted in the death of his opponent, a gentleman of noble birth, and had compelled L'Estrange to flee from his native land, never to return.

As fencing instructor of the Midwestern A. A., L'Estrange soon succeeded in arousing great interest in the graceful accomplishment, and he quickly developed a number of surprisingly clever pupils. In this manner fencing came to be held in high esteem by the organization and was a feature of nearly all indoor contests.

At first Omaha did not appeal to Frank; but he quickly found the people of the city were frank, unreserved, genial, and friendly, and after all, a person learns to like a place mainly through the character of its inhabitants.

At the rooms of the Midwestern, Merry and his comrades met a fine lot of young men, nearly all of whom made an effort to entertain the boys. The visitors were quickly convinced that they were welcome at the club and that they could make themselves at home there without offending any conservative and hidebound old fogies. Although the Midwestern was cautious and discreet in regard to admitting members, and it was necessary for visitors to obtain admittance in the proper manner, once inside its portals a person immediately sensed an air of liberty that was most agreeable.

"The forming of cliques in this club has been frowned down," Hugh Morton explained. "I have visited clubs of similar standing in the East and found them full of cliques and restless with petty jealousies and personal dislikes. We hope to suppress such things here, although I regret to say that of late the club has seemed to be gradually dividing into two parties. Thus far everything has been good-natured and unruffled; but I fear that I see a pernicious undercurrent. I may be wrong; I hope I am."

The morning after Merry's arrival in the city the Bee noted the fact, giving him half a column and speaking of him as "that wonderful young American athlete who had maintained and added to his reputation since leaving college, yet who had persistently abstained from professionalism." A list of his contests and victories during his Western tour was also given.

At ten o'clock that forenoon Frank and Bart Hodge met Hugh Morton by appointment in the reception room of the Midwestern. Morton rose and advanced to meet them, smiling a welcome.

"Look here," said Frank, when they had shaken hands, "I don't feel just right about this."

"About what?" questioned the Omaha man.

"Taking you from your business this way. When I accepted your invitation to stop off here, I didn't expect you to waste your time on us. Business is business, and——"

"Don't you worry. My business is fixed so it will not suffer if I leave it. I'm delighted with this opportunity. Yesterday I gave you a look at the stockyards and the city. To-day, you told me, you wanted to take things easy and just loaf around. I'm more than willing to loaf with you. And my business will go on just the same."

"All right," smiled Frank. "You know your own affairs, and we're glad to have you with us. Bart and I were talking about fencing on our way here. We've been wondering how much we have deteriorated in the art since quitting active practice. It has surprised us—and stirred us up somewhat—to find the sport features in this club. Bart has challenged me to give him a go at it. If we can have a set of foils and——"

"Just follow me," invited Morton. "I'll fix you out."

As they were about to leave the room a tall, slender, dark man of thirty-six or thirty-seven entered. Immediately Morton paused, saying:

"Mr. Merriwell and Mr. Hodge, I am sure you will appreciate the honor of meeting our fencing instructor, Monsieur L'Estrange. Monsieur L'Estrange, this is Frank Merriwell, the most famous American amateur athlete of the present day."

The Frenchman accepted Frank's proffered hand. He was as graceful in his movements as a jungle panther. About him there was an air of conscious strength and superiority, and instantly he struck Frank as a person who could not do an awkward thing or fall into an ungainly pose. His training was such, that grace and ease had become a part of his nature—not second nature, but nature itself.

"Monsieur Merriwell," he breathed softly, "it gives me ze very great pleasure to meet wiz you, sare. I have meet very many of your famous American athletes. Eet is ze grand passion in this country. Eet is good in some ways, but eet nevare make ze feenished gentleman—nevare."

"I agree with you on that point, monsieur," confessed Frank; "but it fits a man for the struggle of life—it prepares him to combat with the world, and you know the success and survival of the fittest was never more in evidence, as the thing of vital importance, than at the present time."

The eyes of the Frenchman glistened.

"Very true, sare; but mere brute strength can nevare make any man ze fittest—nevare. You theenk so? You are wrong—pardone me eef I speak ze truth plainly."

"But I do not think so, monsieur. It takes a combination of strength and brains to make a well-balanced man."

"And skeel—do not forget skeel. Eet is ze most important of all, sare."

"Brains give ability, strength gives power to exercise that ability."

"And skeel defeats ze man with strength and brains. Oh, eet does! Ze man with too much strength, with ze beeg muscles; he ees handicap against ze man with just ze propare development and no more. His beeg muscles tie him, make him awkward."

"Again I am compelled to agree with you," smiled Frank; "and I confess that I consider fencing the most perfect method of developing ease, grace, quickness and skill—attributes essential to any man who desires to reach the highest pinnacle of development."

"You have ze unusual wisdom on zat point, sare," acknowledged L'Estrange. "Eet is strange, for seldom have I met ze great athlete who did not theenk himself superior to ze expert fencer. Eet is plain you know your weakness, sare."

Bart Hodge opened his lips to say something, but Merry checked him with a quick look.

"I have fenced a little, monsieur," explained Frank—"enough to get an idea of its value and importance."

"Zat ees goode. You take eet up at school—at college?"

"Yes, first at Fardale, and later I followed it up at Yale."

"Ah! but you could not have ze propare instruction—no! no! Ze American instructor he seldom know very much about eet. He ees crude; but he have ze—ze—what you call eet? Ze swell head. He theenk he knows eet all. Oui!"

"That is a fact in many instances," acknowledged Merriwell.

At this point Morton whispered in Bart Hodge's ear:

"L'Estrange is started and he will bore Merriwell with talk about fencing, unless we find a way to interrupt it and break away. We must be careful not to offend him."

There was a strange, half-hidden smile on Bart's lips as he turned to their host.

"Let the man talk," he said, in a low tone. "Before he is through Merry will give him the call. You may not believe it, but I doubt if the Frenchman can tell Frank anything new about fencing."

"Oh, L'Estrange is a graduate of Joinville-le-Pont, the great government school of France."

Morton said this as if it settled a point, and Hodge knew the man thought him presuming in fancying Frank's information on fencing was to be compared with that of the great French master of the art.

In the meantime, all his enthusiasm aroused, L'Estrange ardently continued:

"You speak of ze brain, sare. When you fence, ze brain ees prompted to act without a moment of ze hesitation. To hesitate means to make ze failure. Ze fencer must be readee with hees wit, skill, and action, like ze flash of lightning. So ze fencer fits himself for ze struggle of life. He is full of ze resource, he is queek to detec' ze strength or ze weakness, of an argument or situation, and he acts like electricity, sweeft and unerring. Zis make him a bettair business man zan other men."

"Every word of this is true," nodded Merry.

"In societee he is at perfect ease; in business he can stand ze great strain. His blood ees fresh, his tissues are firm and he has ze grand enthusiasm."

"And enthusiasm is absolutely necessary for a man to make the best of himself," said Frank. "The man who goes at any task with indifference is inviting failure. No matter how well he may think he knows his work, he must keep up his enthusiasm unless he is willing to see that work deteriorate. Lack of enthusiasm causes thousands to fail and fall by the wayside every year."

"True, true, sare. I see you have ze enthusiasm of ze boy steel with you. You have nevare met with anything to dull eet."

"Not yet; and I hope I never may."

"To keep eet you should fence, Monsieur Merriwell. Some time eet may safe your life. Oui! Once since I come to zis country I hear a noise in ze night. I rise and go to discovare ze matter. I find ze burglaire. He attack me wiz ze knife. He was beeg and strong—ze brute! I see ze umbrellare in ze corner. I seize eet. I keep ze burglaire off. I punish heem. I thrust, hit him in ze face. I give eet to him hard. Soon he try to get away. He rush for ze door. I sprang between. I continue to administaire ze punishment. I make him drop ze knife. Ze noise have aroused ze rest of ze house. Ze police come. Ze burglaire ees marched to ze jail. Ha! If I had been ze athlete, like you, zen with hees knife ze burglaire he cut me to pieces—he keel me."

"That was fine work," agreed Frank.

"Not yet you are too old to acquire ze skeel. You know a leetale about eet now. That help you. Find ze French master and keep at eet. Take no one but ze French master. Ze Italian style is not so good. That has been proved many time. Ze Frenchman is cool and he stands on guard with ease. Ze Italian he will move all ze time. He jump here, there, everywhere. He crouch, he stand straight, he dodge. Every minute he seem ready to jump. He makes strange sounds in hees throat; but he is not dangerous as he seem. Did you ever hear of Jean Louis?"

"Yes; he was a famous French duelist."

"Oui, oui! When ze French army invade Spain, in 1814, Jean Louis keeled thirteen Italian fencing masters, one after ze other. Zat profe ze superiority of ze French method, sare. Ze Italian believe strength is needed to make ze perfect fencer. That is wrong. In France manee persons of ze highest rank are wondairefully skillful in ze art, yet they are not remarkable for strength. Eet is ze light touch, ze grace, ze art, ze composure, ze ready wit that count."

"How about duels at German colleges, like Leipzig and Heidelberg?"

"Oh, no, no, no! The German have a mixture of ze French and ze Italian method. Zey are fightaires, but zey count on ze strength, too. Years ago fencing was ze study paramount at ze great German colleges; but too manee students they are killed at eet. Ze most peaceable never was he sure of his life for one day. Later ze method change, and now eet is to cut and scar ze face of ze adversary. Ze German never have ze grace of ze French.

"You stay here, Monsieur Merriwell—you see ze finals? Well, zen you see my greatest pupil, Fred Darleton, defeat his opponent. Of Monsieur Darleton I am very proud. Oui! He is a wondaire. I belief he can defeat any American in ze country."

Hodge made a protesting sound in his throat; but again Frank shot Bart a glance of warning.

"I shall be delighted to witness the work of Mr. Darleton," said Merry. "It has been some time since I have fenced, Monsieur L'Estrange, and I know I must be very rusty at it; but you have reawakened my enthusiasm for the sport, and I feel like taking up the foils again. If I were to remain in Omaha any length of time, I would seek to become one of your pupils."

L'Estrange bowed with graciousness.

"Eet would give me pleasure to instruct you, sare," he said. "Eet would give me delight to show you ze real superiority of ze duelist, ze fencer, over ze athlete. You watch ze work of Fred Darleton to-night. Eet will delight you."

As Morton led them away, he said:

"You got off easy, Merriwell. Once get L'Estrange aroused and he can talk a blue streak about fencing for hours. He's really a wizard with the foils, and this fellow Darleton, of whom he spoke, is likewise a wonder. Darleton is not popular with many members

12

in the club; but I believe that is because of his remarkable skill at cards."

"He is a successful card player, is he?" questioned Frank.

"Altogether too successful. He makes his spending money at the game."

"What game."

"Poker."

"Do you permit gambling for stakes in this club?"

"It is permitted," confessed Morton, flushing slightly. "Of course gambling is not open here. We have a private card room for those who wish to play for stakes."

Merry said nothing more, but he was thinking that the practice of gambling was a bad thing for any organization of that sort. It was not his place, however, to express such an opinion.

A short time later Merry and Bart were fitted out with foils, masks, and plastrons, and they prepared for a bout, both eager to discover if they retained their old-time skill at the art.

CHAPTER II

THRUST AND RIPOSTE.

That Frank retained all his old-time skill he soon demonstrated. Hodge was not in bad form, but Merry was far and away his superior, and he toyed with Bart. Morton looked on in some surprise.

"Why, say," he cried, "both of you chaps know the game all right! You could cut some ice at it."

Bart smiled.

"I could have told you that Merry knew it," he said.

"L'Estrange could make an expert of him," declared Morton.

"Perhaps he might surprise L'Estrange," said Hodge.

"I think he would," nodded the host, without detecting Bart's real meaning.

Frank and Bart went at it again. In the midst of the bout two young men sauntered up and paused, watching them with interest.

"Why," said one, "they really know how to fence, Fred!"

"That's right," nodded the other. "They are not novices."

Morton quickly stepped to the side of the two.

"These are my guests, gentlemen," he said.

"Oh," said the taller and darker chap, "I understand you have Merriwell and his friends in town. Is either of these fellows——"

"Yes, that one there is Frank Merriwell."

"Introduce me when they are through. I am interested in him as an athlete, although I may not be as a fencer. Evidently he thinks himself pretty clever at this trick, but his form is not correct, and he makes a number of false moves."

Bart Hodge heard these words distinctly, and he lowered his foil, turning to survey the speaker.

"You see, Darleton!" muttered Morton resentfully. "They have heard you!"

Darleton shrugged his shoulders.

To cover his confusion, Morton hastened to introduce Darleton and his companion, Grant Hardy, to Frank and Bart.

"Mr. Darleton," said Merry, "glad to know you. I've just been hearing about you from your fencing instructor."

"Have you?" said Darleton, with a quite superior air. "I'm afraid Monsieur L'Estrange has been boasting about me, as usual. Just because I happened to be particularly apt as a pupil, he is inclined to puff me on every occasion. I don't fancy it, you know, but I can't seem to prevent it. People will begin to think me quite a wonder if he doesn't stop overrating me."

"But he doesn't overrate you, my dear fellow," quickly put in Grant Hardy. "I've seen you hold L'Estrange himself at something like even play, and he is a wizard."

Hodge laughed a bit.

"Why do you laugh?" asked Hardy, with a flash of resentment. "Do you think——"

"I laughed over Mr. Darleton's modesty," said Hodge. "It is useless for him to seek to conceal the truth from us in that manner. He is quite the wonder of this club."

Hardy missed the sarcasm hidden in Bart's words and his face cleared.

Darleton, however, was not so obtuse, and he surveyed Bart searchingly, a flush creeping into his cheeks.

"I observe that you fence after a fashion, Mr. Hodge," said Darleton, and the passing breath of insult lay in his manner of saying "after a fashion."

"Oh, not at all!" protested Hodge; "but I assure you that my friend Merriwell can put up something of an argument at it when he is in his best form."

"Indeed?" smiled Darleton, lifting his eyebrows. "Then I am led to infer that he is not in his best form just now."

"What leads you to infer that?"

"Oh, your manner of speaking the words, of course. I would not comment on what I have seen him do."

"Wouldn't you?"

"No, indeed."

"Sometimes our ears deceive us," said Bart; "but I fancied I did hear you—never mind that."

He broke off abruptly, but he had informed Darleton that his words, spoken when he first appeared on the scene, had been overheard.

Darleton shrugged his shoulders, a gesture he had caught from his French instructor.

"Fancy leads us into grave mistakes at times," he said. "It should not be permitted to run away with us. Now, I have known fellows who fancied they could fence, but very few of them have been able to make much of a go at it."

This was a sly thrust at Merry. Frank looked pleasant and nodded.

"I have even known instructors to be deceived in the skill of their pupils," he remarked, reaching home and scoring heavily.

This reply brought the blood flashing once more to Darleton's cheeks.

"In case you were the pupil," said the fencer, instantly, "no instructor could feel the least doubt in regard to your skill."

His words plainly implied that he meant lack of skill, although he was not that blunt.

"Although you are not inclined to comment on the work of another," returned Merry; "it is evident that your observation is keen, and with you, one's back might not be as safe as his face."

This was a coup, for Darleton lost his temper, showing how sharply he had been hit.

"I'll not pass words with you, Mr. Merriwell," he exclaimed, "as I am not inclined to waste my breath uselessly. If at any time while you are here you feel inclined to demonstrate what you can really do—or think you can do—you will find me at your service."

Hodge stiffened. It was a challenge.

"Thank you for your kindness," smiled Frank, perfectly at his ease. "I may take you at your word later on."

Darleton and Hardy turned away.

"He may," observed Hardy, speaking to his companion, but making sure Frank could not fail to hear, "yet I doubt it."

Hodge seized Frank's arm, fairly quivering with excitement.

"You're challenged, Merry!" he panted. "You must accept! Don't let him off! Teach the fellow a lesson!"

"Steady, Bart," said Merriwell softly. "There is plenty of time. Don't fly up like this. Do you want to see me defeated?"

"No! He can't defeat you!"

"How do you know?"

Hodge stared at Frank in doubt and astonishment.

"Is it possible you are afraid to face him?" he gasped.

"I don't think so; but you should remember that he is in perfect form and condition, while I am rusty. In order to meet him and do my best I must practice. That I shall do. Wait. I promise you satisfaction—and Mr. Darleton the same!"

CHAPTER III

GETTING INTO TRIM.

art Hodge was not aware that Frank had been so thoroughly aroused; but when he was called to Merry's room in the hotel that day after lunch and found two complete fencing outfits there—foils, masks, jackets, and gauntlet gloves—he realized that there was "something doing."

Frank closed and locked the door.

"Strip down and make ready," he said grimly. "I'm going to brush up and get in condition, and you are the victim."

"I'm happy to be the victim now," declared Bart; "in case Mr. Darleton is the victim later."

Something more than an hour later the comrades were resting after a bath and rub down. Bart's eyes shone and his dark, handsome face wore an expression of great satisfaction.

"You may be rusty, Merry," he observed; "but I fail to see it. I swear you fenced better to-day than ever before in all your life."

"You think so, Bart; but I can't believe that. A man can't be at his best at fencing, any more than at billiards, unless he is in constant practice."

"Oh, I know I've gone back; but you have not. I'll wager my life you can give Fred Darleton all he is looking for."

"It would be a pleasure to me," confessed Frank. "Somehow he irritated me strangely."

"I'd never supposed it by your manner."

"If I had lost my temper I should have been defeated. Mr. Darleton has a temper, and I shall count on it leading to his downfall, in case we meet."

"You'll meet, for you are challenged. He thinks you a mark, Merry. He'll be overconfident."

"Another thing I count on as aiding me. Overconfidence is quite as bad as lack of confidence. Darleton has been praised too much, and he believes he is very nearly perfect as a fencer. A defeat now will either make or mar him. If defeated, he will either set about working harder to acquire further accomplishment, or he will quit."

"I believe he'll quit."

"I don't know."

"I don't like him, Merry."

"There is something about him that I do not fancy, myself. I've not seen him enough to judge what it is. I've tried to think it might be his freshness in shooting his mouth the way he did; but something asserts that I should have disliked him had he kept his mouth closed. He has an air of directness; but behind it there is a touch of cunning and craft that stamps him as crooked. I may sympathize with a weak chap who goes crooked through temptation; but I have no sympathy for a sly rascal who is dishonest with deliberation. If Darleton is naturally honest, I have misjudged him."

There came a heavy knock on the door and the sound of voices outside.

Bart unlocked the door, and Joe Gamp stalked in, followed by Jack Ready, Hans Dunnerwurst, and Jim Stretcher, all of Merriwell's party.

"Ding this tut-tut-tut-tut-tut——" began Joe.

"Tut, tut!" interrupted Jack. "Eliminate repetitions from your profuse flow of language, Joseph."

Gamp flourished his fist in the air and began again:

"Ding this tut-tut-tut-tut-tut-tut——"

"Whistle, Joe—whistle!" advised Frank.

Whereupon the tall chap recommenced:

"Ding this tut-tut-tut—whistle—town! It's all up hill and dud-dud-dud—whistle—down!"

"Oh, Joseph, you're a poet!" exclaimed Ready.

"Yah," said Dunnerwurst gravely, "oudt uf him boetry flows like a sbarkling rifer."

"We have decided in solemn conclave," said Ready, "that the streets of this prosperous Western burgh are exceedingly soiled."

"Und some of them been stood their end onto," put in Hans.

"It's hard to keep your fuf-fuf-fuf—whistle—feet from slipping in the sus-sus-sus—whistle—street," added Gamp.

"There he goes again!" burst from Ready. "I never suspected it of him. Crown him with laurels and adorn him with bays."

"What is the difference between the bay and the laurel, Jack?"

laughed Frank.

"Ask me not at this unpropitious moment," entreated the odd fellow. "We have been meandering hither and yon over Omaha— yea verily, we have been even as far as the stockyards of South Omaha. We have waded across streets that were guiltless of being cleaned even since the day they were paved. We have ascended streets which led into the clouds, and we have descended others which led into the gorges and valleys. We have gazed in awe upon the courthouse, with blind justice standing on its battlements, balances in hand. We have seen the post office and expressed our admiration. Alas and alack, we are wearied! We fain would rest. Omaha is all right for those who think so; but some day she will rise and butcher her street-cleaning department. She will be justified. I have spoke."

With this he dropped on a chair and fanned himself weakly.

"What have you fellows been dud-dud-doing?" inquired Gamp, noticing for the first time that the boys were in bath robes and that fencing paraphernalia was scattered about the room.

Frank explained that they had been fencing.

"Jee-whickers!" cried Joe. "You used to be pretty good at it when you were at cuc-cuc-college. You were the champion fuf-fuf-fuf-fencer at Yale, all right."

"He's just as good to-day as he ever was," declared Bart; "and Mr. Darleton will find out that is good enough."

"Who's Darleton?" asked Stretcher.

Then they were told about the affair at the club, which quickly awoke their interest.

"Omaha takes on new fascination for me," averred Ready. "I felt like folding my tent and stealing away a short time ago; but if Merry is going against some gentleman with the inflated cranium in this burgh, I shall linger with great glee to watch the outcome."

"You talk the way a cub reporter writes, Ready," said Stretcher. "Big words sound good to you, but if you know what you're saying you'll have to show me."

"I shall refrain from exerting myself to that extent, my boy," retorted Jack. "It's not worth while."

"Where are the rest of the boys?" asked Frank.

"Scattered broadcast over the mountains and valleys of Omaha," answered Ready. "Fear not for them; they will return in due time."

"How does Omaha strike you, Jim?" inquired Merriwell.

"She ain't in it much compared with Kansas City," said Stretcher. "We have some hills there, you know. I've yet to see any coun-

19

try that can get away from old Missouri. When you get ahead of Missouri, you'll have to hurry."

"It does me good to see a chap who will stand up for his native State," said Merry, winking at some of the others but maintaining a grave face before Stretcher. "Of course Missouri may have her drawbacks, but we all know she is a land of fertility and——"

"Fertility!" cried Jim enthusiastically. "You bet! Crops grow overnight there. Yes, sir, that's straight. It's perfectly astonishing how things grow. As an illustration, when I was about seven years old my mother gave me some morning-glory seeds to plant. I always did love the morning-glory flower. I thought it would be a grand thing to plant the seeds beneath my chamber window, where I could look forth each morning on rising and revel in the beauty of the purple blossoms. I got busy and stuck the seeds into the ground one afternoon about five o'clock. I knew the soil was particularly rich right there, and I counted on the vines growing fast, so I lost no time in stringing a number of cords from the ground right up to my window.

"That night when I went to bed I wondered if the seeds would be sprouted when I rose the following morning. It was warm weather, and I slept with my window open. I suppose I kicked the bedclothes off. Some time in the night I felt something pushing me, but I was too sleepy to wake up. About daylight I woke up suddenly, for something pushed me out of bed onto the floor. I jumped up and looked to see what was the matter. Fellows, you won't believe it, but the vine—or, rather, a profusion of vines— had grown all the way up to my window in the night, had found the window open, had come into the room, and, being tired from its exertion in growing so hard, I presume, had climbed into my bed and pushed me out."

A profound silence was broken by Dunnerwurst, who gurgled:

"Uf I faint, vill somebody blease throw me on some vater!"

"Stretcher," said Merry, "I don't suppose there is ever anything in your State that is not grand and superior? There are no drawbacks to Missouri? Soil, climate, people—all are of the first quality?"

"Oh," said Jim, with an air of modesty, "I presume any part of the country has its drawbacks. The soil of Missouri is magnificent and the climate superb—as a rule. I presume there are sterile spots within the boundaries of the State, and I have experienced some unpleasant weather. The winter that old Jake died was unusually severe."

"Who was Jake?"

"A mule, and the dumb companion of my innocent boyhood. You see, I always wanted a dog. Lots of boys I knew had dogs. Tom Jones had a shepherd, Pete Boogers had a collie, Muck Robbins had a yaller cur, and Runt Hatch had two bull purps. I pestered paw for a dog. He didn't have any use for dogs, and he wouldn't give me one. I told him I must have a pet of some kind. 'All right, Jim,' says he, 'if you want a pet, there's Jake, our old mule, you may have him.' Now, Jake was pretty well used up. He was spavined and chest foundered and so thin his slats were coming through his hide. He wasn't beautiful, but he had been a faithful old creature, and paw was disinclined to kill him. He thought it was a great joke to give me Jake for a pet; but I was just yearning for something on which I could lavish my affection, and I began to pour it out on Jake.

"I petted the old boy, gave him good feed, took him into the cowshed nights, and did my best to make him generally comfortable. Jake appreciated it. You may think dumb creatures, and mules in particular, have no sense of gratitude, but such is not the case. Jake understood me, and I did him. I could actually read his thoughts. Yes, sir, it's a fact. At first paw grinned over it and tried to joke me about Jake; but after a while he got tired of having his best feed given that old mule and finding the animal bedded down in the cowshed. He said it would have to stop. Then he got mad and turned Jake out to pick for himself. I brought Jake back twice, but both times paw raised a fuss, and the last time, he got so blazing mad he swore he'd knock the mule in the head if I did it again.

"That was in the fall, with winter coming on. I tried to plead with paw; but it was no go. He said Jake would have to shift for himself in the open. Jake used to come up to the lower fence and call to me melodiously in the gloaming, and I would slip down and pat him and talk to him and sympathize with him. But I didn't dare do anything more. Well, that winter was a tough one. Never had so much cold weather packed into one winter before that. Jake suffered from exposure, and my heart bled for him. He grew thinner and thinner and sadder and sadder. Paw's heart was like flint, and I couldn't do anything. Jake hated snowstorms. Every time one came he thought it would be his last; but somehow he worried through them all until the snow went off and spring set in. Then Jake brightened up some and seemed more like himself.

"But late in the spring another cold spell struck in. It was near the first of May. In the midst of that cold spell our barn got afire one night. When Jake saw that fire, he says to himself, 'Here's my chance to get warm all the way through.' He found a weak spot in the fence and got over it, after which he waltzed up to the barn and stood there, warming first one side and then the other by the heat and enjoying himself.

"We had a heap of corn stored in the barn. After a while the roof of the barn burned off and the fire got to the corn. When this happened the corn began to pop and fly into the air. It popped faster and faster and flew high into the air, coming down in a great shower. Jake looked up and saw the air plumb full of great, white flakes of popped corn. The poor, old mule gave a great groan of anguish. 'I've lasted through twenty-one snowstorms this winter,' says he, with tears in his eyes; 'but this one is my finish.' Then he lay right down where he was and gave up the struggle. In the morning we found him frozen stiff."

Ready sobbed and wiped his eyes.

"How pathetic!" he exclaimed chokingly.

"Poor Shake!" gurgled Hans.

"That story should be entitled 'The Tale of a Mule,'" observed Frank.

"It is evident," said Bart, "that Missouri mules are sometimes more intelligent than the inhabitants of the State."

"Oh, we have some dull people, of course," admitted Jim. "I remember the janitor at our old school—he was a trifle dull. Poor old Mullen! One day he threw up his job. They asked him why he did it. Says he: 'I'm honest, and I won't stand being slurred.' He was pressed to explain. 'Why,' he exclaimed, 'when I'm sweeping out, if I happen to find a handkerchief or any little thing, I hang it up, like an honest man. Every now and then the teacher, or somebody who hasn't the nerve to face me, gives me a slur. A few days ago I come in one mornin' and I seen writ on the blackboard: "Find the least common multiple." Well, I just went searching the place over from top to bottom, but I couldn't find a sign of the old thing anywhere. I don't believe nobody lost it. That made me sore, but I stood for it all right. Yesterday mornin' in great big letters there was writ on the blackboard: "Find the greatest common divisor." Says I to myself: "Now, both of them blamed things is lost, and I'll be charged with swipin' 'em." And I throwed up my job.'"

They laughed heartily over this story, and, having aroused their risibilities at last, Jim seemed satisfied.

CHAPTER IV

DARLETON'S CHALLENGE.

It was the night of the "finals" at the Midwestern, and the clubrooms were thronged. Frank and all his friends were there. Morton had introduced them to many well-known young men of the prosperous Nebraska city, and they were being made to feel quite at home.

Much of the general conversation concerned the coming bouts. Opinions were freely expressed as to the abilities and merits of different contestants and there was much good-natured argument and banter.

There was also not a little quiet betting.

In one of the big main rooms of the club, Merry met three Yale men, who expressed their delight at seeing him there. While he was talking with them François L'Estrange came up. The Frenchman knew them also, and he paused to shake hands all round.

"What's the matter, L'Estrange?" asked one. "You seem rather downcast and troubled over something."

The fencing master shrugged his shoulders.

"Eet is unfortunate," he declared. "I haf to geef you ze information zat there will be no fencing zis night."

"Why, how is that?" they exclaimed.

"Meestare Marlowe, who was to meet Meestare Darleton, ees not here."

"Not here?"

"No."

"Where is he?"

"He haf sent ze word zat he is very ill."

"Cold feet!" cried one of the gentlemen. "That's what's the matter! Marlowe squeals!"

"Sure thing!" agreed another. "It's a shame, but he has made a clean backdown."

"He was all right last night. I saw him then," put in the third gentleman.

"Eet is very strange," said L'Estrange regretfully. "I understand eet not why he should haf ze cold feet and be ill. I suppose ze cold feet ees unpleasant, but zey should not make him squeal."

"What we mean," explained the first gentleman, "is that he is afraid to meet Darleton. He has defeated every opponent in the contests, and it has been his boast that he would defeat Darleton. His nerve failed him."

"Eet ruin ze sport for zis night," declared the fencing master. "Zere ees no one who is for Meestare Darleton ze efen match, so zere will be no fencing."

At this point Darleton himself, accompanied as usual by his chum, Grant Hardy, came pushing through the throng, espied L'Estrange and hurried up.

"I've been looking for you, professor!" he exclaimed. "What's this about Marlowe? Is it true that he has quit?"

"Eet is true."

"Well, that's just about the sort I took him to be!" cried Darleton angrily. "He's a great case of bluff! He's a bag of wind! He's a quitter! He knew I'd defeat him. Now, what are we going to do?"

"Zere is nothing we can do," answered the fencing master regretfully.

"And our go was to be the feature to-night. Every one will be disappointed. It's a shame. Besides that, Marlowe had no right not to give me a chance to show him up. I meant to put it all over him, the slob!"

Darleton's chagrin over his lost opportunity to "put it all over" the other fellow seemed to lead him into a complete loss of temper, and he indulged in language which on any occasion he would have condemned in another.

Suddenly his eyes fell on Frank Merriwell, and a peculiar expression came to his face.

"Why, here is the great athlete who fancies he is something of a fencer," he said. "Good evening, Mr. Merriwell. I suppose you came to see me outpoint Marlowe? Well, you will be disappointed, I regret to say."

Hodge was near, and the words and manner of Darleton had caused him to bridle until he was on the point of exploding.

"I regret very much," said Merry quietly, "that we shall not have the pleasure of witnessing the fencing bout between you and Mr. Marlowe, sir."

He was calm, polite, and reserved.

L'Estrange spoke up:

"I suppose we might geef ze exhibition ourselves, Meestare Darleton," he said. "Zat might please ze spectators bettaire than nothing."

"But it would not be like a bout in which there was an element of uncertainty. Every one would know you could defeat me easily if you cared to. If I counted on you I'd win no credit, for they would say you permitted me to do it."

The desire of the fellow for applause and his thirst to display his skill by defeating some one was all too evident.

Suddenly he turned sharply to again face Frank.

"How about you?" he asked.

Merry lifted his eyebrows.

Hodge felt a tingling, for he realized that an open challenge was coming.

"About me?" repeated Frank questioningly.

"Yes, how about you? You think you can fence."

"I have fenced—a little."

"I was told to-day that you are a champion at everything you undertake. That's ridiculous if you undertake many things. You have undertaken fencing. Well, I'd like to convince some people that there is one thing at which you are not much of a champion."

"Would you?" asked Merry, smiling pleasantly.

"Indeed I would. The crowd wants to see a fencing bout to-night. Marlowe has taken water. He isn't here. You are here. Of course we can't fence for honors in the series, as you have not been engaged in previous contests. All the same, we can give an exhibition go. There will be an element of uncertainty about it. What do you say?"

"Why, I don't know——" came slowly from Merry, as if he hesitated over it.

"Oh, if you're afraid," sneered Darleton—"if you haven't the nerve, that's different."

A strange, smothered growl was choked back in the throat of Bart Hodge.

"I don't believe I am afraid of you," said Frank, with the same deliberate manner. "I was thinking that such an affair would be quite irregular if interpolated with the finals."

"Don't worry about that. If you are willing to meet me, I'll fix it."

"Of course I'm willing, but——"

"That settles it!" cried Darleton triumphantly. "You hear him, gentlemen. He's ready to fence me. He can't back out."

"As if he would want to back out!" muttered Bart Hodge softly. "You'll get all you're looking for to-night, Mr. Darleton."

CHAPTER V

THE FENCING BOUT.

On guard, gentlemen!"

It was the voice of François L'Estrange.

The regular finals were over. As a finish to the evening's entertainment, the announcer had stated that, in order not to disappoint those who had expected to witness a fencing contest, an arrangement had been made whereby Frank Merriwell, a guest of the club, would meet the club's champion, Fred Darleton.

Darleton had appeared first on the raised platform and had been greeted by hearty applause.

Then came Merriwell, and the applause accorded him was no less generous.

The preliminaries were quickly arranged.

L'Estrange was agreed on as the referee.

"On guard, gentlemen!" he commanded.

At the word the contestants faced each other, and then they went through the graceful movements of coming on guard, their foils sweeping through the air. Simultaneously they advanced their right feet and were ready.

"Engage!"

The foils met with a soft clash and the bout had begun.

The great gathering of spectators packed on the four sides of the raised platform were hushed and breathless. They saw before them two splendid specimens of youthful manhood. Between them it was indeed no easy thing to make a hasty choice. Both were graceful as panthers and both seemed perfectly at home and fully confident. Frank's face was grave and pleasant, while Darleton wore a faint smile that bespoke his perfect trust in himself.

Frank's friends were all together in a body. Among them Harry Rattleton was the only one who expressed anxiety.

"I know Merry could do that fellow ordinarily," said Rattles, in a whisper; "but I fear he's out of trim now. Darleton is in perfect practice, and he will bet the guest of Merry—I mean get the best of him!"

"Don't you believe it!" hissed Hodge. "Don't you ever think such a thing for a second! Merry may not be at his best, but he is that fellow's master. He has enough skill to hold Darleton even, and he has the master mind. The master mind will conquer."

"I hope you're right," said Harry; "but I'm afraid."

"Don't be afraid!" growled Browning, also aroused. "You make me tired!"

Thus crushed, Rattles relapsed into silence, but he watched with great anxiety, fearing the outcome.

At the outset the two fencers seemed "feeling each other"—that is, each tried to test the skill, technique and versatility of his opponent. Both were calm, cool and calculating, yet quick as a flash to meet and checkmate any fresh mode of attack.

Ordinarily the spectators might have become impatient over this "fiddling," but on this occasion all seemed to realize the fencers were working up to the point of genuine struggle by exploring each other's methods. Besides that the two displayed variety and change enough to maintain unwearied interest in these preliminaries to the real struggle.

The eyes of François L'Estrange took on a light of keener interest as the bout progressed. He watched the stranger from the first, having confidence in the ability of his pupil, and silently praying from the outset that Merriwell would not be too easily overcome. Satisfaction, not anxiety, took possession of him as he began to realize that Frank possessed unusual knowledge of the art, and was capable of putting that knowledge to clever use. The Frenchman continued to believe that Darleton would finish the victor.

The two young men advanced, retreated, circled, feinted, engaged, disengaged—all the time on the alert for the moment when one or the other should launch himself into the encounter in earnest. The foils clicked and hissed, now high, now low. At intervals the fencers stamped lightly with the foot advanced.

"Mon Dieu!" muttered L'Estrange, still watching Merriwell. "Who taught him so much!"

Suddenly, like a throb of electricity, Darleton made a direct lunge—and the real engagement was on.

L'Estrange's pupil was led into the lunge through the belief that Merry had exposed himself unconsciously in the line in which he was engaged.

Quick as the fellow was, it seemed that Frank had known what to expect. He made no sweeping parry, but, quicker than the eye could follow, he altered the position of his foil by fingering and turned Darleton's lunge. Following this with almost incredible swiftness, Merry scored fair and full in quinte.

L'Estrange suppressed an exclamation of displeasure, for he realized his pupil had been decoyed and led to expose himself. Too much confidence in himself and too little regard for the skill of his opponent had caused Darleton to give Merry this chance to score.

"Touch!" exclaimed Darleton, with a mingling of surprise and dismay.

He recovered instantly, a bitter expression settling about his tightened lips.

"So you fooled me!" he thought. "I'll pay you for that! It may be your undoing, Mr. Merriwell!"

He believed Frank would become overconfident through this early success; but he did not know Merriwell, whose observation and experience had long ago told him that overconfidence was the rock on which many a chap has stranded in sight of victory.

Darleton was in earnest, now; there was no more fooling. He sought for an opening. Failing to find it, he tried to lead Frank into attacking and leaving an opening.

Merry pretended to attack, but it was only a feint. When Darleton parried and tried the riposte, his thrust was met and turned. Then Frank attacked in earnest, and his button caught his opponent in tierce.

Darleton leaped away, but did not acknowledge the touch. Instead, he claimed that Merriwell had simply reached his right shoulder, which did not count.

L'Estrange's pupil was white to the lips now. He could not understand why he had failed, and he felt that there must be many among the spectators who would maintain that he had been unfair in claiming he was not fairly touched the second time.

The dismay of the pupil was no greater than that of his instructor. L'Estrange was angry. In French he hissed a warning at Darleton, urging him to be more cautious and to try his antagonist in another style.

Frank understood French even better than Darleton, and he was warned of what to expect.

Therefore when the Midwestern man sought an opening by "absence," Merry declined to spring into the trap and expose himself. To many it seemed that the visitor lost a chance to score, but all were aware that he prevented Darleton from counting when the latter followed the "absence" by a flashing thrust. This thrust was turned, but Darleton had learned his lesson, and he recovered and was on guard so suddenly Frank found no advantageous opening.

Although his pupil had failed to score, L'Estrange showed some satisfaction, for he saw that Darleton was now awake to the danger of failing to cover himself instantly after an attack of any kind. At last the Omaha man knew he would have to exert himself to the utmost to defeat the stranger he had held in scornful contempt.

"Now he knows!" whispered L'Estrange to himself. "Now he will defeat Merriwell with ease!"

A moment later Darleton met and turned a fierce attack. Then he counted cleanly.

"Touch!" cried Frank promptly.

Harry Rattleton gave a gasp of dismay.

"I knew it!" he palpitated. "You see I'm right! He'll win over Merry!"

"You'd better go die!" grated Hodge. "Frank has counted on him twice already!"

"Only once."

"Only once acknowledged, but Merry counted twice, just the same."

"Either time," declared Morgan, "would have ended the affair in a genuine duel."

"Sure!" growled Browning.

"But not in this sort of an encounter," said Harry. "Here a touch is a touch, and Darleton is on even terms with Merry now."

After this none of them paid much attention to Harry's fears, as he expressed them. They were wholly absorbed in the cleverness of the two young men on the platform, who were circling, feinting, attacking, parrying and constantly watching for an opening or seeking to create one through some trick or artifice.

Three times Darleton sought to reach Frank and failed, but each time he prevented a successful riposte on the part of Merry. He was at his very best, and for a few moments his skill seemed superior to that of the visitor.

The shadow that had clouded the face of L'Estrange passed away. Confidence came to him. Once he had feared that his pupil might be outmatched, but this fear troubled him no longer. Darleton was forcing the work, but he was keeping himself well in hand and effectually covered all the while.

Finally the Midwestern man made a flashing cut-over and scored.

"Touch!" cried Merry again.

"I knew it!" half sobbed Rattleton.

A bit later the timekeeper announced the expiration of two minutes, whereupon Merry and Darleton changed positions.

During the first half of the bout, according to acknowledged touches, Darleton had taken the lead.

The Midwestern man began the second half by pressing Frank. He was satisfied that he could win, although experience had warned him that he could not win as easily as he had fancied before the engagement began.

For at least thirty seconds he kept Merry busy, and in that time he secured another touch.

Rattleton was almost in tears. He felt that he must leave the room. He could not bear to remain and see Frank defeated.

Darleton believed he had sounded Merry thoroughly and knew his style. He was on guard for every method displayed by the visitor up to this point.

But now, of a sudden, Frank attacked in a new line. He seemed to attempt a "beat." When Darleton parried the first light thrust following the "beat," Frank quickly changed to another point of attack and made a "re-beat" as his opponent met him. He followed with a second stroke that was quicker and harder than the first and reached home effectively.

Darleton showed a slight trace of confusion, but he was compelled to acknowledge the touch.

They now engaged in tierce; but in a twinkling Merry executed a double. He feinted a disengage into quinte. Darleton executed a counter, upon which Merry lifted the point of his weapon and circled round his opponent's counter with a counter disengage, which brought him back into quinte, the line from which it was intended that he should be shut. Only by marvelously swift work did Darleton prevent himself from being scored upon.

Right on top of this Merry again executed the "re-beat" and scored.

The face of the Midwestern man flamed scarlet and then grew pale. His eyes burned with a light of anger that he could repress only with difficulty. Twice he had been outgeneraled, and he knew it.

In a twinkling the cloud returned to the face of François L'Estrange. His lips parted, but he did not speak.

"I knew he would do it!" muttered Bart Hodge, in satisfaction. "Keep your eyes on Merry! He's getting there now!"

Darleton realized that he was losing his advantage. He sought to recover by feinting in high lines and attacking instantly in low lines. In this effort he placed himself at a disadvantage, for Merry seemed to read his mind and met him effectively.

Again Frank scored, but, in getting away, he appeared to lose his balance.

Darleton followed up.

Down went Merry, falling on his left hand, and Darleton uttered an exclamation of triumph as he attempted to count.

With a twist of his wrist, Frank parried the stroke. His left arm flung him up with a spring.

Dismayed and annoyed by his failure to improve such an opening, Darleton closed in and the fencers came corps-a-corps.

Immediately L'Estrange separated them.

Merriwell won a great burst of applause by the clever manner in which he had extricated himself from a position that seemed almost defenseless.

L'Estrange said nothing to his pupil, but their eyes met, and something in that glance stirred all the resentment in Darleton's soul. It was a reproof. He saw that the fencing master was disappointed in him.

A concentrated fury took possession of Darleton. He went after Frank as if thirsting for his gore. The savageness of his attack would have overcome one less skillful and self-poised.

It did not overcome Frank. On the other hand, Merry turned his opponent's fierceness to a disadvantage. He was not flustered or worried. He met every attack, and in rapid succession he began counting on the Midwestern man.

Darleton closed his lips and refused to acknowledge a touch.

Seeing this, L'Estrange finally began declaring each touch as two for the visitor.

The superiority of Merriwell was now apparent to every spectator who was not prejudiced, and round after round of applause greeted his beautiful work.

Darleton thrust furiously. Down went Frank, but he dropped lightly after having retreated. His right foot had made a long forward step, and barely two fingers of his left hand touched the floor. At the same moment he thrust and reached his opponent. In a twinkling he was erect and ready, if Darleton sought to secure a riposte.

From apprehension and fear Rattleton turned to delight and exultation.

"Frank is winning!" he exclaimed joyously. "He's the best man!"

"Shut up!" hissed Hodge. "Don't let everybody know you had any doubt about it!"

31

"Of course he's the best man," grunted Browning.

The real truth was that in mere knowledge of fencing Merry was not greatly Darleton's superior, but in strategy, originality and mastery of himself he was far and away the superior. As well as a finely trained body, he had a finely trained mind. It was this master mind that was conquering.

Merry had not only probed Darleton's weaknesses in the art of fencing, he had at the same time discovered his weaknesses in the art of self-mastery. And no man who cannot master himself can hope to master others of equal mental and physical equipment.

Merriwell had perfected his plan of campaign, as a great general prepares and perfects a plan of battle.

This he had done after sounding the strength and limitations of his antagonist. This plan in one or two details did not work out as prepared; but, like a successful general, he was resourceful, and when one style of assault was repulsed he changed swiftly, almost instantly, to another style that surprised and confounded the enemy and brought about the desired result.

In this manner he soon turned Darleton's attack into defense, while he became the real assailant. He resorted to all the arts of which he felt himself the master. The failure of one method of assault did not lead him to permanently abandon that method, although he quickly turned to some other. At an unexpected moment he returned to the first attempted effort, making the change when least expected, and, in most cases, was successful the second time.

His success confounded and infuriated Darleton, who had entered into the contest in perfect belief that the outcome would be applause and glory for himself. The confidence of the Midwestern man fled from him and left him trembling with rage and chagrin.

At first on realizing that Merriwell was getting the best of the match toward the close, Darleton had fancied he might put up such defense that the visitor would be held in check to some extent, thinking if he did this that L'Estrange, out of self-pride and disinclination to confess his pupil outmatched, would give him the decision.

But when the spectators began to shout and cheer for Merriwell, Darleton realized that his case was hopeless. In the face of all this the fencing master could not give him the decision.

From this time to the finish, Merriwell seemed able to count on his antagonist at will. Frank gave the fellow no chance to recover, but pressed him persistently to the finish. Before the engagement was over Darleton quite lost his form and sought to score by stabbing and jabbing much like a beginner.

The timekeeper announced the finish.

Frank lowered his foil.

With savage fury, Darleton swung and slapped him across the mask, using such force that Merry was staggered.

From the witnesses a shout arose, followed by a volley of hisses and cries of, "Shame! shame! Dirty work!"

François L'Estrange sprang forward and snatched the bent foil from his pupil's hand. Then he faced the audience and made a gesture that silenced their cries.

"Gentlemen," he said, "I make not ze excuse for Meestare Darleton. He met ze defeat by Meestare Merriwell, an' ze loss of his tempare made him forget to be ze gentleman. Meestare Merriwell is ze very fine fencer. He win ze match."

Saying which, he wheeled and grasped Frank's hand, which he shook heartily, while the room resounded with a thunder of applause.

33

CHAPTER VI

A FORCED APOLOGY.

Merriwell, you astounded this club to-night," said Hugh Morton, as Frank was finishing dressing, after a shower and rub down. "No one here expected you to defeat Fred Darleton. Any member of the club would have wagered two to one on Darleton. He acted like a cur when he struck you with his foil. Every one, except his own particular clique, is down on him for that. We regret very much that it happened, and the president of the club is waiting to offer apologies."

"I'm not looking for apologies," smiled Merry. "The club was not responsible for Darleton's act."

"But we feel greatly humiliated by it. He will be severely censured. He may be expelled."

"Oh, that's too much! I must protest against such an extreme measure."

"He deserves to be expelled," put in Hodge.

"You are right," agreed Morton. "Between us, I believe it would be a good thing for the club."

"How so?"

"I'll tell you later."

In the reception room of the club there was a great gathering waiting to get another look at Frank. The president of the club met him as he appeared and hastened to express regrets over the action of Darleton at the finish of the bout. Frank was sincere in making excuses for his late antagonist.

"But Darleton must apologize," declared the president. "We cannot have any visitor insulted in such a manner without seeing that an apology is made."

"I haven't asked for an apology on my account."

"We demand it on our own account. He has been told that he

must apologize publicly, as the insult was offered publicly."

"Well, he'll find me ready to pardon him freely and just as willing to forget the occurrence."

"You are generous, Mr. Merriwell."

During the next thirty minutes Merry was kept busy shaking hands with those who were eager to express their good will.

That night in Omaha he made a host of admirers and friends who would never forget him, and who would ever stand ready to uphold him on any occasion.

Many of those present seemed lingering for something. A few departed, but the majority waited on.

Finally Fred Darleton, accompanied by Grant Hardy and followed by a number of boon companions, entered the room.

Darleton was pale and nervous. He glanced about the place, and an expression of resentment passed over his face as he noted the number who had lingered. For a moment he seemed to hesitate; then he advanced toward Frank, who sat near the centre of the room, with his comrades and the club members about him.

Merry rose as he saw his late opponent.

"Mr. Merriwell," said Darleton, in a low tone, his words being almost inaudible at a distance of ten feet, "I have to offer you an apology for my hasty act of anger in striking you across the mask with my foil."

"That's all right," declared Frank. "Forget it, Darleton."

Merry offered his hand.

Darleton pretended he did not see this, and turned away at once.

Frank smiled and dropped his hand; but Bart Hodge gave vent to a suppressed exclamation of anger.

The action of the defeated fencer in declining to shake hands with his conqueror was noted by all in the room, and most of them felt annoyed and disgusted by this added slight after the forced apology.

Darleton left the room, without glancing to the right or left, and his companions followed closely.

"I knew he was a cur!" said Hodge, in a low, harsh tone.

The president and other members were annoyed and chagrined, but Frank found a method of passing the matter over by quickly awakening a discussion concerning the bouts of the finals.

A few minutes later François L'Estrange appeared. He advanced swiftly and grasped Frank's hand.

"My dear sare," he cried, "you give me ze very great astonishment to-night. You are ze—ze—what you call it?—ze Jim Dandy! Oui! You nevare learn so much about ze foil in ze American college. Eet is impossible!"

"Well," smiled Merry, "I don't think I told you I obtained all my knowledge and skill at college."

"You mention ze school first. You begin young. Zat ees good! Zat is splendid! Zat ees ze way to make ze feenish fencer, ze same as ze feenish musician or ze feenish beelyarde player. But ze school, ze college, both together zey never gif you all you know. You have ze command, ze skill, ze technique! Eef you choose, sare, you make ze master fencer."

"Thank you, professor," said Merry. "I fear you are flattering me."

"O-oo, no, no! I spik ze truth! You have traveled?"

"Yes."

"You have visited France?"

"Yes."

"I knew eet! In France you take ze fencing lesson from some famous master of ze art. You have ze French method. I do not say you have eet yet to completeness. I belief I could advance you to ze very great extent. But before you had finished ze engagement I knew you had received instruction from ze French master."

"But not in France."

"No? Zen where?"

"In New York."

"O-oo!" L'Estrange threw up his hands. "Zen I know! Oui! Oui! Zere ees but one man—Pierre Lafont. You have from me ze congratulation, sare. I know Pierre Lafont in France. He fight three duel, and in not one did he get even ze scratch. Each time he seriously disable his antagonist. But his son, Louis—zey say he ees ze wondaire."

For a time the professor rattled on in this enthusiastic manner, and his talk was very interesting. Although it was known to every one that he felt deep chagrin over the defeat of his finest pupil, he was now the soul of generosity in his behavior toward the victor. His manner was greatly in contrast to that of the churlish Darleton.

Before departing L'Estrange made an appointment to meet Merry in the club the following afternoon for the purpose of fencing with him.

"I wish to make ze test of your full ability, Meestare Merriwell," smiled the affable Frenchman. "I theenk I discovaire one or two little weaknesses in your style zat may be corrected quickly. Eet will give me pleasure to make ze improvement in you—if you wish eet."

"I'm always anxious to learn, professor," answered Merry.

CHAPTER VII

THE ADMIRATION OF L'ESTRANGE.

ondaireful! wondaireful!" cried L'Estrange. "You are so ready to—to—what you call eet?—to catch on!"

The time was mid afternoon following the evening when the finals were "pulled off" at the great Omaha athletic club. Frank had met the fencing master, according to agreement, and for some time they had been engaged with the foils, Hugh Morton being the only witness. They were resting now.

"Look you, sare," said the enthusiastic Frenchman, "in six month I could make you ze greatest fencer in ze country—in one year ze champion of ze world! Yes, sare—of ze world!"

"I fear you are putting it a little too strong, professor," laughed Frank.

"O-oo, no, no! I did think Meestare Darleton very clever, but you are a perfect wondaire. You catch ze idea like ze flash of lightning. You try ze execution once, twice, three time—perhaps—and you have eet. Zen eet is only to make eet perfect and to combine eet with othaire work and othaire ideas. Three time this day you touch me by ze strategy. You work ze surprise. Twice I touch you in one way; but after that I touch you not in that way at all. I tried to do it, but you had learned ze lesson. I did not have to tell you how to protect yourself."

"He seemed to hold you pretty well, professor," put in Morton.

"Oui! oui!" cried L'Estrange, without hesitation. "He put me on ze mettle. Meestare Merriwell, let me make you ze greatest fencer in ze world. I can do eet."

Merry smilingly shook his head.

"I am afraid I haven't the time," he said.

"One year is all eet will take, at ze most—only one little year."

"Too long."

"Nine month."

"Still too long."

"Zen I try to do eet in six month!" desperately said the fencing master. "In six month I have you so you can toy with me—so you can beat me at my own game. I know how to teach you to do that. You doubt eet?"

"Well, I don't know about——"

"Eet can be done. You know ze man who teach ze actor to act on ze stage? He make of him ze great actor, still perhaps ze teacher he cannot act at all. He know how eet should be done. I am better teacher than zat, for I can fence; but I know ze way to teach you more zan I can accomplish. You have ze physique, ze brain, ze nerve, ze heart, ze youth—everything. In six month I do it."

"But I could not think of giving six months of my time to such as acquirement."

"You make reputation and fortune if you follow eet up."

"And that is the very thing I could not do, professor."

"Why not? You take ze interest in ze amateur sport. You follow eet."

"Not all the time, professor. I have other business."

"You have money? You are reech?"

"I am comfortably fixed; but I have business interests of such a nature that it would be folly for me to give six months over to the acquiring of skill in fencing."

"What your business?"

"Mining."

"O-oo; you have ze mine?"

"Yes."

"Where?"

"One in Arizona and one in Mexico. I must soon look after those mines. I have been away from them a long time. All reports have been favorable, but a great company is soon to begin building a railroad in Mexico that will open up the country in which my mine is located. The mine is rich enough to enable me to work it and pack ore a great distance. When the railroad is completed I shall have one of the best paying mines on this continent. You will see from this explanation that I am not in a position to spend months in acquiring perfection in the art of fencing, and that it would be of little advantage to me in case I did acquire such a degree of skill."

L'Estrange looked disappointed.

"I thought you were ze reech gentleman of leisure," he explained.

"I am not a gentleman of leisure, although I occasionally take time to enjoy myself. When I work, I work hard; when I play, I play just as hard. I have been playing lately, but the end is near. I thank you, professor, for your interest in me and your offer; but I cannot accept."

"Eet is a shame so great a fencer is lost to ze world," sighed the Frenchman. "Steel, sare, if you evaire have cause to defend your life in a duel, I theenk you will be successful."

Nearly an hour later Morton and Merriwell entered the card room of the club—not the general card room, but the one where games were played for stakes.

Two games were in progress. Several of the players had met Frank the night before, and they greeted him pleasantly.

Among the few spectators was Fred Darleton.

"I observe Darleton is not playing," said Frank, in a low tone, to his companion.

"He never plays in the daytime," answered Morton.

"Never in the daytime?"

"No."

"But he does play at night?"

"Almost every night."

"What game?"

"Poker. He is an expert. I'll tell you something about it later. He's looking this way."

Darleton sauntered over.

"I presume you are quite elated about your victory over me, Merriwell?" he said unpleasantly.

"Oh, not at all," answered Merry, annoyed. "It was not anything to feel elated about."

"You are right," said Darleton. "If we were to meet again to-night the result would be quite different. I confess that you gave me a surprise; but I was in my very poorest form last night. I am confident it would be a simple matter for me to defeat you if we fenced again."

"Want of conceit does not seem to be one of your failings."

The fellow flushed.

"I presume you are one of those perfect chaps with no failings," he retorted. "At least, you are, in your own estimation. You are very chesty since you secured the decision over me."

"My dear man," smiled Merry pityingly, "that was a victory so trivial that I have almost forgotten it already."

This cut Darleton still more deeply.

"Oh, you put on a fine air, but you'll get that taken out of you if you remain in Omaha long. I shall not forget you!"

"You are welcome to remember as long as you like."

"And you'll receive something that will cause you to remember me, sir!"

"Look here," said Frank earnestly, "I do not fancy your veiled threats! If you are a man, you'll speak out what you mean."

"I fancy I am quite as much a man as you are. You're a bag of wind, and I will let down your inflation."

"Hold on, Darleton!" warmly exclaimed Morton. "This won't do! Mr. Merriwell is the guest of the club, and——"

"You brought him here, Morton—that will be remembered, also!"

"If you threaten me——"

"I am not threatening."

"You hadn't better! Perhaps you mean that you intend to lay for me and beat me up. Well, sir, I go armed, and I'll shoot if any one tries to jump me. If you want a whole skin——"

"What's this talk about beating and shooting?" interrupted one of the members. "It's fine talk to hear in these rooms! Drop it! If we have any one in the club who can't take an honorable defeat in a square contest of any sort, it's time that person took himself out of our ranks. I reckon that is straight enough."

"Quite straight enough, Mr. Robbins," bowed Darleton; "but it doesn't touch me. I can stand defeat; but I am seldom satisfied with one trial. The first trial may be for sport, but with me the second is for blood."

Having said this, he wheeled and stalked out of the room.

"We'll never have peace in this club while he continues to be a member," asserted Hugh Morton earnestly.

"I beg your pardon!" exclaimed one of the card players. "Don't forget that Mr. Darleton is my friend, sir!"

"I've not said anything behind his back that I am not ready to repeat to his face," flung back Morton.

"Well, you'd better be careful. He can fight."

"I think this is quite enough of this fighting talk!" said the man called Robbins sternly.

"That's right!"

"Quit it!"

"Choke off!"

"It's getting tiresome!"

These exclamations came from various persons, and Darleton's friend closed up at once.

Morton looked both provoked and disgusted.

"This is what the Darleton crowd is bringing us to," he said, addressing Frank, in a low tone. "They have formed a clique and introduced the first jarring element into the club. In the end they'll all get fired out on their necks."

Frank and Morton sat down in a corner by one of the round card tables.

"I don't mind Darleton's talk," protested Hugh, "for I reckon him as a big case of bluff. You called him last night, and he's sore over it. Usually he makes his bluffs go at poker. He'll find he can't always make a bluff go in real life."

"You say he is a clever poker player."

"Clever or crooked."

"Is there a question in regard to his honesty?"

"In some minds it's more than a question."

"Is that right?"

"That's straight."

"Well, in that case, it doesn't seem to me that it should be a very hard case to get rid of him."

"You mean——"

"Crooks are not generally permitted in clubs for gentlemen."

"But no one has been able to catch him."

"Oh; then it is not positively known that he is crooked?"

"Well, I am confident that there is something peculiar about his playing, and I'm not the only one who is confident. He wins right along."

"Never loses?"

"Never more than a few dollars, while he frequently wins several hundred at a sitting."

"It seems to me that catching a dishonest poker player should not be such a difficult thing out in this country."

"We've had some of our cleverest card men watching him, and all have given it up. They say he may be crooked, but they can't detect how he works the trick."

"You stated, I believe, that he never plays in the daytime."

"Never."

"Have you noted any other peculiar thing about his playing?"

"No, nothing unless—unless——"

"Unless what?"

"Unless it is his style of wearing smoked glasses."

"He wears smoked glasses when he plays?"

"Yes."

"Why?"

"Well, he claims the lights here hurt his eyes."

"That seems a very good reason why he should choose to play

41

by day."

"Yes; but he always has an excuse when asked into a game in the daytime."

Merriwell's face wore an expression of deep thought.

"It seems to have the elements of a Sherlock Holmes case," he finally remarked. "I'd like to be present when Darleton is playing. I think it is possible I might detect his trick, in case there is any trick about it."

"Are you a card expert?"

"I make no pretensions of being anything of the sort," answered Merry promptly. "Still I know something about the game of poker, and I did succeed in exposing card crooks, both at Fardale and at Yale."

Morton shook his head.

"I think I'm ordinarily shrewd in regard to cards," he said; "but I haven't been able to find out his secret. I don't believe you would have any success, Mr. Merriwell."

Merry persisted.

"There is no harm in letting me try, is there?"

"The only harm would be to arouse Darleton's suspicion if he caught you rubbering at him. I know he has thought himself watched at various times."

"Leave it to me," urged Frank. "I'll not arouse his suspicions."

"But it won't do a bit of good."

"If he is cheating, I'll detect him," asserted Merry, finding that it was necessary to make a positive declaration of that sort, in order to move Morton.

Hugh looked at him incredulously.

"You're a dandy fencer, old man," he laughed; "but you mustn't get a fancy that you're just as clever at everything. Still, as long as you are so insistent, I'll give you a trial. Meet me in the billiard room at eight o'clock this evening. Play seldom begins here before eight-thirty or nine."

"I'll be there," promised Frank, satisfied.

CHAPTER VIII

AROUSED BY A MYSTERY.

It was nine o'clock that evening when Morton and Merriwell strolled into the card room. They seemed to be wandering around in search of some amusement to pass away the time.

"Come on here, Morton," called a player. "Bring your friend into this game. It will make just enough."

Hugh shook his head.

"No cards for me to-night," he said. "My luck is too poor. Dropped more than enough to satisfy me last week."

"The place to find your money is where you lost it," said another player.

"I'm willing to let it rest where it is a while. I have a severe touch of cold feet."

"How about your friend?"

"He may do as he likes."

"I know so little about cards—so very little," protested Frank. "What are you playing?"

"Poker."

He shook his head.

"I have played euchre," he said.

"Quite a difference in the games," laughed a man. "I suppose you have played old maid, also?"

"Yes," answered Merry innocently, "I have. Do you play that?"

"He'll spoil your game, fellows," laughed Morton quickly.

"How do you know I would?" exclaimed Merry resentfully.

"Reckon Hugh is right, Mr. Merriwell," laughed the one who had invited Frank. "You had better keep out of the game."

Fred Darleton was playing at one of the tables. He regarded Frank with a sneer on his face.

"An innocent stiff," he commented, in a low tone. "They say he never takes a drink, never swears, never does anything naughty."

"He's rather naughty at fencing," reminded a man jokingly; but Darleton saw nothing to laugh at in the remark.

Morton was heard informing Merry that he must not ask questions about the game while play was in progress, as by so doing he might seem to give away some player's hand.

"Oh, I can keep still," assured Frank smilingly. "I've seen them play poker before."

"No one would ever suspect it," sneered Darleton under his breath.

This fellow was wearing dark-colored glasses, after his usual custom.

Merry found an opportunity to inspect the lights. While they were sufficiently bright for all purposes, they were shaded in such a manner that Darleton's excuse for wearing smoked glasses seemed a paltry one.

"His real reason is not because the lights hurt his eyes," decided Frank.

What was the fellow's real reason? Merriwell hoped to discover before the evening was over. He seemed to take interest in the play first at one table and then at another, but finally settled on the one at which Darleton was seated.

As usual, Darleton was winning. He had a lot of chips stacked up before him.

"Why did you drop your hand after opening that last jack pot, Darleton?" inquired one of the players.

"Because I was satisfied that you had me beaten," was the answer.

"You had two pairs to open on, and you drew only one card."

"What of that?"

"I took three cards."

"I remember."

"Well, you wouldn't bet your two pairs, and I raked in the pot. How did it happen?"

"I decided that you bettered your hand. My pairs were small."

"I did better my hand," confessed the man; "but I swear you have a queer method of playing poker! I don't understand it."

"My method suits me," laughed Darleton, fingering his chips.

"It is a successful one, all right; but I never lay down two pairs after opening a jack pot, especially if the only player who stays in with me draws three cards."

"You lose oftener than I do."

"No question about that."

"Then my judgment must be better than yours. Let it go at that."

Frank had listened to all this, and he, likewise, was puzzled to understand why Darleton had decided not to risk a bet after the draw. It happened that Merry had stood where he could look into the other man's hand. The man held up a pair of kings on the deal and drew another king when cards were given out. His three kings were better than Darleton's two pairs; but Darleton knew he had the man beaten before the draw. How did he come to believe the man had him beaten after the draw?

Frank found an opportunity to look round for mirrors. There were none in the room.

Darleton was not working with an accomplice who could look into the other man's hand. Merry was the only person able to see the man's cards as he picked them up.

"I don't believe he'll suspect me of being Darleton's accomplice," thought Frank.

This was only one of the things which increased the mystery of Darleton's playing. The fellow seemed to know exactly when to bet a hand for all it was worth, and once he persisted in raising a player who was bluffing recklessly. Finally the bluffer became angry and called.

"I have a pair of seven spots, Darleton? What have you got? I don't believe you have much of anything."

"Why, I have a pair of ten spots, and they win," was the smiling retort.

"Bluffers, both of you!" cried another player. "But I swear this is the first time I've ever known Darleton to bluff at poker. And he got away with it on a show-down!"

The entire party regarded Darleton with wonderment, but the winner simply smiled a bit behind his dark goggles.

Morton glanced swiftly at Frank, as if to say: "You see how it goes, but you can't make anything of it."

Merriwell was perplexed, but this perplexity served as a spur to urge him forward in his desire to solve the mystery. For mystery about Darleton's success there certainly seemed to be.

With an inquiring and searching mind, Merry was one who disliked to be baffled by anything in the form of mystery that might be legitimately investigated. A mystery amid common things and common events aroused him to insistent investigation, for he knew there should be no mystery, and that which was baffling should, in case it was natural, eventually develop to be simple indeed.

He now felt himself fully aroused, for he did not believe it possible that by any occult power or discernment Darleton was capable of reading the minds of his companions at the card table and thus learning when to drop two pairs and when to bet one very ordinary pair to a finish.

"The cards must be marked," decided Frank.

At this juncture the player who had called Darleton asked for a fresh pack.

Merry saw the cards brought in by a colored boy. They were still sealed. He saw the seal broken, the joker removed from the pack, the cards shuffled, cut, and dealt.

"Now we'll note if Darleton continues to win," thought Merry.

He knew the fresh pack could not be marked. They were sealed, just as purchased from the dealer, when thrown on the table.

Morton spoke to Frank.

"Are you getting tired?" he asked.

"Oh, no," was the immediate reply. "I am enjoying watching this game. I have nothing else to do to-night."

Hugh pushed along a chair, and urged Merry to sit down. Frank accepted the chair. Without appearing to do so, he continued to watch Darleton.

Morton leaned on the back of Frank's chair.

"Have they ever looked for marked cards after playing with Darleton?" asked Frank, in such a low tone that no one save Hugh could hear and understand him.

"Frequently."

"Never found them marked?"

"Never. They are not marked. I fancied you might think they were. We've had experts, regular card sharps, examine packs used in games when he has won heavily."

Still Merry was not satisfied on this point.

"If they are not marked," he thought, "Darleton must have an accomplice who gives him tips. The latter seems utterly impossible, and, therefore, the cards must be marked."

Occasionally Darleton glanced at Merriwell, but every time it seemed that Frank was giving him no attention at all.

Yet every move on the part of the successful player was watched by the young man who had resolved to solve the mystery.

For some time after the appearance of the fresh pack of cards Darleton did little betting. Still he seemed to examine each hand dealt him, and his manner of examining the hands was very critical, as if weighing their value. The cards interested him greatly, although he did not bet.

"Your luck has turned," cried one of the players. "You haven't done a thing since the fresh pack was brought."

"Oh, I'll get after you again directly," smiled Darleton. "I'm waiting for the psychological moment, that's all."

Frank noted that the fellow frequently put his hand into the side pocket of his coat. Although he did this, he did not seem to take anything out of that pocket. Still, after a while, the watcher began to fancy these careless, but often repeated movements had something to do with the mystery.

At last, Darleton seemed to get a hand to his liking. It was on his own deal, and two other players held good hands, one a straight and the other a flush.

When Darleton was finally called he exhibited a full hand and raked in the money.

"You see!" muttered Morton, in Merry's ear.

"No, I don't see," admitted Frank; "but I mean to."

Morton was growing tired. He yawned, straightened up and sauntered about.

Frank rose, stretched himself a little, looked on at another table a few moments, and finally brought himself to a position behind Darleton's chair without attracting Darleton's attention.

From this point he once more began to watch the playing in which he was so keenly interested.

Morton observed this change, but said nothing, although to him it seemed like wasted time on Frank's part.

From his new position Merriwell was able to see into Darleton's hands, and the style of play followed by the fellow surprised him even more. At the very outset he saw Darleton drop two pairs, kings up, without attempting to bet them and without even showing them to any one. In the end it developed that another player held winning cards, having three five spots; but this player had drawn three cards, and before the betting began there seemed nothing to indicate that he could beat kings up.

On the very next hand something still more remarkable happened. The first man after the age stayed in and all the others remained. Observing Darleton's cards, Merry saw he held the deuce, six, seven, and king of diamonds and the seven of spades. He split his pair, casting aside the seven of spades, and drew to the four diamonds.

The card that came in was the ace of diamonds, giving him an ace-high flush.

Two of the other players took two cards each; but Merry decided that one of them was holding up a "kicker"—that is, an odd card with his pair. This estimation of his hand Frank formed from the fact that the man had not raised the original bettor before the draw, although sitting in a fine position to do so. Had the man held threes he would have raised. It was likely he had a small pair and an ace, and also that he knew the style of play of the original bettor and believed this person was likewise holding a "kicker," probably for the purpose of leading the other players into fancying he had threes.

This being the case, Darleton's ace-high was a fancy hand and would be almost certain to rake down the pot.

Even supposing it possible that both players who called for two cards held three of a kind, it was not, in the natural run of the game, at all likely they had improved their hands.

Still when the original bettor tossed four blue chips into the pot and one of the others called, Darleton dropped his handsome flush, declining to come in and, remarking:

"I didn't catch."

He lied, for he had "caught" and filled a flush.

What was his object in lying?

A moment later the original bettor lay down three jacks and a pair of nine spots.

The hand was superior to Darleton's flush.

Beyond question Darleton knew he was beaten, and therefore he chose to pretend he had not filled his hand.

But how did he know?

CHAPTER IX

THE TRICK EXPOSED.

he cards must be marked!" was the thought that again flashed through Frank Merriwell's mind.

But if they were marked and it was impossible to detect the fact, there was no way of exposing the crooked player. If they were marked, however, Merry believed there must be some way of detecting it.

Frank kept very still. Slipping his hand into an inner pocket, he brought forth something he had purchased that very afternoon, after talking with Morton concerning Darleton's success at poker and his methods. Quietly he adjusted his purchase to the bridge of his nose.

He had bought a pair of smoked glass goggles!

The cards were being shuffled. The goggles changed the aspect of the room, causing everything to look dim and dusky.

The man who was dealing tossed the cards round to the different players. As this was being done, Frank detected something hitherto unseen upon the cards.

On the backs of many of them were strange luminous designs, crosses, spots, circles, and straight lines. These marks could be distinctly seen with the aid of the smoked glasses.

Lifting his hand, Merry raised the glasses.

The glowing marks vanished! A feeling of satisfaction shot through the discoverer.

"I have him!" he mentally exclaimed. "I have detected his clever little trick!"

It happened that Darleton received a pair of jacks and a pair of sixes on the deal.

One of the players "stayed" and Darleton "came up."

On the draw Darleton caught another six spot, giving him a full hand.

He seemed to be looking at his cards intently, but Frank observed that he had watched every card as it was dealt.

In the betting that followed Darleton pressed it every time. At the call he displayed the winning hand.

But just as he reached to pull in the chips his wrist was clutched by a grip of iron.

Frank Merriwell had grasped and checked him.

"Gentlemen," cried Merry, "you are playing with a crook! You are being cheated!"

Instantly there was a great stir in the room. Men sprang up from their chairs.

Darleton uttered an exclamation of fury.

"What do you mean, you duffer?" he snarled. "Let go!"

Instead of obeying, Merry pinned him fast in his chair, so he could not move.

"Yes, what do you mean?" shouted one of Darleton's friends, leaping from another table and endeavoring to reach Frank. "Let go, or I'll——"

Hugh Morton grappled with the fellow.

"I wouldn't do anything if I were you," he said. "Take it easy, Higgins. We'll find out what he means in a minute."

"Find out!" roared Higgins. "You bet! He'll get all that's coming to him for this!"

"Explain yourself, Mr. Merriwell," urged one of the players. "This is a very grave charge. If you cannot substantiate it——"

"I can, sir."

"Do so at once."

"These cards are marked."

"It's a lie!" raged Darleton.

"You must prove that the cards are marked, Mr. Merriwell," said another player. "They were but lately unsealed, and it seems impossible."

"They have been marked since they were opened."

"How?"

"With the aid of luminous marking fluid of some sort, carried in this man's pocket. I have watched him marking them."

"Liar!" came from the fellow accused; but he choked over the word, and he was white to the lips, for he had discovered that Merry was wearing smoked goggles, like his own.

"Let me get at him!" panted Darleton's friend; but Morton continued, with the assistance of another man, to hold the fellow in check.

"Under ordinary conditions," said Frank coolly, "the marking cannot be detected. Mr. Darleton has pretended it was necessary for him to wear dark-colored goggles in order to protect his eyes from the lights. Why didn't he play in the daytime? Because he would then have no excuse for using the goggles, which he does not wear as a rule. With the aid of the goggles he is able to see and understand the marking on the backs of the cards. This makes it possible for him to tell what every man round the table holds. No wonder he knows when to bet and when to drop his cards!"

"It's false!" muttered the accused weakly.

"If any one doubts that I speak the truth," said Merry, "let him feel in Mr. Darleton's coat pocket on the right-hand side."

A man did so at once, bringing forth a little, tin box, minus the lid, which contained a yellowish, paste-like substance.

"That is the luminous paint," said Frank.

"Further doubts will be settled by taking my goggles, with which I detected the fraud, and examining the backs of the cards."

He handed the goggles over, releasing his hold on Darleton, who seemed for the moment incapable of action.

The excited players tried the goggles and examined the cards, one after another. All saw the marks distinctly with the aid of the smoke-colored glasses. They discovered that the four aces were marked, each card with a single dot, the kings bore two dots, the queens three dots and the jacks four dots. The ten spot was indicated by a cross, the nine spot showed two crosses, the eight a straight line, the seven two parallel lines, the six a circle, and there the marking stopped. Evidently Darleton had not found time to finish his work on the remainder of the pack.

And now Darleton found himself regarded with intense indignation and disgust by all save the fellow who had attempted to come to his aid. Indeed, the indignation of the men was such that they threatened personal violence to the exposed rascal.

It seemed that the fellow would not escape from the room without being handled roughly. Before the outburst of indignation, his bravado and nerve wilted, and he became very humble and apprehensive.

No wonder he was alarmed for his own safety. Several of those present had lost heavily to him, and they demanded satisfaction of some sort.

"He has skinned me out of hundreds!" snarled one man. "I'll take it out of his hide! I'll break every bone in his dishonest body!"

Two men placed themselves before the infuriated one and tried to reason with him.

"What are you going to do?" he shouted. "Are you going to let him off without doing anything?"

"We'll make him fork over what he has won to-night."

"Little satisfaction that will be!"

"We'll find how much money he has on his person and make him give that up."

"That doesn't satisfy me!"

"Then we'll expel him in disgrace from the club."

"That sounds better, but it isn't enough. Just step out of the room, all of you, and leave him to me. While you're outside, you had better call an ambulance for him."

"I warn you not to offer me personal violence," said Darleton, his lips quivering and his voice unsteady.

"You warn us, you cur!" snarled one, shaking his fist under the rascal's nose. "Why, do you know what you deserve and what you would get in some places? You deserve to be lynched! There was a time in this town when you would have been shot."

Frank stood back and let matters take their course. He had done his part, and he felt that he had done well in exposing the scoundrel. It was not for him to say how the man should be dealt with by the club.

Darleton drew forth a pocketbook and flung it on the table.

"There's my money," he said. "Go ahead and take it."

"You bet we will!" was the instant response.

The money was taken and divided before his eyes.

Then the men of cooler judgment prevailed over their more excitable companions, whom they persuaded to let Darleton depart in disgrace.

The fellow was only too glad to get off in that manner, and he hastily slunk to the door.

There he paused and looked around. His eyes met those of Frank Merriwell, and the look he gave was pregnant with malignant hatred of the most murderous nature.

The Midwestern lost little time in calling a meeting for the purpose of considering Darleton's case. In short order the fellow was declared expelled in disgrace from the organization. Following this, it was agreed that Frank Merriwell should be tendered a vote of thanks for his service to the club.

The outcome of the affair gave all of Merry's friends a feeling of satisfaction, for they believed that the scoundrel had received his just deserts.

Bart Hodge expressed a feeling of intense regret because he had not been present to witness Darleton's humiliation.

"I sized him up at the start," declared Bart. "I knew he was a crook, and I knew no crook could defeat Merry."

That afternoon Frank came face to face with Darleton in front of the post office. The fellow stopped short, the glare of a panther that has been wounded leaping into his eyes.

"You—you—you meddling dog!" he panted huskily.

Frank would have passed on without speaking, but the rascal stepped before him.

"Kindly stand aside," said Merry. "I don't wish to soil my hands on you."

"Oh, you're very fine and lofty! You think you have done a grand thing in putting this disgrace on me, I suppose."

"I'm not at all proud of it; but I did my duty."

"Your duty! Bah!"

"It is the duty of any man to expose a rascal when he can do so."

"Bah! You did not do that from a sense of duty, but to win applause and lead people to think you very cunning and clever. You're a notoriety seeker."

"I don't care to waste words with you."

"You have ruined my good name!"

"You ruined it yourself by your crookedness. Don't try to put the blame on me."

"You did it!" panted Darleton; "but you shall suffer for it!"

"If you make too many threats, I'll call a policeman and turn you over to him."

"No doubt of it! That's the way you'll try to hide behind a bluecoat! You're a coward, Frank Merriwell!"

"Your opinion of me does not disturb me in the least, sir."

"I'll disturb you before I am through with you! You have ruined me; but I'll square it!"

"I don't care to be seen talking with you."

"One moment more. I'll have my say! You triumphed and gloated over me when I was humbled at the club."

"I never gloat over the fallen."

"Oh, you are very fine and lofty in sentiment! You try to make people believe you are a goody-goody. You play a part, and play it well enough to deceive most persons; but I'll wager there are spots in your career that will not bear investigation. If some of your admirers knew all about you they would turn from you in disgust. I've seen chaps like you before, and they're always disgusting, for they are always hypocrites. You pretend that you do not play cards! How was it that you were clever enough to detect my methods? You claim you do not drink, but I'll bet my life you do drink on the sly.

"You seem to have no vices, but no chap travels about as you do and keeps free from little vices. Small vices make men more manly. The fellow who has no vices is either cold-blooded or more than human. If I had time I'd follow you up and expose you. Then I'd strike you as you have struck me. But I haven't the time. Still you needn't think you're going to get off. I'll strike just the same, and I'll strike you good and sufficient! When I land you'll know it, and I'll land in a hurry.

"That's all. I don't care to say anything more. I have some friends who will stick to me. Don't fancy for a moment that I am friendless. I'll see you again. If you get frightened and hike out of Omaha, I'll follow. I'll follow until I get my opportunity!"

Having expressed himself in this manner, he stepped aside and walked swiftly away.

"He's the sort of chap to strike at an enemy's back," thought Merry.

That evening Frank took dinner with Morton at the latter's home. He met Hugh's mother and sister, and found them refined and pleasant people. After dinner he remained for two hours or more, chatting with them and enjoying himself.

Kate Morton was a cultured girl, having attended college in the East. She talked of books, music, and art, yet she was not stilted and conventional in her conversation, and she proved that she had thoughts and ideas of her own.

When he finally arose to leave, Merry felt that he had passed a most agreeable and profitable evening. He had met a girl who thought of something besides dress, society, and frivolity, yet who must appear at advantage in the very best society, and who undoubtedly enjoyed the pastimes which most girls enjoy.

Hugh was inclined to accompany Frank, but Merry dissuaded him, saying he would catch a car at the first corner and ride within a block of the hotel.

Merriwell whistled as he sauntered along the street. His first warning of danger was when he heard a rustle close behind his back. Before he could turn something smote him down.

CHAPTER X

STEEL MEETS STEEL.

Here we are," said a low voice.

The hack had stopped. Several persons sprang down from the top. The door was flung open and others issued from within.

"Drag him out."

At this command a helpless figure was pulled forth.

The night was dark and the place the outskirts of the city of Omaha. Near at hand rose the black hulk of a silent and apparently deserted building.

"All right, driver."

The door of the hack slammed, the driver whipped up his horses, and the men were left with the helpless one in their midst.

"Make him walk," said the first speaker. "He's conscious, for he tried to get his hands free inside."

They moved, forcing along their captive. Close up to the wall to the wall of the building they halted.

"Have you the key?" asked one.

"Yes; here it is."

"Open the door. Hurry up. The watchman may see us, and it will be all off."

"That's right," put in another. "You know somebody tried to burn this place a week ago."

Soon the man with the key opened a door and the captive was pushed into the building. Every man followed, and the door was closed.

Ten minutes later all were assembled in a bare room of the old building. One of them had brought a number of torches, which were now lighted. The light showed that there were ten of them in all, and with the exception of the captive, whose hands were tied behind his back and whose jaws were distended by a gag, they wore masks which effectually concealed their features.

The captive was Frank Merriwell.

One of the men stepped before Frank.

"Well, how do you like it?" he asked tauntingly. "What do you think is going to happen to you?"

It was impossible for Merry to reply.

"Remove that gag," directed the taunting chap. "Let him talk. Let him yell, if he wants to. No one can hear him now."

The mask was removed from between Frank's teeth.

"Thank you," said Merry, after a moment. "That's a great relief to my jaws."

"Oh, it hurt you, did it?" sneered the taunting fellow. "Well, you may get hurt worse than that before the night is over."

"I suppose you contemplate murdering me, Darleton," said Frank, his voice steady.

Immediately the other snatched off his mask, exposing the face of Fred Darleton.

"I'm willing you should know me," he said. "You do not know any of the others."

"I am quite confident that your chum, Grant Hardy, is one of them."

"You can't pick him out. You couldn't swear to it."

"If you put me out of the way, like the brave men you are, I'll not be able to swear to anything."

"Oh, we're not going to murder you, you fool!"

"You surprise me!"

"But I have had you brought here in order that I may square my account with you."

"In what manner? Are you going to mutilate me?"

"I may carve you up some before I am through with you. You think you are a great fencer, but I am satisfied that you are a coward. If you were forced to fight for your life you would show the white feather."

"Do you think so?"

"I know it."

"Give me half an opportunity."

"I will, and you shall fight me!" cried Darleton viciously. "You did some very fancy work on exhibition. Now you can show what you're capable of doing when your handsome body is at stake."

"What do you mean?"

Darleton turned to his companion.

"Where are the rapiers?" he asked.

One of the masked men held out something wrapped in a black

cloth.

"Here they are."

"All right. Set him free. He can't get away. Release his hands."

A moment later Frank's hands were freed.

"Strip down for business, Merriwell," commanded Darleton, flinging aside his coat and vest and removing his collar. "You are going to fight me with rapiers."

"A genuine duel?" asked Merry.

"That's what it will be."

Frank did not hesitate. He flung aside his coat and vest, removed his collar and necktie, and rolled back the shirt sleeve of his right arm.

The readiness with which he accepted the situation and prepared for business, surprised some of the masked men.

Before long Darleton and Frank were ready.

In the meantime, the cloth had been removed from the rapiers, revealing two long, glittering weapons.

"Give him the choice," cried Darleton, with a flourish.

The man with the weapons stepped forward, holding them by the blades and having them crossed. Frank accepted the first that came to his hand. His enemy took the other.

"On guard!" cried Darleton savagely; "on guard, and defend your life!"

Steel met steel with a deadly click.

There was no fooling about that encounter. From the very start it was deadly and thrilling in its every aspect. The duelists went at it keyed to the highest tension.

Merry saw a deadly purpose in Fred Darleton's eyes, and he knew the fellow longed to run him through.

On the other hand, only as a last resort to save himself did Frank wish to seriously wound his enemy.

Aroused by his fancied wrongs, Darleton handled the rapier with consummate skill. He watched for an opening, and he was ready to take advantage of the slightest mistake on the part of his opponent.

The torches flared and smoked, casting a weird glow over the scene. The fighters advanced and retreated. The rapiers glinted and flashed.

"Do your best, Merriwell!" hissed Darleton.

Frank was kept busy meeting the swiftly shifting attacks of the fellow, who was seeking to confuse him.

"I know your style," declared the vengeful chap. "You can't work the tricks you played on me at the Midwestern. Try any of them—try them all!"

Frank made no retort. He was watching for a chance to try quite a different trick.

Suddenly the opening came. He closed in. The rapiers slipped past until hilt met hilt. With a snapping twist Frank tore the weapon from the fingers of his foe and sent it spinning aside.

Darleton was at Merry's mercy. Frank had been forced into this engagement in a way that made it something entirely different from an ordinary affair of honor. He was surrounded by enemies. No friends were present. He could have ended Fred Darleton's life with a single stroke.

Instead of that, he stepped quickly aside, picked up the rapier and offered it to his foe, hilt first.

Chagrined by what had happened, Darleton snatched it and made a quick thrust at Merry's throat.

By a backward spring, Merry escaped being killed.

Instantly a wonderful change came over Frank. He closed in and became the assailant. Twice he thrust for Darleton. He was parried, but he guarded instantly and prevented the fellow from securing a riposte.

Merry's third attempt was more successful.

He caught Darleton in the shoulder and inflicted a superficial but somewhat painful wound.

Exclamations came from the masked witnesses.

Infuriated by his poor success and the wound, Darleton threw caution to the winds and sailed into Merry like a tornado.

"It's your life or mine!" he panted, as he made a vicious thrust at Frank's heart.

The thrust was turned.

Then a cry of horror broke from the spectators, for Frank seemed to have run his antagonist clean through the body.

Darleton fell. One of the masked men, who seemed to be a surgeon, knelt at once to examine the wound.

"I'm sorry," said Frank grimly; "but I call on you all to bear witness that he forced me to it. As he said, it was his life or mine."

The following day Frank visited Darleton in the hospital whither the unfortunate fellow had been taken. The wounded man's injury had been pronounced very serious, but not necessarily fatal. The course of the steel had been changed by a rib, and only Darleton's right side had been pierced.

The moment they were left alone, Darleton said:

"You did the trick, Merriwell. I didn't believe you could, but you were justified in defending yourself. I made every man there take a solemn oath that he would keep silent no matter what happened."

"I have been expecting and waiting for arrest," said Frank. "I supposed you would have me arrested."

"You're wrong. You'll never be arrested for this affair unless you go to the police and peach on yourself. They say I'll get well, all right. I want to. Do you know what I mean to do?"

"No."

"I'm going to practice until I can defeat you with the rapiers, if it takes me years. When I am confident that I can do the trick, I'm going to find you, force you to fight again and kill you. It would be no satisfaction to me to see you arrested for last night's work. Unless you're a fool, you'll not be arrested. If you were arrested and told the truth, you could not be punished for defending yourself."

"That's the way I feel about it," said Frank; "but I regret that you still thirst for my blood. I came here to find out if there is anything I can do for you."

"I wouldn't take a favor from you for worlds. I know I'm in the wrong, but that makes me hate you none the less. Go now. But expect to face me again some day and fight for your life."

And thus they parted, still deadly enemies, much to Frank's regret, for, in spite of Darleton's dishonesty, there was a certain something in the make-up of the man that had won for him a feeling of sympathy in Merry's heart. More than that, the courage displayed by Darleton in the duel caused Frank to think of him in a light of mingled admiration and regret. Although a scoundrel, not all the elements of his nature were unworthy.

CHAPTER XI

THE RECEPTION AT CARTERSVILLE.

he town of Cartersville is situated in the southern part of the State of Iowa. This was the first stop Frank and his party made after leaving Omaha. Their first view of the town was not particularly inviting, as the railway station, after the disagreeable habit of nearly all railway stations, was situated in the most unsightly and forbidding portion of the place. In the immediate vicinity were unpainted, ramshackle buildings, saloons, cheap stores and hovel-like houses. In front of the saloons and stores lounged a few slovenly, ambition-lacking loafers, while slatternly women and dirty children were seen in the doorways or leaning from the open windows of the wretched houses.

On the station platform had gathered the usual crowd, including those who came to the train from necessity and those drawn thither by curiosity. There was also a surprisingly large gathering of boys of various ages, from six to eighteen.

Frank walked briskly along to the baggage car and noted that the baggage belonging to his party was put off there. Then he glanced around, as if in search of some one.

"I wonder where Mr. Gaddis is?" he said. "He was to meet us at the station."

A big, hulking six-footer, with ham-like hands and a thick neck, stepped forward from the van of a mixed crowd of about twenty tough-looking young fellows who had flocked down the platform behind Merry and his party.

"Are you Frank Merriwell?" asked the huge chap, who was about twenty years old, as he held the butt of a half-smoked cheroot in the corner of his capacious mouth.

"Yes, sir," answered Merry promptly. "Do you represent Joseph Gaddis?"

"I should say not!" was the retort. "Not by a blame sight."

"I thought not," said Frank.

"Oh, ye did? What made ye think not, hey?"

"You are not just the sort of man I expected to meet. Do you know Mr. Gaddis?"

"Do I? Some!"

"Isn't he here?"

"I reckon not."

"Where is he?"

"Ask me!"

Although the manner of the big fellow was openly insolent, Merry did not seem to notice it.

The motley crowd accompanying this man were grinning or scowling at Merriwell and his friends, while some of them made half-audible comments of an unflattering sort. They were tall, short, stout, and thin, but one and all they carried the atmosphere of tough characters.

"It's rather odd, Bart," said Frank, speaking to Hodge, who was surveying the crowd with dark disapproval, "that Gaddis should fail to keep his appointment to meet us here."

"No it ain't odd," contradicted the big chap. "He knowed better than to be here. You made some sort of arrangement with him to play a game of baseball in this town, didn't ye?"

"Yes."

"Well, fergit it."

"What do you mean?"

"Fergit it. You'll be wastin' a whole lot of time if you stop here, an' you'll put yourselves to a heap of inconvenience. You won't play no baseball with Gaddis' team, so you'd better hop right back onter the train and continue your ride."

Merry now surveyed the speaker from his head to his feet.

"I happen to have a contract with Mr. Gaddis," he said. "How is it that you have so much authority? Who are you?"

"I'm Mat Madison, and I happen to know what I'm talkin' about. Joe Gaddis has changed his mind about playin' baseball with you. He ain't goin' to play baseball no more this season."

"Did he send you here to tell me this?" demanded Frank, his eyes beginning to gleam with an ominous light.

"No, he didn't send me; I come myself."

"Then you haven't any real authority."

"Is that so! You bet I have! I'm giving it to you on the level when I say you won't play no baseball game in Cartersville, and the wisest thing you can do is to step right back onter this train and

61

git out. In short, I'm here to see that you do git back onter the train, and I brought my backers. If you don't git we'll have to make ye git."

By this time Frank's friends were gathered at his back, ready for anything that might happen. They scented trouble, although they could not understand the cause of it.

"I have no idea of leaving Cartersville until I see Mr. Gaddis," said Merry, with cool determination. "If he fails to keep his agreement with me, I propose to collect one hundred and fifty dollars forfeit money."

"Oh, haw! haw! You do, do ye? Well, when you collect a hundred and fifty from Joe Gaddis you'll be bald-headed. There ain't no time for foolin'. The train will pull out pretty soon, so you want to hop right back onto it and go along. If you don't, I'll make you hop. Git that?"

"If you bother me I'll feel it my duty to make you regret your action. Get that?"

"Why, you thunderin' fool, you don't mean to fight, do ye? I'll knock the head off your shoulders!"

"I don't think you will."

"Then take this!"

As he snarled forth the words, Madison struck viciously at Frank's face with his right fist.

Merry ducked like a flash, at the same time throwing up his left hand and catching the fellow's wrist. With this hold, he gave a strong, sharp pull in the same direction that Madison had started, at the same time jerking the fellow's arm downward. While doing this, Merry stooped and thrust his right arm between the ruffian's legs, grasping Madison's right leg back of the knee. In this manner he brought the bruiser across his back and shoulders in such a way that the fellow had no time to recover and was losing his balance when Frank suddenly straightened up with a heaving surge.

To the amazement of Madison's friends, the fellow was sent flying through the air clear of the platform, striking the ground on his head and shoulders.

Merry calmly turned to look after the baggage, not giving his late assailant as much as a glance after the latter struck the ground.

Madison was somewhat stunned. He sat up, holding his hands to his head and looking bewildered. A number of his friends sprang from the platform and gathered around him.

The young toughs were astounded by the manner in which Merry had met Madison's assault. If before that they had contemplated an attack on Frank and his party, the sudden disposal of their leader caused them to falter and change their plan.

Hans Dunnerwurst chuckled as he looked after Madison.

"Maype you vill holdt that for a vile," he observed.

"There is something wrong about this business here in Carters-ville, fellows," said Frank; "but we'll find out what it is. If Gaddis squeals on his contract with me, I'm going to see if he cannot be compelled to pay the forfeit."

"That's business," nodded Hodge. "I'll wager he sent these thugs to frighten us away, so he wouldn't be compelled to pay the money. If we didn't stop, he could get out of it."

"Whereupon we'll linger," murmured Jack Ready.

"Somebody's gug-gug-going to fuf-fuf-find out we mean bub-bub-business!" stuttered Gamp.

"I opine one chap has found it out already," observed Buck Badger dryly.

"It must have been a shock to him," said Dade Morgan, a gleam of satisfaction in his dark eyes.

"Glad he tackled Frank," yawned Browning, with a wearied air. "I don't feel like exerting myself after that infernally uncomfort-able car ride."

"The gentleman experienced a taste of jutsuju—I mean jujutsu," laughed Harry Rattleton.

"Sorry Merry had to soil his hands on the big loafer," said Dick Starbright, taking off his hat and tossing back his mane of golden hair.

"It was a clever piece of business," admitted Jim Stretcher; "but two years ago, at a fair in Tipton, Missouri, I saw a little piece of business that——"

"Don't tell it—don't dare to tell it!" exclaimed Badger. "I'm from Kansas, and I'm sick of hearing these powerful extravagant tales about Missouri. If you mention Missouri in my hearing for the next three days you'll be in danger of sudden destruction. That's whatever!"

"You're jealous, and I don't blame you," said Jim. "If I lived in Kansas I'd never acknowledge it. It was the last place created, and made out of mighty poor material. Everybody in Kansas worth knowing has moved out."

"Which is a genuine Irish bull," said Morgan.

"All aboard," called the conductor.

A few moments later the train pulled out.

In the meantime, Mat Madison had recovered and regained his feet. The result of his attack on Merriwell had astonished him no less than it did his followers. Even after recovering from the shock he could not understand just what had happened to him, although he realized that, in some manner, he had been sent spinning through the air. It had dazed him. After regaining his feet he asked one of the young toughs what had happened.

"Why," was the answer, "he just grabbed you and throwed you, that's all."

"Oh, he throwed me, did he?" growled Madison, a vicious look on his face. "Well, I ruther think I'll throw him next time. He'll git all that's coming now!"

"That's right, Mad!" encouraged his followers. "You didn't hit him because he dodged. Go for him again. Grab him this time before he can grab you."

"Just watch me," advised the thug, as he sprang to the platform.

Without warning, Madison came quickly up behind Merry, throwing his arms round Frank, in this manner pinning the arms of the latter to his sides.

"Now I've got ye, burn your hide!" snarled the ruffian. "You worked a slick trick on me t'other time, but you can't do it aga——"

He did not finish; Frank gave him no further time for speech.

Down Merry dropped to one knee, causing the man's arms to slip up about his neck. Before Madison could get a strangle hold, even as he dropped to his knee, Frank caught the ruffian's right hand and twisted it outward, bringing the palm upward. With his other hand Frank secured a hold on Madison's wrist, and then he jerked downward, bending far forward.

Mat Madison's feet left the ground, his heels flew through the air and he went turning over Merry's head, landing flat on his back in front of the undisturbed young man.

The town toughs, who had fancied their leader had the stranger foul, were even more astonished than by Madison's first failure.

Merriwell rose to his feet, stood with his hands on his hips and regarded his fallen assailant with a pitying smile.

Frank's friends—the most of them—seemed amused over the affair, and either smiled broadly or laughed outright. Hodge and Morgan were the only ones who betrayed no mirth.

"Jee-roo-sa-lum!" cried one of the tough youngsters. "Did you see that, fellers?"

"How did he do it?" gasped another.

"Why, he throws Mad just as e-e-easy!"

"He's a slippery chap!"

"Slippery! He's quicker'n lightnin'!"

"Strong as a bull!"

"Full of slick tricks!"

The astonishment of Madison's friends was somewhat ludicrous. They had expected the bully to handle the clean, quiet young man with perfect ease, especially when he seemed to obtain such a great advantage by seizing Merry from the rear.

Madison's arm had been given a severe wrench, but the fellow rose quickly, not yet subdued or satisfied.

"I ain't done with ye," he snarled; "I ain't done yet!"

"That's unfortunate—for you," declared Frank, wholly undisturbed.

"I'll kill ye yet!"

"You frighten me."

But the tone of voice in which Merriwell spoke the words told he was not frightened in the least.

Madison was breathing heavily, his huge breast heaving, as he rose and confronted Frank. With his hands hanging at his sides, the young man who had twice taken a fall out of the bully seemed utterly off his guard and unable to defend himself quickly.

The thug stepped in, suddenly shooting out his left fist toward Merry's solar plexus, hoping to get in a knockout blow.

Merriwell sidestepped in a manner that caused the bruiser to miss entirely. With his right hand Frank caught the fellow's left wrist, giving the middle of his arm a sharp rap with the side of his left hand, thus causing it to bend. Instantly twisting the man's arm outward and bending it backward, Frank placed his left hand against Madison's elbow and pushed toward the thug's right side. In the meantime, Merry had placed his right foot squarely behind Madison's left. Madison found himself utterly unable to resist, and, almost before he realized that he was helpless, he was hurled over backward with great violence.

"Maype dot blatform vill lay sdill on you a vile," observed Dunnerwurst, as Madison fell with a terrible thud.

"Three times and out," murmured Jack Ready.

"It ain't no use!" exclaimed one of Madison's backers. "Mat can't do this chap on ther level. He's up against a better man."

Madison thought so, too. He was beginning to realize that he had encountered his master, although the thought filled him with rage he could not express. For some time he had been the bully of Cartersville, universally feared by the younger set of hoodlums, and in that period he had not encountered any one who could give him anything like an argument in a fight. He had expected to handle Merriwell with ease, and the ease with which he was defeated made the whole affair seem like an unreal and unpleasant dream. Furthermore, he knew that never after this would he be regarded with the same degree of respect and awe by the young ruffians of the town. Having seen him handled in such a simple manner by a calm, smiling stranger, they would never again look on him as invincible.

The encounter had been witnessed by others besides those immediately interested. Madison was well known and feared in Cartersville, and the loafers about the station, as well as those who had business there, saw him defeated for the first time in his career of terrorism. Although some of them rejoiced over it, yet nearly all were still too much awed by his record to express themselves.

The treatment he had received at the hands of Merriwell had wrenched and bruised the ruffian, whose arms and shoulders felt as if they had been twisted nearly out of their joints. The fellow got up slowly after the third fall.

Some fancied he would attempt to get at Merriwell again, but he had been checked and cowed most effectively. He stood beyond Frank's reach and glared, his face showing his fury, while his huge hands twitched convulsively.

The language that flowed from the lips of the ruffian was of a character to make any hearer shudder in case he possessed any degree of decency.

"That will do!" interrupted Merry sharply, the pleasant expression leaving his face. "Not another word of it! Close up instantly!"

"What if I don't?" demanded Madison.

"Then what you have received from me is a mere taste beside what you'll get," promised Frank.

Madison turned to his followers.

"What's the matter with you?" he snarled. "What made you stand round and see him do stunts with me? Why didn't you light on him, you muckers?"

"We were waiting and pining for them to make some such movement, gentle sir," observed Jack Ready.

"Yah!" cried Dunnerwurst. "Id vould haf peen very bleasing for us to seen id did."

"You told us you'd do ther whole thing when we came down to the station, Mad," reminded one of the gang.

"We was waitin' for ye to do it," said another grimly.

"Of vaiting you haf become tiredness," observed Hans. "You don'd blame me vor dot."

Madison started to pour forth vile language again, but Merry took a single step in his direction and he stopped, lifting his hands to defend himself.

"I don't care to touch you again," said Frank; "but if I hear two more words of that character from your lips I'll take another fall out of you."

"You're mighty brave now!" muttered the tough; "but I ain't done with ye. No man ever flung Mat Madison round like a bag of rags and didn't regret it. You'd been better off if you'd took my advice and left on that train. Now you can't leave before to-morrer, and I'm going to square up with you before you git away."

"I don't fancy your threats, any more than your vile language. I'll take neither from you. We came to this town to play baseball, and we propose to do so—or know the reason why."

"You won't play no baseball here, and don't you think ye will. That's all settled. There won't be no more baseball in this town as long as Joe Gaddis tries to run things."

"What's the matter with Gaddis?"

"You'll find out—mebbe. There ain't no baseball team here now."

"No ball team?"

"No."

"I don't believe that."

"It don't make no difference whether you believe it or not. You go ahead and investigate. Mebbe you'll have a good time stopping in Cartersville, but I don't think it."

"Oh, they'll have fun!" sneered one of the crowd.

"Carey Cameron will see about that."

"Shut up, Bilker!" snapped Madison. "You ain't to call no names."

"Who is Carey Cameron?" asked Merry promptly.

But no one would answer the question.

Madison turned away, after giving Merriwell another glaring look of hatred, and the young ruffians flocked after him.

"Well," said Merry, "that incident is closed for the present. Now we'll find a hotel and secure accommodations."

CHAPTER XII

TURNED DOWN.

It was not a difficult thing to find a hotel. Inquiry enabled them to reach the Hall House, which was the nearest public house after leaving the station. It was not a particularly inviting house on the outside, being sadly in need of paint. It was a frame building, standing on a corner, and a number of loafers were sitting about in front, smoking, chewing tobacco, and gossiping. They stared curiously at the boys.

Frank led the way into the office.

Two men, one in his shirt sleeves and the other looking like a countryman, were talking politics. They stopped and turned to look the strangers over.

"Where is the proprietor?" inquired Frank, as he stepped briskly up to the desk.

The man in his shirt sleeves drawled:

"What yer want o' him?"

"We want to put up here."

"Can't do it."

"Can't?"

"Nope."

"Why not?"

"I reckon you're ball players, ain't ye?"

"Yes, sir."

"This house don't accommerdate no ball players."

"But we are gentlemen, and we——"

"I tell you this house don't accommerdate no ball players. That ought to be plain ernough for ye. Go on about your business."

"This is a public house, isn't it?"

"Ye-ah."

"Well, I demand to see the proprietor."

"You're lookin' at him. Help yourself."

"Are you the proprietor?"

"You bet!"

"And you refuse to give us accommodations in your hotel?"

"You bet!"

"All right. Your only reason for doing so is because we are baseball players, is it?"

"I didn't say so," answered the man shrewdly.

"But you inferred it."

"Did I?"

"It sounded that way."

"Well, there may be a dozen other reasons, young feller. I've been in the hotel business ten years, an' you can't trap me. We ain't prepared to accommerdate ye. You didn't notify us you was comin', an' so we made no special preparations. Our help is short, there's a case of typhus fever in the house, my wife is down with the lumbago, and I'm some broke up myself with the chills. So you see there ain't no need to discuss the matter further. We can't take ye in. Good day. The Mansion House is up the street three squares."

"That inn did not appeal to my æsthetic sense of refinement, anyhow," observed Ready, as they filed out onto the street with their hand bags and grips. "It looked somewhat soiled and out of condition. The Mansion House seems far more alluring."

"I don't think much of being turned down in that manner," said Merry. "It is irritating."

The Mansion House proved to be a brick building near the centre of the business section of the place.

"I'm glad we were turned down back there," said Morgan. "This looks better to me."

"Yah, I pelief id does haf a petterment look," agreed Dunnerwurst. "I think we vill peen accommodationed mit superiority here."

The office was empty. They waited a few moments and no one appeared. Then Frank found a bell on the desk and rang it. After another period of waiting and a second ringing of the bell, a sleepy-eyed fat boy came in, dragging his feet and looking both tired and disturbed.

"Here, boy!" exclaimed Merry; "what's the matter with this place? We want to stop here."

"You'll ha-ve t-o s-ee Mr. Jones," declared the boy, drawling forth his words with a great effort.

"Who is Mr. Jones?"

"He's th-e pro-pri-e-tor."

"Well, where is he?"

"I do-n't kno-ow."

"Stick a pup-pup-pin into him and wa-wa-wake him up, Ready!" cried Joe Gamp.

"Do-n't yo-ou lar-a-rfe a-ut me-e-e!" said the fat boy, still in that weary drawl. "I do-n't li-ke to ha-ave a pi-un stu-ck in-to me-e-e."

Rattleton dropped on a chair and began to laugh.

"He cakes the take—no, takes the cake!" cried Harry. "He don't li-i-ike to ha-ave a pi-un stu-ck in-to he-e-e-um. Ha! ha! ha!"

"Do-n't yo-ou lar-r-rfe a-ut me-e-e!" said the fat boy resentfully.

"This is a fine hotel!" exploded Hodge.

Dunnerwurst waddled over to the fat boy.

"Look ad myseluf," he commanded. "We vish to pecome the jests uf the house."

"Guests, Hans," corrected Frank, laughing.

"Yah, so id vos I said id. Ve vant to pecome der jests uf der house. Der money we vill paid vor dot, und we haf id readiness. Now on yourseluf got a mofement und pring righdt avay quick der brobrietor. Id is our urchent objection to registrate righdt off before soon und to our rooms got assignments. Yah!"

"Why-y do-n't yo-ou ta-a-alk E-e-eng-lish?" inquired the fat boy.

"Vot?" squawled Hans excitedly. "Vot dit you hear me say? Vy don't Enklish talk me? Vot dit you caldt id? Dit you pelief I vos Irish talking alretty now? Chust you got a viggle on und pring der chentleman by der name of Chones vot this hodel runs."

He gave the fat boy a push, and the sleepy-eyed chap disappeared through the door by which he had entered, muttering:

"So-ome fo-o-olks are al-wus in a naw-ful hur-ry."

Five minutes later an undersized man with a reddish mustache came pudging into the room. He was smoking a huge, black cigar, which he held slanted upward in a comical manner. His hands were in his pockets.

"What do you fellers want?" he asked, in a voice like the yapping of a small dog.

"Are you Mr. Jones?" asked Merry.

"That's my name," yapped the little man.

"Well, my name is Frank Merriwell, and these are members of my baseball team. We would like to know your rates."

"Won't do ye any good to know."

"Why not?"

"My house is full, an' I can't accommodate ye."

"Oh, come!" exclaimed Frank; "we'll pay in advance."

"That don't make no difference. Can't take ye."

70

"We'll put up with accommodations of any sort."

"Ain't got any sort for ye. I tell ye the house is full an' runnin' over. That settles it."

"Where can we find accommodations in this town?"

"Can't say."

Frank was holding himself well in hand, although burning with indignation.

"We would like to know the meaning of this," he said. "Do the hotels in this town ever accommodate transient guests?"

"Certain they do."

"There are only two hotels here."

"That's correct."

"Well, we have applied to both, and neither will take us in. Where are we to go?"

"That ain't none o' my business, is it?" yapped the landlord. "If my place is full you can't force me to take ye in. Git out! I can't bother with ye."

Merriwell felt like making trouble, but knew it would do no good and might do a great deal of harm. He longed to talk straight to the insolent little man who snapped like a bad-natured dog; but that, too, he believed would be a mistake, and so he turned to his companions, saying:

"Come on, boys."

"Wait!" cried Bart Hodge, his dark eyes blazing—"wait until I tell this imitation of a real man a few things!"

Before Bart could express himself, however, Frank had him by the arm.

"Keep still, Hodge," he commanded, in a low tone of authority. "It will be a mistake. Come away quietly."

Although he felt like rebelling, Bart submitted in mute protest, giving Jones one contemptuous look, and they all left the Mansion House.

"Vasn't id a sadness to haf der coldt und empty vorld turned oudt indo us!" sobbed Hans Dunnerwurst, as they paused in front of the hotel.

Jack Ready sang:

I ain't got no reg'ler place that I can call my home,
I mark each back-yard gate as through this world I roam;
Portland, Maine, is just the same as sunny Tennessee,

And any old place that I hang up my hat is home, sweet home to me.

"Don'd dood id! Don'd dood id!" implored Dunnerwurst. "Id gifes me such a melancholery. I vish I vouldt be more thought-

71

lesss uf your feelings!"

Browning growled and grumbled.

"I'm mighty tired of this business!" he declared. "We're having a fine time playing baseball in this town! I'm sick of this baseball business, anyhow. It's too much trouble. There's always something doing. I'm going to swear off and never play the game any more."

Dick Starbright laughed and slapped Bruce on the shoulder.

"You're a great bluffer, old chap," he said. "You've been swearing off ever since I knew you, but I'll bet you'll stick to the game until you weigh three hundred pounds."

"When I reach the three-hundred-pound mark I'm going to commit suicide."

"Then you haven't long to live."

Frank stepped out and spoke to a man who was passing, inquiring about boarding houses. The man was rather surly, but he told Merry of a house kept by Mrs. Walker, and soon the party was on the way thither.

Mrs. Walker's house proved to be a long, rambling, frame building, about which hovered an atmosphere of poverty. They were met at the door by a sharp-nosed, belligerent-appearing woman, who placed her hands on her hips and demanded to know who they were and what they wanted.

Removing his hat and bowing low with grace and politeness, Merry explained that they were looking for a place to stop overnight, at least, and he hastened to add that they were willing to pay in advance, emphasizing this statement by producing a roll of bills.

The eyes of the woman glittered as she saw the money.

"Are you baseball players?" she inquired.

Merry confessed that they were, whereupon she shook her head with an air of regret.

"Then I can't have anything to do with ye," she declared.

"What difference does that make, if we are quiet and gentlemanly and pay our bills in advance?" inquired Merriwell.

"It makes a heap of difference. I can't take ye in."

"I wish you would be kind enough to give a satisfactory reason for refusing us, madam."

"I ain't giving any reasons, and I ain't talking too much. You can't stop here."

"Not if we pay double rates for transients and pay in advance, Mrs. Walker?"

"Not if you pay ten times regler rates and pay in advance," was the grim answer. "I judge that's plain enough for you."

"It's plain enough, but still we cannot understand your reasons. I wish you would——"

"It ain't any use making further talk. You've got my answer, and that settles it."

Saying which, she retreated into the house and slammed the door in their faces.

"I'm so lonesome, oh, I'm so lonesome!" sang Jack Ready. "Children, we are cast adrift in the cold and cruel world. We are stranded in the wilds of Iowa, far from home and kindred. Permit me to shed a few briny tears."

"This thing is getting me blazing mad!" grated Bart Hodge. "What do you think about it, Merry?"

"There seems to exist a peculiar prejudice against baseball teams in this town," said Frank.

"This makes me think of a little experience of mine in Missouri two years ago," began Stretcher.

But Buck Badger suddenly placed a clenched fist right under Jim's nose, which caused the boy from Missouri to dodge backward, exclaiming:

"I beg your pardon! I'll tell you about that some other time."

"What can we do?" exclaimed Morgan. "We seem to be up against it."

"Perhaps we can get into a private house somewhere if we pay enough," suggested Rattleton. "I'm willing to doff the coe—I mean cough the dough."

"We'll have to try it," said Frank.

They did try it, with the result that they were promptly refused at three houses, although Merry resorted to all the diplomacy at his command.

They turned back into the main part of the town.

"What will you do now, Frank?" asked Morgan.

"I'm going to try to get track of Mr. Joseph Gaddis," answered Merriwell grimly. "When I do——"

The manner in which he paused and failed to complete the sentence was very expressive.

"I don't blame you!" cried Hodge. "Mr. Gaddis must explain why we have been treated in this outrageous manner. He agreed to meet us at the station and have accommodations for us at the best hotel in town. He has broken his contract, and I'd like to break his face!"

"That wouldn't help matters much, Bart."

"But it would relieve my feelings in a wonderful manner."

"There is something behind this affair that we do not understand," said Merry. "In order to understand it we'll have to learn the facts."

"You're sure Gaddis was in earnest when he made that contract with you in Omaha?" questioned Rattleton.

"If ever I saw a man who seemed to be in earnest, Mr. Gaddis was such a man. He witnessed our great seventeen-inning game with the Nebraska Indians and lost no time after that in seeking to arrange a game with us to be played here. Stated that his team had beaten the Indians twice out of three times last season, and Green, the manager of the Indians, acknowledged that it was so. The inducements offered were satisfactory. We could reach this town without going out of our way on the trip East, and I finally made a contract with him. Here we are."

"And where, oh! where is Gaddis?" sighed Ready.

Reaching the main street of the town, they entered a drug store and inquired for Mr. Gaddis. The druggist looked them over in a peculiar manner. He knew Gaddis very well, he said. Gaddis was out of town. Left suddenly that very morning for Des Moines.

At this moment a handsome open carriage, in which sat a woman heavily veiled, drew up before the door. The lady waited until the druggist's clerk stepped out to see what she wanted. A moment later the clerk re-entered the store and asked if Mr. Merriwell was there.

"That is my name," said Frank.

"The lady in the carriage wishes to speak to you," said the clerk.

"What's this? what's this?" muttered Jack Ready. "How could she miss me? My ravishing beauty should have appealed to her. I am fast coming to the conclusion that beauty like mine is a decided disadvantage. It awes the fair sex."

Wondering who the unknown woman could be and what she wanted, Merry left the store.

"Are you Mr. Merriwell?" inquired the woman, as Frank stepped up to the carriage and lifted his hat.

"I am—miss."

He had quickly decided that she was young, and diplomacy led him in his uncertainty to address her as miss instead of madam.

Her veil was so heavy that it was absolutely baffling, permitting him to obtain no view of her features that would give him a conception of her looks. Her voice was musical and low and filled with strange, sweet sadness.

There was about her an air of mystery that struck Frank at once.

"I believe you are looking for some place to stop while in town?"

she observed questioningly.

"That is quite true, and thus far I have looked in vain."

"It is a shame that a stranger here should be treated thus. The hotels have declined to take you in?"

"Yes, miss; likewise the only boarding house and several private houses where we have made application."

"If you will depend on me I'll find accommodations for you and your friends."

Merry's surprise increased. His face cleared and he gave her one of those rare, manly smiles that made him so wonderfully attractive.

"You are very kind, but I fear——"

"Do not fear anything. I live here, and this outrage upon strangers has awakened my indignation. If you will enter my carriage and ask your friends to follow us I'll see that you are taken care of."

"I hope you will not be putting yourself to any inconvenience in this——"

"Not at all; it gives me pleasure and satisfaction. Do not hesitate. Speak to your friends at once."

Thus urged, Merry called his followers from the store and made known the offer he had received from the unknown woman. Hodge surveyed her suspiciously and then found an opportunity to whisper in Frank's ear without being observed:

"Look out for some kind of a trick, Merry."

"Nonsense!" laughed Frank. "Come on."

He entered the carriage and took a seat beside the lady, who made room for him. Thus they were driven away along the street, the others following on the sidewalk.

"You appeared just in time to save us, miss," said Merry. "We were beginning to get desperate."

She urged him to tell her just what had happened, which he did, passing over the attack upon him by the ruffian Madison.

"It's all very mysterious to me," admitted Frank. "I wonder if you can throw any light on the situation."

"All I know is that there is trouble in town over baseball affairs. During a number of seasons, and up to last season, baseball here was conducted by the cheapest element in the town, and the place acquired a very bad reputation. Outside teams, I have heard, were robbed and mobbed here. It became so bad that no manager who knew the exact condition of affairs would bring his team here. Last season a number of people who enjoy clean baseball resolved to put a stop to the hoodlumism. They secured the ball ground through some stratagem, and the tough characters found themselves out in the cold. A baseball association of respectable people was formed and Mr. Gaddis was chosen manager. The ruffians made him a lot of trouble, but he ran a team through the season. This year he was warned that he would not be permitted to conduct a team here. He paid no attention to the warning, but went ahead and made up his team. Immediately there was trouble, and it became evident that an attempt would be made to drive Gaddis out of baseball. The same ruffianly element that had predominated before his appearance started to make it warm for him. In doing this the whole place has been terrorized into backing up the ruffians. No one seems to dare to do anything different. Another man by the name of——"

She seemed to hesitate over the name, but quickly resumed:

"A man by the name of Cameron has organized a baseball team here. He has announced that he will take possession of the ball ground to-morrow, and that Gaddis will not be permitted to hold it longer. The members of Gaddis' team have been intimidated and driven out of town, Gaddis himself has been threatened with personal violence. Without doubt, the hotel keepers and people of the place were warned in advance to have nothing to do with any ball team that came here to play with Gaddis' team. Your team was chosen in particular, as it happened to be the first to arrive here after—after Cameron came out boldly and announced his intention. That is about all there is to it. At least, it is all I know about it."

"Well," cried Merry, in surprise, "it certainly is astonishing that a whole town can be intimidated in such a manner by a set of ruffians. Is there no law here?"

"If so, there is little danger that it will be enforced against the scoundrel Cameron!" she exclaimed, with surprising bitterness, all the music and sweetness gone from her voice. "He is a wretch who finds methods of evading the law, even when he commits the most heinous crimes! But vengeance will fall on him in the end! He cannot always escape!"

The depth of feeling betrayed by the mysterious woman told Frank that she was the implacable enemy of Cameron and that she had reasons for hating the man most intensely.

As they were passing the Mansion House two men came out and paused on the steps.

One of them was the bruiser, Mat Madison.

The other was a slender, red-lipped, dark man of thirty-five or more, dressed stylishly and smoking a cigarette.

"There is Carey Cameron!" hissed the veiled woman.

For all of her evident hatred of Cameron, the mysterious woman made no outward demonstration that could lead either of the men on the steps of the hotel to suppose she had as much as noticed them. If her face expressed the passion of hatred that was betokened by her voice, the veil effectually concealed the fact, and apparently she sat looking straight ahead without even turning her eyes in the direction of the hotel.

The two men who had chanced to come out upon the steps at that moment quickly discovered Merriwell in the carriage and saw the others of Frank's team following on the sidewalk.

"What in blazes does that mean, Madison?" exclaimed Cameron.

"You know as well as I do, boss," answered the bruiser.

"Who is that chap in the carriage with the woman?"

"That's the feller I was just telling you about—the one who downed me at the station."

"Frank Merriwell himself, eh?"

"Yes, boss."

"Well, I swear he doesn't look very much like a fighter. You should handle a smooth-faced chap like that with ease. I'm disgusted with you. Where is he going with that woman?"

"I judge she's taking him to her house, and it looks like the rest of the bunch is bound for the same place. They couldn't git no accommodations at hotels or other places, so she's goin' to take them in."

Carey Cameron flung aside his cigarette.

"Hasn't she been warned?" he asked.

"No, for nobody reckoned she would be taking strangers in, as she's been so haughty and high-headed since comin' here that she's scarce spoke to anybody, and she don't have any dealings with the people in the town."

Instantly Cameron descended the steps and hastened to the street, where he planted himself in front of the horse, commanding the driver to stop.

"Madam," he said, "it's likely you don't understand what you are doing. I am led to suppose that you contemplate taking your companion and his crowd into your house and giving them shelter. If such is the case you had better change your mind instantly, or you will find yourself in serious trouble."

The woman did not answer, but, rising slightly from her seat, she hissed at the driver:

"Whip up! Drive over that man!"

The driver's whip was in his hand, but he hesitated about obeying the order. Turning his head, he answered, in a low tone:

"I dare not, Miss Blake. He——"

Instantly she sprang erect, snatched the whip and, reaching over the driver's seat, hit the horse such a cut that the fiery animal instantly leaped forward.

By an agile spring, Cameron succeeded in escaping, although he barely avoided the wheels of the carriage. His hand went to his hip as he glared after the woman, but he did not draw a weapon.

Frank's friends had seen this, but were not given time to come up and take any part in the affair. Hodge was inclined to pitch into Cameron, but the others advised against it, and all hurried along after the carriage.

There was a glare of fury in the eyes of Carey Cameron as he stood in the street looking after the mysterious woman who had dared defy him.

Madison hurried up.

"Why didn't you stop her, boss?" he asked.

Cameron turned on him, blazing with wrath.

"You idiot, didn't you see what she did? She tried to run over me!"

"I should say she did, boss."

"Confound her! I'll make her regret it! She doesn't know me! She doesn't know my influence in this town. I'll drive her out of Cartersville!"

"Are you goin' to let her take Merriwell's crowd in?"

"I could stop it, but what's the good? We've done enough, I fancy. Gaddis is out of baseball, and the fine crowd that was backing him have taken to cover. I don't believe they'll dare butt against us after this. I wanted to show them just what we could do when we wished, and I believe they understand. Half our new players are here now, and the rest will arrive in the morning. The new Cartersville baseball team will take the field the following day. Old Martin, who owns the field, is so well cowed that he has told me to go ahead and use it, although Gaddis holds a receipt for the season's rent, which he has paid. I have no particular quarrel with the Merriwell crowd."

"Well, I have!" snarled Madison; "and I'm going to get a crack at Merriwell before they pull out of Cartersville!"

"Go ahead," nodded Cameron, as he took a gold cigarette case, decorated with diamonds, from his pocket, and selected a fresh cigarette. "You have my permission; but, according to your own story you'll have to catch him off his guard and lay him out stiff before he has a chance to recover."

"Leave it to me!" growled the bruiser.

CHAPTER XIII

THE HOUSE AMID THE TREES.

The gloved hands of the woman quivered as she restored the whip to the driver. She did not look back, although an expression of disappointment came from her hidden lips.

"Lucky for him he moved lively," said Frank, as she sank down at his side.

"Some evil charm protects him!" breathed the mysterious woman. "I did not wish to kill him—then. I hoped to drive over him and maim him!"

"It is plain that you have no liking for the man."

"Like him? I loathe and detest the sight of his wicked face, his treacherous eyes and his cruel mouth! When I behold him something in my heart struggles and burns until it is only by the utmost restraint that I keep myself from flying at him."

"He has done you a great wrong?"

"Yes, me and one dearest to me in all the world."

"He knows you, and that is why you keep yourself veiled?"

"He has never seen my face."

By the time the driver had quieted and restrained the frightened horse, and Merry looked back. He saw at a distance his companions making all haste in that direction, and he knew Cameron had not interfered with them, which gave him a feeling of relief.

"The boys are coming," he said. "I thought that man might try to stop them."

The woman directed the driver to pull the horse down to a walk, which he succeeded in doing.

"I do not wish to seem inquisitive," said Merry; "but it is no more than natural that I should be greatly interested in Carey Cameron after what has happened."

"Quite natural," admitted the woman. "He is a gambler."

"I thought it by his appearance."

"He has traveled much, making his living by gambling. His former home was here, and he returned here a few months ago. As a boy he was a baseball enthusiast, and that explains his wonderful interest in the game. When he came back here he sided with the vicious element, and I believe he has been appointed manager of the team they mean to put in the place of the one organized by Gaddis. I do not know much about it, but I have learned that they believe this team will be able to defeat anything in these parts. He has secured a number of players blacklisted in the big leagues. Cameron will run the team to make money for himself."

"How can he make money out of baseball in a town like this?"

"He will gamble on the games."

"But if he has a team that is far superior to any team it meets he'll find no one to bet on the other teams."

"When that happens he will bet on the other teams himself."

"You mean——"

"That I know his treacherous nature. He will betray his friends. He'll not wager money openly on an opposing team. It is likely he will openly bet small sums on his own team. His supposed-to-be friends will do the betting. Some agent of Cameron will bet Cameron's money, and you may be sure that his team will lose that game."

"In short, he will double-cross his friends, and that is the worst form of treachery."

"That man is capable of anything, Mr. Merriwell! To carry out his ends he would commit murder!"

"He'll reach the end of his rope some day."

"I trust that day is not far in the future!"

By this time they had reached the outskirts of the town. The road led up a low hill, near the crest of which, set back amid some trees, could be seen a rather gloomy-looking house. This house the mysterious woman indicated with a slight gesture, explaining that they were bound thither.

"It is your home?" questioned Merry.

"For the time being it serves me as home," she replied. "I have occupied it two months."

"You do not belong in this town?"

"No; before coming here two months ago I had never seen the place. I shall be happy when I leave it to return no more."

"You do not like Cartersville?"

"I detest the place! It is run by hoodlums and ruffians. There are some respectable people here, but the vicious element predominates, and respectable people are afraid to stand up for their rights."

"A fine place in which to play baseball!" laughed Merry.

"No worse place in Iowa."

"Perhaps it is just as well that we are not going to play here."

"You are better off."

The boys were not far behind when they reached the gate and turned into the grounds surrounding the gloomy house amid the trees. The house was shuttered, and many of the shutters were closed.

At the front step Merry sprang from the carriage and assisted his strange companion to alight.

As the others of his party came up Frank said:

"Fellows, although this lady has been kind enough to offer us the shelter of her house, I fear we are intruding in a certain way. I am sure we are putting her to great inconvenience, and I wish to——"

"Mr. Merriwell," interrupted the veiled woman, "I have tried to make it plain that you are not placing me at any inconvenience. I will add that my circumstances are such that the sum you may pay me for the accommodation of yourself and friends will be very acceptable. Oh! I'm going to take pay! You may give whatever sum you choose; I am satisfied that it will be satisfactory. I think this should put you more at your ease."

"To a certain extent it does," admitted Merry.

"Then come in."

The woman turned toward the door, which opened at once. As Merry followed her he saw the door had been opened by a singularly grave-looking Chinaman.

"John," said the mysterious woman, "these are my guests."

"Velly well, miss," nodded the Celestial.

"They will remain as long as they choose and are to have the best the house affords while here."

"Velly well, miss."

"Take them upstairs and let them select their own rooms."

"Velly well, miss."

Then, turning to Frank, the woman said:

"Dinner will be served in an hour. I think you will be ready by that time."

"Yah," muttered Hans. "I vos readiness alretty soon."

"If you wish to send to the station for anything in the way of baggage I will call a man to attend to that."

"There is nothing at the station that we shall need to-night," said Frank. "We had better leave our stuff there. We have everything necessary for present wants in our hand bags."

"Show them up, John."

"Velly well, miss."

They followed the Chinaman of the solemn and respectful manner and the limited vocabulary.

CHAPTER XIV

MATTERS OF UNCERTAINTY.

ell, this is not half bad," grunted Browning, as he stretched himself on one of the double beds which had delighted his eyes. "It's a lot better than camping outdoors overnight."

"Thou speakest truly, weary knight," said Ready. "The prospect of a supperless bed on the greensward was not at all cheerful to me, and the lady with the somber drop curtain over her radiant features came to our rescue at the proper time."

"This is the experience of a lifetime," put in Morgan. "I'm wondering over it yet. Can you shed any light on the subject, Frank?"

Merry told them what he had learned while in the carriage with the mysterious woman.

"Well," smiled Starbright, as he finished, "we can thank our stars that she has no use for Mr. Carey Cameron. Evidently she has offered us this hospitality because we seem to be the special objects of Mr. Cameron's spite."

"She did come plenty near hiking over Cameron when he tried to hold her up," said Badger. "It sure was a close call for that gent. Way he acted after that, I thought he was going to pull a gun and try to pot you both."

"And then I th-th-thought he was going to cuc-cuc-come at us," observed Gamp.

"It was lucky for him that he decided to let us alone," declared Hodge.

"Yah!" cried Hans. "You bet my life he vos luckiness!"

"This whole affair is most peculiar from start to finish," said Dade Morgan. "It has many mysterious features, and not the least mysterious is this strange young woman who keeps her face hidden by a heavy veil and who lives here in this gloomy house. Who is she? and what is she?"

"I scarcely think you will find any one in Cartersville who can answer those questions," said Frank. "It is not for us to be too inquisitive while accepting her hospitality."

"In one sense, we are not exactly accepting hospitality," asserted Stretcher. "What we receive we're going to pay for."

"It is hospitality none the less."

"I dud-dud-don't believe she tut-tut-took us in because she needs the mum-mum-money," declared Gamp.

"That was a bluff," nodded Hodge.

"She made that assertion," said Frank, "in order that we might accept her kindness with greater freedom. It was very good of her to attempt to make us feel more at home and less like intruders by giving us a chance to pay for what we shall obtain."

"Vainly I speculate upon her looks," murmured Ready. "I wonder be she dark or be she light?"

"Young or old?" came from Badger.

"Plain or pretty?" put in Rattleton.

"Sus-she's a bub-blonde," declared Gamp positively.

"Nix; she vos a prunette," said Hans, just as positively.

"She's about thirty-five years old," guessed Starbright.

"Not a day over twenty," asserted Morgan.

"I'll guarantee she's as homely as a hitching post," grunted Browning.

"I would like to make a wager that she is exceptionally good-looking," said Stretcher.

"All this speculation about her leads to nothing," interrupted Frank. "Besides that, as long as we are beneath this roof too much curiosity concerning her is a matter of poor taste. It's up to us to accept what she has provided, pay for it liberally, and be very grateful for her kindness. That she is a person of courage she has demonstrated by defying the ruffianly element of the town, which has the entire place subjugated and trembling beneath a reign of terror. I admire her nerve, and I am ready to render her assistance or give her protection if occasion arises."

"You are mit me in dot!" exclaimed Dunnerwurst. "I vill stood by her vid my last drop uf gore. How apoudt you, Choe? Speech up und declaration yourseluf."

"I gug-gug-guess she can depend on the whole of us to bub-bub-back her," said Gamp.

"We're still in the land of the hostiles," reminded Jack Ready. "His nibs, Mattie Madison, must still be smarting a trifle over what happened to him when he endeavored to lay violent hands on our leader, and it is probable that he will seek retaliation."

"Besides that," smiled Badger, "Carey Cameron must be some sore because he failed to hold Merry up and the lady whipped the horse in an attempt to run him down. I have a notion we'll hear further from him. That's whatever."

Darkness came on slowly. The rooms were supplied with oil lamps, which the boys lighted. They prepared for dinner, and at the expiration of an hour after they entered the house a set of chimes in the lower hall summoned them.

They filed down and were conducted to the dining room by the same solemn Chinaman who had admitted them to the house.

The dining room was almost severe in its plainness, but a long table was tastefully spread and decorated, being lighted by lamps and candles. They began to find seats around it before they discovered there were only eleven chairs.

"It's all right," said Merry, in a low tone. "It's plain we're not to enjoy the society of our hostess during this meal."

When they were seated two women in black, with white aprons, appeared and served soup.

At first the boys were somewhat oppressed by the situation, but Merry soon started things up with a jest and they began to enjoy themselves.

"Although we met a warm reception in this town," said Frank, "it was not much worse than the reception given Ready the first time he visited Niagara Falls. When Jack stepped off the trolley he found several carriages waiting for passengers. He capered over to one of them and asked the man to drive him to the falls. The man said he would be pleased to drive him there, but he didn't have a harness that would fit him."

"That man was a trifle nearsighted," declared Jack, good-naturedly taking the laugh this had aroused. "He failed to note my marvelous beauty, and he thought he could get gay with me. He lost as much as fifty small coins of the realm by that joke."

"You should remember, Jack," said Rattleton, "that beauty is only din skeep—er, that is skin deep."

"But I'm very thick-skinned," retorted Ready promptly. "Trala-la!"

"Vale, in Puffalo," said Dunnerwurst, "I vos consulted."

"Insulted, Hans," corrected Morgan.

"Shoot yourseluf apoudt der bronunciation," gurgled Hans. "Dese vos der vay in vich id habbened. A street car vos riding on me ven a chent who vos intoxicated came apoard. A numper uf laties peen on dot car, und I thought id vos a shame. I rose me up und caldt to der corn doctor. Says I to dot corn doctor: 'Do you bermit intoxicationed men to ride der cars ondo?' 'Yah,' saidt der corn doctor. 'Sid down und shut up und nopody vill know you vos drunk.' Dot made a seddlement by me, und don'd you vorget him."

"Did you notice that terrible thing about the epidemic in Chicago?" asked Frank seriously.

"The epidemic? What epidemic?" asked Rattleton instantly.

"Why, the whole city is sick. I saw it in the newspaper this morning. The first words I read in the paper were: 'Chicago, Ill.'"

Somebody groaned. It was Browning, who had dropped his fork and seemed about to collapse.

"That makes me ill myself!" he gasped huskily. "I never thought it of you, Merry! You are rapidly descending to the level of such buffoons as Ready and his kind."

"I admit it was a bad one," smiled Frank, "and I promise not to do it again."

In this manner they caused the meal to pass off merrily, and an excellent meal it proved to be. All were hungry, but when the dessert was over even Dunnerwurst confessed that he was more than satisfied.

As they were leaving the dining room Frank was about to ask for the hostess, when she appeared. Merry again protested that they feared they were causing her great inconvenience.

"Not at all," she declared. "I shall not be home to-night, and I decided to caution you before leaving the house. At the top of the stairs and at the rear there is a room with a black door. Although you have perfect liberty in the rest of the house, I wish it understood that you are to keep away from that room with the black door."

"You may depend on it that we'll not go near the room," pledged Merry instantly.

"And should you hear strange sounds in the night there will be no cause for alarm. Pay no attention to anything you may hear. That is all. I shall return before you leave in the morning."

She then bade them good night in a pleasant manner, and, being dressed for the street and still heavily veiled, left at once.

"More mystery!" grunted Browning, as they were once more gathered in the big room upstairs.

"A room with a bub-bub-bub-black door!" exploded Gamp.

"Und stranch noises may hear us in der nighdt!" cried Dunnerwurst. "Poys, you vos indo a haunted house!"

"La! la!" said Jack Ready easily. "I am ne'er disturbed by departed spirits. They alarm me not."

"Why did she go out to-night?" questioned Hodge.

"It is my idea," laughed Frank, "that we will occupy about all the beds in the house. Quite likely she went out to find a place to sleep. I feel guilty over it, but she insisted that we were putting her to no inconvenience."

"And prevaricated like a lady," said Ready.

"There isn't a bub-bub-bit of danger that I'll go poking round on the top floor looking for a room with a bub-bub-black door," declared Gamp.

"I'm afraid I'll not sleep very well to-night," acknowledged Rattleton.

"I vos anodder," confessed Hans. "Vrankie, vos ghosts afraidt uf you?"

"Not that I know of," answered Merry.

"Vale, in der room vich you haf selectioned dere vos a couch, as vell as a ped."

"Yes."

"Couldt you bermit dot couch to sleep on me?"

"You want to sleep on the couch in that room?"

"Yah."

"All right; I'm willing."

"But don't you dare to snore," warned Hodge. "I'm going to sleep with Frank, and I can't sleep when I hear any one snoring."

"I vill nod dood id," promised the Dutchman. "I vill nod snore so loudt as a visper."

"All right," nodded Bart; "the couch for you."

"If we escape from this town with our lives I'll be thankful," said Harry.

"Lo, and behold! you are exceedingly timid," mocked Ready.

They soon fell to joking and laughing, after their usual manner, and, in spite of the mystery which seemed to hover near, the evening passed pleasantly.

Some time in the night Frank was awakened by something that caused him to lift his head from the pillow and listen.

At first he could not make out what it was, but after a while he decided that it was some person singing somewhere in the house. Finally the singing became somewhat more distinct, and he decided that it was the voice of a woman. The song, as best he could determine, was a lullaby, such as a mother might croon above the crib of her sleeping babe. It was strangely pathetic and gave Frank a peculiar sensation of sadness. To him it seemed as if the person who sang that song had met with a terrible affliction and was thus softly pouring forth the grief of a broken heart.

Merry thought of the warning of the mysterious veiled woman and how she had cautioned them to pay no attention to anything they might hear. Still he could not resist the impulse to slip softly from the bed, steal to the door, open it and listen.

The singing seemed to come from the upper part of the house. A moment after he opened the door it stopped, and, although he remained there for fully ten minutes, he heard it no more.

Hodge was sleeping soundly, and Dunnerwurst breathing heavily, on the verge of snoring, when Merry crept back into bed.

It was some time after that before Merriwell again closed his eyes in sleep. He longed to investigate the mystery, but the promise made to the veiled woman restrained him. He was inclined to fancy he had not slept at all when he was once more awakened.

Something soft and cold, almost clammy, was touching his cheek gently with a patting motion.

In a twinkling he was wide awake, but he did not stir.

He felt a presence near him and knew some one or something was bending over the bed!

A chill ran over him.

The touch on his cheek was like the cold hand of a dead person!

Then he heard a voice—that of a woman—which softly murmured:

"Sleep, my baby—sleep! Mother is near!"

Fear passed from Frank in a twinkling, and he stirred, making a grab at the hand that had touched him.

Quick as he was, he was not quick enough, although he barely missed as the hand was snatched away.

Springing up, he saw a shadowy figure in white gliding toward the door.

At that moment Dunnerwurst awoke and beheld the figure as it flitted past the couch.

Uttering a squawk of terror, the Dutchman rolled off the couch with a crash.

Hodge leaped from the bed and grappled with Frank as Merry came round the foot in pursuit of the mysterious visitor. Before he could realize his mistake Hans had clutched them both round the legs, chattering:

"Safe me from der ghost! Safe me! safe me!"

Frank broke away, but the visitor was gone. Merry rushed out of the room, but he was too late.

This racket had aroused the others, and they came flocking from their rooms, demanding the cause of the trouble.

"Hans had a bad case of nightmare, I think," said Merry.

They found the Dutchman with his head under the couch, whither he had attempted to crawl. Bart struck a light and Merry pulled Dunnerwurst out.

"Vos der ghost gone alretty yet?" asked Hans, his teeth chattering.

"There was no ghost," assured Frank.

"Don'd you toldt me so!" palpitated the frightened fellow. "Der ghost seen me mit my own eyes! Yah!"

"Nonsense," said Merriwell. "I tell you there was no ghost."

"Vot vos id dot seen me all in vite?" demanded Hans.

"That was either Bart or myself. If you're going to kick up such a disturbance you'll have to sleep somewhere else."

It proved no simple matter to convince the Dutchman that he had not seen a ghost. The boys ridiculed him until he relapsed into sulky silence, and finally all went back to bed.

"What was it, Merry?" asked Bart, when they were once more in bed. "Wasn't there some person in this room?"

"Sh!" cautioned Frank. "Don't let Hans hear you. Some one was here."

"I thought so. What happened?"

Merriwell told of hearing the singing and again falling asleep, to be finally aroused by the touch of an ice-cold hand and to hear the voice of a woman who seemed to fancy she was speaking to a sleeping babe.

"I take no stock in spooks," said Hodge; "but I'll be rather pleased when we get out of this ranch."

"On the contrary," averred Merry, "if it were not a breach of hospitality I'd like to remain here for the purpose of solving the mystery."

Ten minutes later he was sound asleep, and he slept soundly until morning.

CHAPTER XV

CAMERON'S CHALLENGE.

he boys were finishing their breakfast when John, the Chinaman, appeared and stated that there was a gentleman at the door who wished to speak with Frank.

Frank left the table and went to the door, Hodge following him, in case there should be trouble.

Carey Cameron was waiting on the step.

"That heathen is decidedly inhospitable," laughed Cameron pleasantly, removing a cigarette from his lips and holding it between a discolored thumb and forefinger. "He left me standing out here, like a huckster. But I understand that visitors—with the exception of yourselves—are not welcome in this house."

Merriwell waited for the man to announce why he had called.

"I presume you're surprised to see me here at this early hour," said the man. "Oh, I'm alone! There's no trickery about it. You need not be alarmed."

"You quite mistake my feelings," assured Merry.

"I have a proposition to make to you."

"Have you?"

"I fancy you think it nervy of me, but I'm willing to explain and apologize. You may have learned of the baseball mix-up in Cartersville."

"I have heard something about it."

"Well, perhaps you know that I am manager of the new Cartersville baseball team. Gaddis and his bunch of stiffs have been put out of business. He has taken to the woods. Two of his best men have signed with me. The others are in retirement."

Merriwell wondered what the man was driving at.

"My team will be complete to-day and every man on hand ready for business. I had arranged to open the season to-morrow with Bloomfield. Received a message late last evening that Bloomfield would not appear. The duffers! They are afraid to come."

"If what I have heard about past methods of conducting base-ball here is true," said Merry, "I don't wonder that Bloomfield canceled."

"Oh, somebody has been giving you a lot of hot air. You can't believe all you hear. It is possible the rooters have been rather rough on visiting teams in the past, but I'm going to cut that out."

"Are you?"

"Sure thing."

"It's a good idea," said Hodge sarcastically.

"There'll be no need of winning games in future by intimidating visitors," said Cameron. "When you learn the line-up of my team you'll agree that I have the players. Among them I have Johnson, the great colored player, formerly of the Chicago Giants. Then there is Moran, from Springfield; Hickey, of Indianapolis; Tonando, with the Kansas City team last season; and Weaver, the great Indian fielder. The others are just as good. I have a team that can defeat anything on the turf in the middle West, and when we get into trim we'll be able to make some of the big leaguers hustle. I'm going to give Cartersville and southern Iowa such baseball as was never before seen in these parts."

"How does this interest me?" inquired Frank.

"I'm coming to that. I presume you're rather hot over your treatment in this town."

"You presume correctly."

"Well, I don't blame you; but you see Gaddis was given fair notice to quit, and he persisted in holding on. He had no business to make a contract with you. At that time he had been told to get out and warned that he would not be able to play after a certain date. He had an idea that the law would support him, and he attempted to fight me and the majority of baseball people in town. We had to make it good and hot for him. We began by driving visiting teams out of the place without giving them a chance to play. We thought Gaddis would throw up the sponge when he found he couldn't get teams here. At last we were compelled to get after Gaddis himself, and yesterday he tumbled and skipped."

"All this explaining does not justify you in the least."

"Perhaps not; but there you are. I'm ready to apologize, if that suits you better."

"Even an apology can't square it," asserted Hodge.

"I'm very sorry," declared Cameron. "I've told the boys that you are to be treated with the utmost courtesy during the rest of your stay in town."

"Which will be very brief," said Frank. "We shall leave on the ten A.M. train to-day."

"I hope not. I am here to offer you inducements to play with my team to-morrow. It will be the opening game, and I know we'll turn out a mob of people."

"When it comes to nerve," said Bart, "that is just about the full limit!"

"If you'll play," Cameron went on, "I'll give you a fixed sum, or I'll pay you two-thirds the net gate receipts, win or lose. Besides that I'll put you up at the Mansion House, and the best Cartersville affords shall be yours. Can you ask for anything fairer?"

"It sounds very fine," laughed Merry; "but what we have seen and heard has taught us the folly of dealing with you and the class of people you represent."

"Then you refuse?"

"Yes, sir!"

"You're afraid! That's what's the matter! You have made a great reputation, and you're afraid of being defeated."

"That is the very least of my fears, sir. We opened in Los Angeles with the Chicago Cubs, defeating them two out of three games. I hardly think we would fear you after that."

"Oh, I don't know! If you had lost all three games to the Chicagos it would have been no disgrace. After your triumphant career this season, you might feel sore if you dropped a game to a new team here in Cartersville."

"As far as possible," said Merry, "I seek to deal with gentlemen."

Cameron flushed the least bit, and a wicked look came to his eyes.

"I don't fancy the insinuation!" he exclaimed. "I have apologized and endeavored to set things straight. If you are looking for further trouble——"

He checked himself, changing his manner in a moment.

"That's nonsense!" he laughed. "I'm sorry you are afraid. I have heard of you, Mr. Merriwell. You have a reputation for nerve, but it seems that you have very little real nerve. You are challenged to play my team. You dare not play! You know I can defeat you. You're a squealer!"

"All that sort of talk never drove me into anything I had decided not to do, and never could," said Frank.

Then, to his surprise, the mysterious woman, still wearing the heavy veil, stepped quickly from the house and placed a hand on his arm.

"Accept the challenge, Mr. Merriwell," exclaimed the lips hidden behind the veil. "Play him for my sake—and defeat him! You can do it!"

"Do you realize, miss, the manner in which we shall be handicapped? We are in a strange town, and a place where there is little chance that we'll be given a fair show. Even the umpire would be against us."

"To satisfy you on that point," cried Cameron, "I'll permit you to select your own umpire. How is that? If you have a man with you who can umpire the game, I'll accept him. You can't squeal— if you have the nerve."

"Play him!" again urged the mysterious woman. "For my sake!"

"With the understanding that I am to furnish the umpire——" began Merry.

"It's a go!" cried Cameron, in satisfaction. "With the team I shall put onto the field, it will be an easy matter to defeat you. There'll be no need of anything but straight and legitimate baseball to do that."

"Very well," said Merry. "We'll play you, Mr. Cameron."

As Cameron departed the strange woman spoke excitedly to Frank.

"You will win!" she declared. "I feel it! I know it! He is confident there is no need to resort to crooked methods to defeat you. He'll try to get bets on the game. I hope he loses heavily. I'll back you! I have money. You shall take it and cover his bets."

"I beg your pardon, miss," protested Frank, "but I have certain scruples about betting. I may have made wagers in the past, but I am sure I shall never again do so, either with my own money or that of another."

"Let her bet on us, if she wants to," urged Hodge warmly. "I, too, feel it in my bones that we'll take a fall out of Cameron's great aggregation. I know every fellow on the team will play as if for his very life."

Merry shook his head.

"I can make no exceptions to the rule I have laid down for myself," he said. "Even if Cameron is confident of success, and begins a square game, he may resort to treachery if he becomes alarmed before the finish. He'll not intend to lose the opening game with his team. That would disgust the tough element that is backing him. He would lose prestige at once."

Frank was immovable on his point.

The boys were greatly surprised when Merry informed them of the challenge and acceptance.

"Py Shimminy!" cried Dunnerwurst. "Ve vill gif them der greatest run their money for that you efer saw. Id vill peen a satisfaction to dood them up. Yah!"

Frank explained that they were to supply the umpire, which caused no small amount of satisfaction.

"We are to move to the Mansion House, fellows," he said. "We'll impose on Miss Blake no longer."

"You have not imposed on me in the least," assured the hostess. "If you defeat Cameron, I shall be more than repaid."

"But we are going to pay you good, cold cash for what we have received. That was the agreement."

She began to demur, but Frank insisted that she had made that a part of the agreement when she took them in, and at last she consented to accept payment.

Having settled by compelling her to take twenty dollars, although she was unwilling to the very last to accept more than ten, the boys picked up and started off gayly for the hotel.

"I toldt you vot," said Hans, as they descended the hill, "I vos glat to got dot house oudt uf. No matteration vot you say, I vos postiveness I seen a ghost last nighdt indo. Id scooted me by like a streak of vind, und id gif me der shiverings all ofer your back. Dot blace been haunted."

Although they laughed at him, the Dutchman continued to insist that he had seen a ghost.

As they marched into town they were observed with curiosity by the people of the place. A mob of youngsters quickly gathered and followed them along the street.

At the Mansion House they found Mat Madison and several of his companions of the previous day standing on the steps. Apparently they had been waiting for Frank and his team to appear.

Madison leered at Merry.

"Say," he cried, "you won't prance with your head so high in the air after our team gits through with you to-morrow. We'll take some of the starch outer you."

"Great blizzards!" exclaimed Badger. "Does that play on Cameron's team?"

"You bet," answered the bruiser. "Cameron signed me for my hittin'. There ain't no pitcher in the business that I can't hit."

"That should make you tremble, Frank," laughed Morgan.

None of the young thugs offered to molest Merry or his party as they entered the hotel.

Cameron was waiting for them in the office.

"Here you are, I see!" he cried. "I was afraid you might back out, after all, and try to skip out of town."

"Your fears were quite groundless," said Merriwell.

"Well, everything is fixed for you here. I told you I'd arrange it. You're to have the very best the house affords, and I'll settle the bills. I can afford to, considering the trimming we're going to hand out to you to-morrow."

"You seem inclined to count your chickens before they are hatched," said Frank.

"Do you have an idea that you'll win?"

"Of course."

"Want to make a little wager?"

"No."

"Why not?"

"I never bet."

"A poor excuse is better than none. Of course, that means you dare not bet."

"It means just what I said—I never bet."

"Oh, well, if any of your bunch feels like sporting a little I'll be open for business up to the time the umpire calls 'Play!' It adds interest to any event to make a little wager on it. I'm not in baseball for my health. We're going to pay you the biggest part of the gate money, and so I'll have to catch some money somehow. Considering your record, there ought to be some sports with nerve enough to take a chance on you."

Cameron's manner was offensive, although it was not likely he meant it to be.

The accommodations at the Mansion House were none too good, and the place seemed poor enough after the plain comforts of the private house they had just left. Nevertheless, they were inclined to make the best of everything, kicking being in disfavor among them.

At the earliest opportunity Merry took occasion to seek information concerning the mysterious woman who lived on the hill; but he soon discovered that no one in the place knew much about her, save that she had appeared some ten weeks before and leased the house for the summer. The place was furnished, its owner having gone abroad after the death of his wife. When Miss Blake moved in, no one seemed to know. Shortly after taking the house she reappeared in Cartersville, and the people of the town discovered that she as occupying the house, together with a number of servants, both male and female.

"No one could be found who had ever seen her without her heavy veil. She had discouraged all efforts at familiarity or friendliness on the part of the villagers. It appeared to be a matter of wonder that Merriwell and his friends had been admitted to the house, as they were the only ones outside the members of her household to cross the threshold since she took possession. One old woman gossip of the town had made repeated attempts to get in on one pretext or another, but had been rebuffed each time. The townspeople were not only piqued and mystified by the woman, they were not a little offended, and the rougher element had threatened to tear the veil from her face in order to see what she looked like."

All this was interesting but unsatisfactory. Merry felt that he would sincerely regret to leave Cartersville without solving the mystery of the veiled woman.

CHAPTER XVI

AN ASTOUNDING WAGER.

he expected members of the new local team arrived before noon that day. In the afternoon Cameron had them out for practice.

They were, indeed, for the most part, well-known players, seven of them, at least, being professionals with records. Several were league men who had been blacklisted for one offense or another. Taken all together, they were a tough set and just the aggregation to win a game by bulldozing when other methods failed. They made a team that was certain to be heartily approved by the local toughs.

These players, the most of them, also stopped at the Mansion House. They looked Frank's team over, with no effort to conceal their merriment and disdain. To them Merry's players were a lot of stripplings.

"We'll eat 'em up," said Big Hickey, the Indianapolis man. "Why, dey won't last t'ree innin's."

"Sho' not," chuckled Wash Johnson, the colored player from the Chicago Giants. "Dey is a lot o' college fellers. Nebber seen none o' dem college fellers dat could play de game wid professionals. No, sar."

"They ain't got-a da nerve," observed Tony Tonando, the Italian from Kansas City. "Sometimes they play one-a, two or three-a inning first-a rate; but they no keep-a it up."

"Easy frightened, easy frightened," grunted Wally Weaver, the Indian. "When they play too well, then jump in and scare them. That's easy."

"Look here, you chaps," said Tunk Moran, who had made a great reputation on the Springfield, Illinois, team, but had been fired for drinking, "I happen to know something about Frank Merriwell, and you're off your trolley if you think you're going to win from him by scaring him. If you beat that chap you'll have to play baseball, and don't you forget it."

The others laughed at this and ridiculed Moran.

"All right," he growled. "Just you wait until after the game and see if you don't agree with me."

The appearance of Cameron's team in suits when they left the hotel to march to the ball ground was the signal for a great demonstration on the part of the youngsters of Cartersville, who were waiting to escort them. The cheering brought a number of the Merries to windows to look out, and they saw their opponents-to-be set off down the street, followed by the admiring crowd.

"Behold the gladiators whom we are to meet in the arena!" cried Jack Ready.

"They're a hot bunch of old-stagers," grunted Browning.

"It will keep us busy to cool them off," said Frank. "Don't get the idea that they are has beens. Half of them could play on fast league teams if they were not crooked and rebellious. They will go after us savage, with the idea of taking the sand out of us at the very start."

"On the other hand," said Rattleton, "if we get a start on them early in the game all the hoodlums will be against us and we'll be in danger of the mob."

"I have thought about that," declared Frank. "I have a plan. Come, fellows, and we'll talk it over."

They gathered in one room, and Merry explained his plan, speaking as follows:

"Rattleton is right in fancying it will not do to get a big lead on those fellows at an early stage in the game. Of course, we might not be able to do so, even if we tried; but should the opportunity offer, we must still refrain from it and take chances on our ability to pull out toward the end. Cameron has no idea of permitting us to take the game under any circumstances. If we started off like winners the hoodlums would be set on us. I've had more than one experience with hoodlums. They can make it hot for any team by crowding down to the base lines, insulting the players, stoning them and doing a hundred things to rattle them. I am confident that, as long as the crowd has a belief that the local team is sure to win it will behave in a fairly decent manner. Cameron will make an effort to hold the toughs in check. Therefore, we must resort to the stratagem of keeping close to the enemy all through the game, with the hope of winning at the very finish by an unexpected spurt that will take them by surprise. Of course, we may lose in this manner; but I am confident it is also our only chance of winning."

"I think you are right, Merry," agreed Hodge. "If you could fix it with Cameron so that we may have our last turn at bat, there is a possible show for us."

"I'll do what I can," assured Merriwell, "although it is possible he will refuse such a request if I make it. If we can't get our last turn at bat we'll have to do the best we can. But I wish you all to keep in mind the scheme I have proposed, and play from the start with the idea of holding them down and keeping close to them, so that we may have a chance at the finish."

To this they agreed readily enough.

During the remainder of the day they saw nothing of the strange woman who had befriended them.

The following morning, directly after breakfast, a stranger appeared at the Mansion House.

He was a quiet, smooth-faced young man, and he registered as "Warren Doom, Chicago."

Doom betrayed interest at once when he learned there was to be a baseball game in town that afternoon, and when he was told that the locals were to meet Frank Merriwell's team, his interest became genuine enthusiasm. He was purchasing a cigar at the counter when he received this bit of information.

"Going to play Merriwell's team?" he cried. "Well, I struck this place at the proper moment! I've seen Merriwell pitch once, and he's a wonder. I've always longed to see him again. Your team hasn't a chance against him."

"What's that?" exclaimed the man behind the counter disdainfully. "I reckon you don't know what you're talking about. We've got a team right here in this town that can skin anything outside the two big leagues. Our players are professionals and crackajacks. This Merriwell bunch looks like a lot of boys. They're amateurs, and Cartersville will bury them up this afternoon."

"Oh, come, come!" smiled Doom. "It's plain you are the one who doesn't know what he's talking about. I don't care how many professionals you have, Merriwell will defeat you. I'll bet on it."

"How much will you bet?" was the hot inquiry.

"Anything from ten dollars to ten thousand."

"That's a bluff."

"Is it? I'll back it up."

"Of course it is a bluff," said another voice, as Carey Cameron, puffing at a cigarette, came sauntering up. "The cocksure gentleman never saw ten thousand dollars."

99

Doom turned with his freshly lighted cigar in his mouth and his hands in his pockets, surveying Cameron critically.

"Who are you?" he inquired. "Why are you so sudden to chip into this?"

"I'm the manager of the Cartersville baseball team, and my name is Cameron. I happened to hear you making a lot of bluff betting talk, which I am positive you can't back up."

"How positive are you?"

"Positive enough to stake ten thousand dollars against a similar sum that Cartersville will win to-day. Put up—or shut up!"

"I don't happen to have ten thousand dollars in cash on my person."

"Of course not!" cried Cameron sneeringly. "Bluffers never are able to make good."

"I believe you have a good bank in town?"

"Yes; the First National."

"Well, I have with me a certified check for ten thousand dollars, and I believe the cashier at your bank will recognize it as good. If you are not running a bluff I'll step out to the bank with you and deposit my check in the hands of one of the bank officials, with the understanding that I am backing Frank Merriwell and you are to put up a similar sum to back your own team. Now you put up—or shut up!"

Cameron was somewhat surprised, but he recovered quickly, still confident that Doom was still bluffing.

"Come on!" he almost shouted. "Come out to the bank! I can raise ten thousand dollars if your old check is good. I'll do it, too! It will be like finding a small fortune."

The man from Chicago was ready to go.

"But wait a moment," said the manager of the local team. "I want to tell you something. I hate to be fooled, and it makes me very disagreeable. In case I accompany you to the bank and find this is what I believe it to be—a bluff—you'll be very sorry. I warn you that you'll leave Cartersville in such a condition that you'll require medical attention for some time to come."

"Come on, man," said Doom, with curling lips. "You are wasting your breath. You'll find I am in earnest, although I fancy you are the one who will squeal."

Together they left the hotel and started for the bank.

The man who had sold Doom a cigar and overheard this conversation ran out after them and told what had happened to a number of loiterers who were in front of the hotel. Immediately these loiterers hustled away after Cameron and Doom, greatly excited over what they had heard.

"Ten thousand dollars!" exclaimed one. "Cameron will make a fortune off this first game!"

"I don't believe it!" declared another. "Nobody is fool enough to bet Cameron ten thousand dollars."

"The man is joking," was the opinion expressed by a third.

"Then it will be a mighty poor joke for him when Carey Cameron is done with him," said the first.

Outside the bank they lingered and waited. Cameron and Doom were inside a full quarter hour, but finally they appeared. Immediately the crowd besieged the manager of the local team to know if such a bet had really been made.

"Sure thing," nodded Cameron, with a smile of confidence. "This gentleman had a certified check that was good, and I covered it. There is a wager of ten thousand dollars on the result of the game to-day."

The report spread like wildfire. In less than an hour, it seemed, every man, woman, and child over six years of age in Cartersville knew of the amazing wager that had been made. The report was wired to surrounding towns and carried into the country in various ways.

By midday people from out of town began to appear in Cartersville. At first they straggled in, but as the time passed they came faster and thicker. They came from the country in conveyances of all sorts, while the 12.48 P.M. train brought at least a hundred. The streets took on a surprising appearance of life. Men gathered in groups and discussed the wonderful bet that had been made. Some were skeptical and pronounced it an advertising dodge on the part of Cameron. Others there were who knew the stakeholder, or knew those who did know him, and they protested that the wager was on the level.

At any rate, never had so much excitement over a game of baseball been aroused in such a brief time in the whole State of Iowa.

A later train brought a still larger number of visitors, and the influx from the country continued up to the hour for the game to begin.

No sooner were the gates opened at the ball ground than the great crowd waiting outside made a push to get in and secure seats. It required the united efforts of a number of local officers, who had been summoned by Cameron for that purpose, to hold the eager people back.

In the meantime Merriwell and his friends had learned of the wager. At first all were inclined to laugh over it, thinking, like many others, that it was an advertising scheme. After a while, however, they began to have reasons to believe there was something of truth in the report.

"By Jove!" cried Morgan. "We'll be playing for a fortune this afternoon, boys!"

"If such a bet has actually been made," said Rattleton, "we won't have any show to win."

"Wh-wh-why not?" demanded Gamp.

"Don't you fancy for a moment that Carey Cameron is the sort to lose that amount of money. He'll fix it somehow so he can win."

"Dost hear the croaker?" inquired Jack Ready. "Rattles, you have a very weak heart."

"See if I'm not right!" exclaimed Harry. "Cameron is no fool."

"I am certain that he depends mainly on the skill of his players," said Frank. "He cannot believe it possible that a lot of amateurs stand a show of downing those professionals. There will be nothing crooked as long as it appears to him that his players have the best chance to take the game. We must fool them, fellows."

"We'll do our best, Frank," was the assurance they gave him.

Never had there been such a wonderful outpouring to witness a baseball game in all that region. When Frank and his players entered the inclosure they found the stand packed, the bleachers black with people, and a great gathering held back by ropes stretched on both sides of the field. Besides that, the officers employed by Cameron were kept busy chasing spectators out of the outfield.

Not only did it seem that all Cartersville was there, but more than a like number of people had come in from outside the town.

The Merries were received with a hearty cheer. They hurried to their bench, lost no time in laying out their bats, pulling off their sweaters, adjusting gloves and preparing for practice. At a word from Frank they trotted briskly onto the field, and practice began.

Merry warmed up with Stretcher as catcher, while Hodge and Starbright batted to the men practicing on the diamond and in the field.

Frank was slow and deliberate in warming up. He did not use speed, but limbered his arm gradually. Toward the last he threw two or three fairly swift ones and let it go at that.

The players, however, went at it in earnest from the very start, and both infield and outfield work was of a snappy and sensational order.

At a quarter to three the local players, with Cameron leading them, appeared. Instantly there was a great uproar from the toughs of the town who had been supporting Cameron. They rose up and yelled like a lot of Indians. Not only that, but they insisted that every one else should yell and threatened those who did not.

"Them's our boys!" they cried. "Cheer, you duffers—cheer!"

If any one declined to cheer he suddenly found himself beaten over the head by two or three of the toughs, who insisted that he must "open up," and this came near causing a general riot.

Not for at least five minutes after the arrival of the Cartersville team did the commotion cease. Even then there were symptoms of anger and resentment in a number of places amid the crowd, and it seemed as if a spark might fire the powder and bring about an explosion.

Frank called his players from the field, and the home team went out for practice.

Merry found an opportunity to speak with Cameron, but the local manager insisted on his privilege of choosing innings, declining to toss a coin for choice.

"All right," smiled Frank. "Take your choice."

Imagine his surprise when Cameron said:

"We'll go to bat first."

"Suit yourself," nodded Frank, with pretended disappointment. Cameron had played into his hands without knowing it.

The practice of the locals was soon over.

Then big Dick Starbright was accepted as the umpire. The time for the game to begin had arrived. Merriwell gave the signal, and his players ran out onto the field, scattering to their different positions.

Frank entered the pitcher's box.

"Play ball!" cried Starbright.

At this point, to the astonishment of Frank, the mysterious veiled woman darted onto the diamond and grasped his arm with her gloved hand.

"Win this game, Frank Merriwell!" she urged huskily. "My fortune—yes, my life—depends upon it!"

CHAPTER XVII

THE VEILED WOMAN'S SECRET.

"I assure you, Miss Blake, that I shall do my best to win," said Merriwell wonderingly; "but I can't understand what you mean by the statement that your fortune and your life depend upon it."

"I am backing you."

"You are?"

"Yes."

"Why, I thought——"

"You know about the bet of ten thousand dollars on the result of this game?"

"Of course. A gentleman from Chicago, by the name of Doom, made that wager with Cameron."

"Doom is my agent," declared the woman.

"Impossible!"

"It is true. He wagered my money. It is all I have in the world. I also happen to know that ten thousand dollars is practically all Carey Cameron possesses. If I win he will be ruined. I must win."

Frank was both perplexed and annoyed.

"I ask your pardon in advance for speaking plainly," he said, "but I must tell you that I think you very foolish to take such a risk. You know all the chances are against us. If we win we must do so by strategy. I cannot understand why you should make such a venture."

"I hate Carey Cameron!" she hissed. "I wish to ruin him—to strip him of his last dollar! He married my sister and treated her in the most brutal and inhuman manner until he forced her to give him all of her fortune, which he squandered in dissipation and gambling. After that he used her in the most inhuman manner, making her a prisoner in her own house. Her baby he starved and abused until the poor thing died. In the end my sister's mind gave way, and he placed her in a madhouse.

"Why shouldn't I hate him? Now you understand my reasons! I have sworn to ruin him, and for that purpose I am living here in Cartersville. He does not know me. He never saw my face, but I bear a strong resemblance to my sister as she looked when he married her, and I fear he might detect the resemblance should he behold me unveiled. For that reason I keep my face hidden constantly.

"You know my secret, Frank Merriwell. You are the first to whom I have revealed it since coming here. I hope to strike a blow at him to-day. If I fail—if you lose the game—my money will be gone, and I shall have no means of keeping up the struggle. What will there be for me then? I might as well be dead!"

At last Frank understood her secret, but that did not relieve him of his vexation on account of her folly, as he considered it. He saw that she was extremely impulsive. She had accepted this crude method of seeking revenge on Cameron, without sufficiently considering the danger that the result might be disastrous to herself; but now, as the struggle was about to begin, a full realization of the peril made her tremble and quake.

There was no rectifying her folly. The only way to save her was to win the game.

"Play ball! play ball!" howled the rough element of the crowed. "Put her off the field!"

"Merriwell has a mash!" shouted a man.

"Do your goo-gooing after the game," advised another.

"Miss Blake," said Frank earnestly, "you may rely on me to do my best; but I warn you in advance that the chances are strongly in favor of Cameron."

"I have confidence in you," she declared. "That is why I made that wager. I have had confidence in you from the moment when I first set eyes on you. Something tells me you are the sort of a man who triumphs. You will win—you must!"

"It would be a great misfortune for me to lose," confessed Frank; "but you will be forced to bear uncertainty until the very end of the game, as we dare not take the lead too soon."

Once more declaring her confidence in him, and seeming not to mind the cries of the crowd, she retired from the diamond and the game began.

Following was the line-up of each team:

CARTERSVILLE.	MERRIES.
Grady, cf.	Ready, 3d b.
Moran, ss.	Morgan, ss.

Johnson, 1st b.	Badger, lf.
Madison, rf.	Hodge, c.
Tonando, 3d b.	Merriwell, p.
Gibson, lf.	Gamp, cf.
Hickey, 2d b.	Browning, 1st b.
Collins, c.	Rattleton, 2d b.
Weaver, p.	Dunnerwurst, rf.

A yell of delight went up from the crowd as Grady met the first ball pitched and drove out a scorching single.

"We're off! we're off!" whooped Gibson, as he capered down to the coaching line back of first. "Keep it going, Moran!"

Moran responded by bunting and attempting to "beat it out."

On the bunt Grady reached second, but Frank got the ball and threw Moran out at first.

"All right, chillun!" grinned Johnson, the colored player, as he ran out to hit. "Why, we's gwine to make a hundred right heah."

Frank gave him a swift inshoot.

"G'way dar, ma-a-an!" shouted Johnson. "Yo'll sho' hurt yo' wing if yo' tries to keep dat speed up."

"One ball," announced Starbright.

"Dat's right, Mistah Umpiah," commented the negro. "Make him git 'em ober de pan. If he do, I's gwine to slam it right ober de fence."

The next one was too far out.

"Two balls."

"Come on, ma-a-an," urged Johnson. "Yo'll nebber fool dis chicken dat way."

Merry tried a high ball, using lots of speed.

The batter hit it fairly and laced it on a line far into the field.

"Yah! yah! yah!" he whooped, as he scooted for first. "Dat pitcher was made fo' me."

Sitting on the bench, Carey Cameron saw Grady come home on the hit, while Johnson reached third base.

"This is going to be too easy," said Cameron, to one of the substitutes. "It won't do to run the score up too high and not give those poor dubs a show, for it will disgust the crowd and hurt baseball here for the rest of the season. I'll have to hold the boys down the moment they get the game well in hand."

The crowd began to ridicule Frank.

"Is that the great pitcher we've heard about?"

"He's a fake!"

"That's not the genuine Frank Merriwell!"

"Take him out!"

"Knock him out of the box!"

"Put him in the stable!"

Mat Madison was the next batter. The big bruiser made an insulting remark to Frank as he took his position at the plate.

"You'll be a puddin' for me," he declared.

Instantly Merry resolved to strike Madison out. He gave Hodge a signal which Bart understood.

Frank began with the double shoot. Madison fancied the first ball pitched was just what he wanted and slashed at it with all his strength.

He missed.

"Strike one!" cried Starbright.

"Accident," said Madison. "I'll hit the next one I go after."

Merry reversed the curve, and Madison missed again, much to his wonderment and disgust.

"Give me another just like that," he urged.

"Here it is," said Merry, and he actually pitched another of the same sort as the last.

"You're out!" declared Starbright, as the bruiser missed the third time.

Madison was astounded and infuriated.

"Wait till my turn comes again!" he snarled, as he flung the bat down.

"Get-a ready to score, you black-a rascal," cried Tonando to Johnson, as he danced out to the plate.

"I's waitin', ma-a-an," retorted Johnson, dancing off third and back again. "Just yo' git any kind of a hit an' see me cleave de air."

Tonando let one pass and then met the next, getting a safe single on a fast grounder that Rattleton failed to touch.

"Just as e-e-easy, chillun!" laughed Johnson, as he came home. "Why, dis is a cinch!"

The crowd now redoubled its ridicule of Merriwell.

Gibson prepared to hit, being overconfident. To his surprise, he missed twice. Then he put up an easy infield fly and was out, which retired the side.

Cartersville had made two runs in the first inning, and every man on the team felt that they might have obtained many more with ease.

Without letting them secure too many runs, Merry had placed them in a frame of mind that would enable him to deceive them for a while, at least, before they awoke to their mistake.

The first three batters for the visitors fanned the air, seeming utterly bewildered by the curves and speed of Weaver, the Indian pitcher.

"Oh, you're pretty stickers!" derided a small boy. "You won't git a hit to-day!"

In the second inning neither team scored, although it seemed more by bungling good fortune than anything else that the Merries held their opponents down.

The fact was that Cameron had warned his players not to get too long a lead. He was perfectly at his ease, fully believing his team quite outclassed the visitors and could win the game by heavy batting in a single inning, if necessary.

In this manner the game slipped along with neither side making further runs until the sixth inning.

In the last of the sixth the visitors sprang a surprise on Cameron's men. Morgan led off with a hit, Badger sacrificed him to second. Hodge sacrificed him to third, and Frank brought him home with a slashing two-bagger.

That made the spectators sit up and take notice.

It also aroused Carey Cameron, causing him to realize the possible danger that the amateurs might make a spurt when such a thing was least expected. He was relieved when Weaver struck Gamp out.

"We must have some more runs, boys," said Cameron, as his players gathered about him. "Jump right in now and make them. Not too many, but enough to have the game safely in hand."

They responded by getting a single score, and it seemed that pure accident prevented the piling up of several more.

In the last of the seventh the Merries did not make a run, Weaver seeming to have them at his mercy.

Again in the eighth, although Cartersville got two men onto the sacks, no scores were made on either side.

The ninth inning opened with the score three to one in favor of the locals.

"That's really lead enough," said Cameron; "but one or two more runs will not spoil the game. I want you to make two scores, boys. You have a fine opening, for Moran starts it."

"I'll agree to get a hit," said Moran, "if they'll just help me circle the bags."

He was positive he could get a hit then, but some of his conceit evaporated when he fanned twice and was fooled both times.

There had not been much complaint against Starbright's work as umpire, for Cartersville was holding the lead and fancied that lead could be increased any time. Just now Moran was unable to kick, as he was swinging at the balls.

Apparently Merriwell put the next ball just where the batter wanted it.

But again Moran missed, greatly to his dismay.

"Oh, you're a mark!" sneered Madison. "Wait till I git at him! I ain't got no hits to-day, but I've been waitin' for this chance."

Johnson was in position to strike.

"Look out fo' me, ma-a-an," he grinned. "Dis time I puts it ober de fence. Allus does it once in a game."

He tried hard—too hard, in fact. Like Moran, he fell an easy victim to Merriwell's arts.

Frank was now pitching in his best form, having thrown off all attempt at deception.

Madison swore he would get a hit. He realized that his reputation as a heavy batter had suffered that day.

The crowd yelled and hooted at Frank, seeking to rattle him, but his face was perfectly grave and he seemed deaf to the uproar. In the stand he saw a veiled woman, who sat silent and rigid, her gloved hands clasped. He knew she was watching him, her heart heavy with despair, for it seemed that the locals had won.

At the beginning of the game Merry had resolved not to let Madison get a hit. Now, as the fellow came up for the last time, Frank pitched with bewildering speed, his curves being sharp and baffling.

Although every ball pitched was a strike, Starbright had confidence in Merry and declared two, at which the batter did not offer, to be "balls."

Then Merry wound up with his surprising slow ball, which seemed to hang in the air, and Madison struck too soon.

"You're out!" cried Starbright.

"Well, it's all right, fellows," laughed Cameron. "You have to hold them down, that's all. It's easy for Weaver. The game is ours."

Frank spoke to his players in low tones as they gathered around him at the bench.

"We must go after it now," he said. "There must be no tie. We must win it in this inning—or lose it. You're the first batter, Bart."

Hodge was grim and determined as he walked to the plate. He let the first ball pass, but hit the second and lined it out.

Hickey made a jump to one side, struck out his glove and caught the ball. It was a handsome catch of what had looked like a safe two-bagger.

Bart's head dropped a moment as he turned back toward the bench, but it came up at once, and he spoke to Frank, making himself heard above the uproar, for the crowd was yelling like madmen:

"You can do it just the same, Frank. That was a case of horse-shoes."

Merry did not try for a long hit. One run would do no good. He attempted to place a safe single, and drove a liner into an opening in right field.

Gamp followed, but the hopes of the visitors sank when Joe fanned out in the most dismal manner.

The only chance now seemed for Browning to make a long, safe hit, and the big fellow tried for it. Instead of hitting as he expected, he sent a slow one rolling toward Moran.

Never in all his life did Bruce cover ground as he did then. Those who fancied him to be a huge, heavy, lazy fellow now saw him fairly fly over the ground, and he reached first a good stride ahead of the ball.

"Safe!" declared Starbright.

Sitting on the bench, Hodge groaned as he saw Rattleton, pale and unsteady, step out to strike.

"It's all off!" Bart muttered. "Harry can't hit that pitching!"

Weaver flashed over a speedy one.

Harry did not move.

"One strike!" declared Starbright, his honesty compelling him to declare it.

Weaver sent in another one.

Rattleton swung.

Crack!

Bart Hodge leaped into the air with a yell of astonishment and joy.

It was the hit of Rattleton's whole career in baseball. Clean over the most distant portion of centre-field fence sailed the ball, disappearing from view.

A second yell escaped Bart's lips, and he began "throwing cartwheels," while Merriwell, Browning, and Rattleton capered round the bases and came home.

The spectators seemed dazed.

No one, however, was more dazed than Carey Cameron. He did not move from the bench.

CHAPTER XVIII

IN THE CLUB CONSERVATORY.

Their experience with the sporting element of Cartersville had been so unpleasant that Frank and his friends had no desire to remain longer in the town. Greatly to their surprise they were not molested in any way by the friends of Carey Cameron, who seemed to have received a knockout blow, and the Merries left the town by the first train for the East.

Their objective point was Ashport, where a gentleman by the name of Robert Ashley had offered a magnificent trophy to be contested for by all legitimate amateurs who wished to enter a cross-country running contest. It was not that Frank, or any of his team, intended to enter the contest that had influenced Merry to take in Ashport on his journey to the East, but he had heard much about the man who was promoting the event, and what he had heard had been favorable.

Ashley was an Englishman, and shortly after graduating from Oxford he had found himself, at the death of his father, left with but a small portion of the fortune he had been led to believe he should inherit. Quickly realizing that the income of this reduced fortune would not support him in the style he desired, he put aside family and caste prejudice against "trade" and formed an unfortunate business alliance with a shrewd rascal, who quickly succeeded by crooked methods in robbing him of what he had left, and then threw him over to face the world.

By the sale of personal effects, Ashley raised something like three hundred pounds, and with this in his pocket he bade farewell to England and turned his face toward America.

There is no need to recount his career in this country, but let it suffice to say that, after many hardships and severe struggles, he "struck it rich" in Colorado. For him "the mining game" was a successful one, and within five years after fortune turned, he retired from the struggle, many times a millionaire. His success in the face of disappointment and hard luck he attributed to his persistence, endurance, and staying power; and many a time he averred that these qualities—to some extent hereditary—had been cultivated, developed, and brought to perfection by such school-day and college sports as cross-country running and hare and hounds.

Ashley had conceived a great admiration and love for the country in which he had retrieved his fallen fortunes. After a visit to his former home in the old country, he returned to the United States and finally settled near Ashport, on the Ohio River. Whether or not he was attracted by the name of the town it is impossible to say; but there he found precisely the sort of country he admired and his fortune permitted him to purchase a large estate.

He soon became actively concerned in many charitable works and he took a great interest in all sorts of healthy outdoor sports, participating in such as were adapted to his years and encouraging those in which he could not longer indulge. He founded the Ashport Amateur Athletic Association, which, although located in the country, was within easy range of many thriving towns and two large and prosperous cities; and, in the two years of its existence, it had made such rapid advancement in membership and achievement that it was regarded as one of the leading organizations of the sort in the country.

Among the members of the club were several former college men of note in athletics, not the least of whom was Carl Prince, who became known as the "Georgetown Wonder" when he had twice broken the American college record in the quarter-mile run.

Other ex-college men who had accomplished things on the track and the cinder path and later joined Ashport were Clifford Clyde, of Yale, and Hugh Sheldon, Michigan's remarkable hurdler and steeplechaser.

Mr. Ashley had a theory that distance running was neglected in America, and he sought to arouse interest in it. For this purpose he had offered a prize to be contested for at Ashport on a certain date, by any and all legitimate amateurs of America who wished to enter the cross-country running contest.

The sporting columns of the newspapers had thoroughly advertised the coming event, and had commented much on the beauty and costliness of the trophy. Having seen these articles in the papers, Frank Merriwell planned to reach Ashport on the trip East with his athletic team in time to witness the contest.

It happened, however, that Paul Proctor, the president of the Ashport A. A., a Harvard grad, knew Merry well and took pains to extend him an invitation to participate in the contest.

Although Frank had not given any thought to a participation in the events, he had gladly accepted Proctor's invitation, and on the day of the tryouts he watched them from the observatory of the clubhouse which was located at the shoulder of an oval mile track that had been constructed for all sorts of foot races. From this observatory could be obtained a clear and complete view of the track and grounds of the Ashport Athletic Association.

Back of the clubhouse and to the east lay Ashport, a thriving, up-to-date village. The river swept in a horseshoe-like curve to the south. To the north was the estate of Robert Ashley, comprising hundreds of acres of green fields, broad meadows, hills, valleys, and wild woodland. On one of the hillsides, surrounded by splendid old trees, stood Ash Hall. In order to build a home to suit himself, Mr. Ashley had razed a house that formerly stood on the same spot.

"Who is the pacemaker?" asked Merry, as he watched the runners through a pair of field glasses.

"That is Carl Prince, of Batavia," answered Paul Proctor.

"Not Prince, the Georgetown Wonder?"

"The same fellow. He's just as fast to-day as he was at college, when he became known as the Georgetown Wonder."

"He was a great quarter-miler," nodded Frank, having lowered the glasses for a moment; "but I don't recall that he ever made a reputation as a long-distance man."

"Not at college," admitted Proctor. "He didn't go in for long-distance work then. He has since becoming a member of the Ashport A. A."

"I am inclined to fancy he has not changed his methods to any great extent, and you know long-distance work is much different from sprinting and dashes. True it is running, but runners are divided into three classes—the sprinters, the middle-distance men, and the long-distance or cross-country men. Those adapted for the second class named, or who have won records or events in that class, find it more easy to become cross-country men than do those of the first class."

"What makes you think Prince has not changed his methods?"

"His stride, his carriage, and his tenseness. Sprinters are under strain from start to finish in a race, and their muscles are taut. They are liable to tie up in long runs. They forget to relax, and their muscles become overstrained. When a man ties up in a long run he's liable not to finish at all. He finds himself run out at a time and point when he should be at his very best."

"Hollingsworth has considerable confidence in Prince."

"Who is Hollingsworth?"

"Our trainer. He's an Englishman, and he knows his business. He was formerly the champion of the Middlesex Cross Country Club, in England. We were lucky to get hold of him here."

"Long-distance and cross-country running seems to be a fad with your club, Proctor."

"Naturally," smiled the president of the club. "Mr. Robert Ashley, who founded the club, gave us our field and track and built this handsome clubhouse for us, is a crank on that sort of sport. In his day, he was the greatest cross-country and hare-and-hounds man in Oxford."

"He is an Englishman?"

"Yes. That is, he was. He's a naturalized American now. Made a fortune in mining and settled here. That splendid house you can see on the hill yonder is where he lives. It is modeled after the old English country mansion, and he calls it Ash Hall. Mr. Ashley claims that cross-country running is the finest sport in the world to develop staying power and endurance in a young man, and he says staying power is what the modern young man needs to make him successful in business. He thinks there are too many sprinters in business, who make a hot dash for a while, but are unable to keep up the pace until successful."

Frank smiled and nodded.

"It is my opinion that Mr. Ashley is a man of wisdom and generosity," he said. "The runners are coming down the straight course to the stand. We can get a better view of them now."

He again lifted the glasses to his eyes, an example followed by several other persons.

CHAPTER XIX

CONFIDENTIAL CRITICISM.

As the runners came nearer, Frank lowered the glasses and watched them with the naked eye.

"Yes," he murmured, "I'm afraid Prince will tie up in a long run. He is inclined to carry his chin a bit too high."

"We are placing a great deal of reliance in him," said Proctor, as if a bit vexed by Merry's criticism. "Hollingsworth has chosen him as a leader to work out the bunch."

"Who is that second fellow—the one with the mop of light hair?"

"That's Tom Bramwell."

"His form is better than that of Prince; but he hasn't the range, and I'm afraid he's a bit too heavy."

"Oh, Bramwell never did anything brilliant in his life. Nobody counts on him."

"He's just the man who's liable to surprise everybody in a match of this sort. There is a pretty runner to the left of him—the slender little chap."

"That's Clifford Clyde, a Yale man."

"Grad?"

"No; he was suspended in his sophomore year and never tried to get back."

"He runs easy, but lifts his feet just a little too high. The man behind him is the best runner in the lot, if he didn't have one bad fault."

"That's Hugh Sheldon, the University of Michigan hurdler. What's the fault?"

"The way he carries his arms. He swings them across his body, and thus fails to get the proper lift of a direct forward swing. There is lost motion in that swing."

"There seems to be something the matter with them all," muttered Proctor, with a disappointed air.

"It is seldom you see a runner without faults," smiled Frank. "And some mighty good men have bad habits in running. Many wonderfully good English long-distance runners have the fault of swinging their arms across their bodies, yet, for all of this, they generally defeat Americans in cross-country running and in other things which demand endurance."

"That's what Mr. Ashley says, except he has made no mention of the bad arm action of the English. If Americans run in better form, why don't they defeat the English?"

"Because they have not the stamina—the stay. They have not been properly trained."

"Oh, do you believe in a rigid form of training for all men?"

"Not at all. I have arrived at a point in life when I firmly believe the old saw: 'What's one man's meat is another man's poison.' You can't put a bunch of men in training and force them all to conform to set and rigid rules with the best result. Above everything else, a runner must have some love for his work and a great ambition to excel. Then he should study himself and find out just the sort of work that agrees with him in training. He should not shirk. He should take all he can stand without injury. He should consult with his trainer, and the trainer must have discernment and sense enough not to underwork or overwork that man. It requires a trainer of mighty keen discernment to determine just what is best for a bunch of five or six men with different natures, different habits, and varying ability. It's likely you have done well in engaging an English trainer, as the English excel in this style of running. How often has he sent the men cross country?"

"Only twice thus far. He says he can get the best out of them by working them on the track where he can watch them. He's a good runner himself, but in going cross country he cannot watch all the men, you know."

Merriwell looked mildly surprised, opened his mouth to speak, then closed his lips and remained silent.

Hodge also betrayed surprise, but maintained the silent demeanor that had made him non-conspicuous since entering the observatory.

Proctor was too shrewd not to note Frank's action.

"What were you thinking of saying, Merriwell?" he asked.

"Oh, not much," answered Frank.

The runners had now turned the shoulder near the clubhouse, and all leaned over the rail to watch them as they passed the long, low bathhouse, which was also the residence of the track master.

After a moment, Proctor said:

"I wish you would tell me what you started to say a bit ago, Merriwell."

"I don't think I had better."

"Why not?"

"It's not the thing for me to come here and criticise the methods of your trainer."

"You may do so privately to me."

Still Frank was disinclined, seeking to divert Proctor from this inquiry by calling his attention to the fact that Bramwell had a beautiful stride and no lost motion.

"If he had more range," said Merry, "he would be the man of that lot to back."

"It's strange Hollingsworth doesn't think so—or, at least, hasn't said anything about it," said Proctor.

"Perhaps Hollingsworth understands Bramwell's disposition and doesn't wish the fellow to get too good an opinion of himself. You know that spoils a runner occasionally."

Proctor slipped over close to Frank. The two men were now at the western side of the observatory, still watching the runners and talking in low tones. Hodge leaned on the southern rail and seemed absorbed in thought.

"What were you going to say about Hollingsworth's methods a short time ago, Merriwell?" persisted the president of the club.

"It is now three days before the great match?"

"Yes."

"Already contestants are coming in. If you will take the pains to look yonder and watch the woods on the side of that hill away there, using the glass, you will soon see three runners emerge and descend the hill. They are some of the men who are going to compete, and they are getting practical cross-country work."

Proctor seized the glass and leveled it as directed. After fifteen or twenty seconds, he muttered:

"You're right! There comes one of them—yes, and there is another! Now I can see all three of them. How in the world did you discover them?"

"Oh, I often look around. I surveyed the country, with the aid of that glass, when we first came up here. There are two more chaps hidden in that valley yonder, while still a third, a solitary fellow, is skirting the bend of the river down yonder. It's likely I have not seen all the men who are out getting practical cross-country work to-day, for we know that at least a dozen are stopping in Ashport."

"Well?"

"Well, here are your men hammering round a fine, smooth track. Why, they should have quit track running long ago. For the past two weeks they should have run cross country at least five times a week, directed by the trainer. One day out of every six in the last two weeks could have been given to work here on the track, where Hollingsworth would be able to watch the men and note their peculiarities and progress. Has Mr. Ashley taken special note of Hollingsworth's methods?"

"No; but he has confidence in Hollingsworth."

"Well, I'm not infallible," laughed Frank. "I'm only giving my ideas; but I have received those ideas from experience and from the suggestion of men of experience. I don't wish to set myself up as authority, Proctor, for I——"

"You might," interrupted Proctor quickly. "You are recognized in this country as authority on most amateur sports."

"But I have never tried for a record in cross-country running."

"Why don't you try in this contest? The champions of the United States will take part. Look at these entries: Harvey Neil, New York Athletic Club; Philip Pope, Bay State A. A., Boston; Arthur Huntley, Bison A. A., Buffalo; Farwell Lyons, of the Chicago Clippers, and many others, among whom are several college grads and ex-collegians of note. It would be a great thing for us to have Frank Merriwell in the contest. Come on, old man! The course has been laid off and will be announced to-morrow. You're in time to go over it with the men before the race."

"But, my dear fellow," smiled Merry, "you seem to forget that I ought to put in two or three weeks of consistent training for such a contest if I meant to enter."

Unheard and unobserved, a red-faced chap in a sweater had mounted the steps to the observatory. He had a Scotch cap pushed back on his head, and he paused with his hands on his hips, surveying Merriwell's back with a look of disapproval, while he listened to the words of Frank and Paul.

"But I have heard it claimed that you keep yourself constantly in training, and you are now finishing a tour with your own athletic team. If you remain here and do not enter, it will be fancied that you were afraid. People will ask why you were present and failed to compete for the splendid Ashley trophy."

"There is another reason why I should not enter," said Merry. "That trophy ought to be won by a member of this club. If I did enter, I'd go after it in earnest as it is my rule never to do a thing unless I do my level best."

"But, according to your criticism, Carl Prince has no chance of winning, our men are being coached wrong, and all of them have faults. We have no real chance of winning, it seems."

"You appear to forget what I have said about Bramwell."

"Even he lacks the range, you have said."

"But I think he has the courage and endurance. It is endurance and heart that count in a contest of this sort, providing the runner has had something like correct training. You pressed me for my idea of your trainer's methods, and what I said was spoken in confidence. I have no desire to injure Hollingsworth, who may be sincere and a very good fellow."

The chap in the sweater smiled disdainfully, continuing to listen, an expression of mingled anger and craft on his unpleasant face.

"Of course if you will not enter that settles it," said Proctor; "but I don't believe Bramwell can defeat Pope, of Boston, or Huntley, of Buffalo."

"How about Neil?"

"He is not the best man from his club."

"Well, I'd like to see one of your men take that trophy, Proctor. I don't want it."

The fellow in the sweater laughed rather harshly and sarcastically, causing every one in the observatory to turn quickly and look at him.

"Hollingsworth!" exclaimed Proctor.

"Mr. Merriwell is very generous," observed the laughing man cuttingly. "It's an easy thing for 'im to be generous in such a manner, and no one will hever suspect 'im of timidness. He can travel on his record. I think he is hextremely wise in keeping hout of this race."

It was Hollingsworth, the English trainer, who betrayed his origin whenever excited in the least by the misuse of the letter "h" in his speech. In ordinary conversation he seldom did this.

Proctor knew at once that the trainer had overheard some of their talk, which threw him into confusion.

Merriwell did not seem disturbed. He surveyed Hollingsworth with quiet interest.

Proctor hastened to introduce them.

Hollingsworth did not remove his hands from his hips, but gave a little jerk of his bullet head in acknowledgment of the introduction.

"I knew it was Mr. Merriwell," he said. "No one helse would think of being so hextremely generous."

These words were meant to be very cutting.

"Besides," continued the Englishman, as Frank did not speak at

119

once, "no one helse is so wonderfully wise."

Bart Hodge was frowning blackly. He had taken an instant dislike to Hollingsworth. He afterward confessed a desire to punch the fellow on sight.

Proctor sought to mediate and pour oil on the waters.

"Mr. Merriwell was speaking in strict confidence to me," he declared. "He did not intend that any one should overhear."

"And," said Frank, "I had no thought that any one would come up behind us with such pantherish steps that we could not know he was listening to conversation not intended for his ears."

The red face of Hollingsworth took on a deeper tinge.

"I 'ave seen these gents who go round offering secret criticisms!" he exclaimed warmly. "They think to do more 'arm that way than by speaking hout with courage; but hoften it is the case that they hinjure no one, as they seldom know what they are talking habout."

This was meant as another deep thrust at Merry.

"You'll get what's coming to you if you keep it up!" thought Hodge. "If Merry doesn't deliver the goods, I will!"

Frank knew Bart would smart under such conditions, and he gave the quick-tempered fellow a glance of warning.

Merriwell was the guest of the Ashport A. A., and he wished no encounter with the trainer.

"I have not the least desire to say anything to injure you, Mr. Hollingsworth," he declared calmly. "On the contrary, I am inclined to give you Englishmen all the credit you deserve in long-distance and cross-country work, and that is a great deal, for you stand at the head."

This seemed to quiet the trainer a little, although it did not wholly satisfy him.

"But you have no call to come here and discuss me with the president of the club," he asserted. "I know my business, sir. If you don't think so, look into the records of Overby and Hare, of the Middlesex Cross Country Club, England. I trained both of those men."

"I know about them. Hare could not defeat Orton, the American, at the steeplechase in your own country. Orton won the championship of England. Already he held the championship of America, and later, at Paris, he became champion of the world."

Hollingsworth flushed again.

"Horton was an accident!" he cried. "You never produced a man like 'im before, and you never will hagain!"

"Oh, I don't know about that," returned Frank, with slightly uplifted eyebrows. "We're just getting into such work in earnest over here. You have been training men for it a long, long time. Generation after generation of long-distance men have followed each other at your colleges. We're beginning to press you hard. Twenty or thirty years from now you'll find yourselves following in our lead."

"Never!" snapped the Englishman. "You Hamericans are conceited, that's what's the matter with you! Heven in this race I wouldn't be surprised to see an Englishman take the trophy."

"But you have no English runner in this club who is formidable."

"No."

"Then it seems you do not expect one of your own runners to win."

"I 'ope one of them will," said Hollingsworth hastily. "I 'ave done my best, but a man can't make champions hout of poor material."

"Occasionally he can," denied Frank.

"Oh, I suppose you might, you 'ave a way of haccomplishing such wonders! Better get hup your courage and henter. I don't think it would be so 'ard for one or two of our members to defeat you."

"You tempt me—really you do," smiled Merriwell.

"You 'aven't the nerve."

"Haven't I?"

"'Ardly. If you did, as sure as my name is 'Erbert 'Ollingsworth, I'd wager you wouldn't finish better than third."

"Just to show you I can finish second, at least," Frank laughed, "I may reconsider my determination and enter for the run. In fact, I think I will."

"I 'ope you don't back hout," sneered Hollingsworth; "but, considering who is hentered already, I fear you will."

Frank had settled his mind.

"Put your fears at rest," he advised.

"Well, if you get shown up after being so critical," said the Englishman, "I shall not shed tears. Mr. Proctor, I wish to see you after training is over. Will you wait for me here, or come over to the baths?"

"I'll see you downstairs, Hollingsworth."

The Englishman nodded to Proctor and the two gentlemen at the west side of the observatory, who had listened to the talk, but had offered to take no part in it, descended the steps, disappearing from view.

"I give you my word, Frank," said Hodge hotly, "that I'd rather punch that fellow than any man I've encountered in a whole year! I simply ached to hit him, but, of course, I wouldn't pick up a quarrel with him here."

"I hope you refrain from picking a quarrel with him anywhere as long as we remain in Ashport."

"But he was so confounded insolent!"

"Which is the manner of some Englishmen of a certain grade. They entertain a contempt for Americans and are unable to conceal it. The better class, like Mr. Ashley, for instance, have come to understand and respect us."

"You seem to be a rather broad-minded young man," said one of the gentlemen. "I observed that you held yourself in perfect restraint throughout that talk with Hollingsworth just now."

"Too much restraint is as bad as none," muttered Hodge.

"That depends on what you consider too much," said Frank, who had caught the words.

"I tell you," said Proctor, speaking to Merry and Bart, "I'm inclined to believe Hollingsworth has not worked our men out properly. He'll have to give them some cross-country work now."

"But it's pretty late," reminded Merriwell. "They must not be overworked. There is danger of overworking them at this stage. Don't let him push them until they go stale on the eve of the contest."

"If one of our men does not win," said Paul, "I hope you get that trophy, Merriwell."

"Thank you. I have decided to try for it, but I still think it should go to a member of this club. Who is the Englishman entered, and where is he from? Hollingsworth said he'd not be a bit surprised to see an Englishman walk off with the trophy."

"He must have been thinking of Arthur Huntley, of Buffalo."

"Is he English?"

"I believe so. I think, though, he is now a naturalized American."

"We'll have to take a little interest in Huntley, Bart," said Frank. "I wish to know why Hollingsworth fancies he may win the trophy."

"Simply because the fellow is an Englishman," said Hodge.

But Merry shook his head.

"Hollingsworth is not a fool, and he knows there will be other good cross-country men in the race. No doubt he sympathizes with Huntley, but Huntley must be unusual in order to lead this man to believe he will win."

At this moment one of the gentlemen called attention to a carriage that was approaching the clubhouse. Immediately Proctor announced that Mr. Ashley was one of the two gentlemen in the carriage.

"He is bringing the trophy!" cried the president of the club, in great eagerness. "He stated he would show it here this afternoon. Come down, gentlemen—come down and see it!"

They descended from the observatory and went down to the parlor, where they found Mr. Ashley had already arrived, the carriage being outside the door.

The gentleman who accompanied Mr. Ashley carried in his hand a leather bag, which seemed quite heavy.

"That bag contains the trophy, I think," said Frank to Bart, as Proctor hastened to speak to Ashley.

The founder of the club was a man of slender, wiry build, an Englishman of the higher grade, who had not acquired that ponderous solemnity most Americans expect to see in Britishers of middle age and of his standing. In many respects he was more like an American than a typical Englishman. His hair and mustache contained a liberal sprinkling of gray. He was plainly dressed in brown.

Mr. Ashley had been expected, and there was a large gathering of members in the parlor. He greeted them in a pleasant manner, yet without elaborate politeness.

"Put the bag on the table in the centre of the room, Mr. Graham," he said, and his companion did as directed.

Herbert Hollingsworth entered and hurried to Mr. Ashley.

"The men have just finished work for the day," he said. "They are in the bathhouse. It will be thirty or forty minutes before they can be here."

"We will wait until they can come before showing the trophy," said Ashley. "How are our boys showing up?"

"Splendidly, sir. Prince and Clyde are in the pink of condition."

"That is good. How about Sheldon and Bramwell?"

"Oh, they will be pretty sure to make a good showing, especially Sheldon. Bramwell is persistent."

Proctor gave Frank and Bart a nod, upon which they approached and were introduced to Mr. Ashley, who shook hands warmly with both of them.

"Mr. Merriwell," he said, "I am particularly glad to meet you. Are you going to enter?"

"Well," smiled Frank, giving Hollingsworth a glance, "I have been persuaded to do so, although I did not contemplate it when

I came here."

"I persuaded him, sir," the trainer hastened to declare. "To me it seemed an opportune time to demonstrate that Mr. Merriwell is not the only one in his class."

Ashley was quick to catch something amiss in the manner of Hollingsworth.

"This contest has been advertised as open for all registered amateurs in this country," he said, at once. "Every one is welcome to compete, and may the best man win."

CHAPTER XX

THE GOLDEN TROPHY.

The parlor of the clubhouse was well filled when Robert Ashley exposed the trophy, which had been placed on the table in the centre of the room and covered with a flag.

First Mr. Ashley made a short speech, in which he explained his object in offering such an award. In substance it was for the purpose of arousing greater interest in cross-country races and thus to develop in American athletes that stamina and endurance essential in the modern man of business.

"American runners are better known for flashing brilliancy than for dogged determination," he said. "In the great race of life, endurance wins far more often than brilliancy, which is not infrequently allied with weakness. But the runner must have a strong heart, else he may become discouraged by the apparent success of some competitor who flashes past him at the start. If he persists doggedly, determinedly, gauging himself properly and making the best of his powers, he may have the satisfaction of passing the brilliant starter, leaving him winded and spent and floundering helplessly in some morass of business or thicket of commerce."

There was a breathless hush when Ashley had finished. Then a signal was given and the flag lifted.

All leaned forward and stared.

Then followed a murmur of admiration and a burst of applause.

It was a statue, the lifelike and natural representation of a diminutive, lithe-limbed runner, being about eight inches in height and molded from a fine quality of gold. The base on which it stood was also of gold.

But the admiration of the beholders was aroused not merely on account of the material from which the trophy had been made and its evident great value; the figure was splendidly and scientifically molded, being so natural in its every pose, resting on the toes of the right foot, with the left leg thrown forward in a fine stride, the knee bent, the naked left arm swung backward on a line and the right arm forward, the hands closed, the head setting perfectly on a slender yet full neck, the face firm and determined, every line from toe to topknot denoting vigorous and easy action—so natural was it that it must have created a sensation even though formed of lead.

Those present crowded about the table. After a little they began to comment wonderingly, not so much on the costliness of the trophy, as on its value as a work of art. There was no one present who did not realize that it must have cost a great sum of money, and was something that the fortunate winner could display throughout the remainder of his life with the utmost pride.

After they had discussed it for a time, Mr. Ashley spoke:

"Gentlemen," he said, "it may seem strange to you that I have not up to the present time made known the exact nature of the trophy I intended to offer. I will explain. It is my belief that the cleanest and most commendable sports are those in which the contestants participate without covetousness or hope of reward other than the glory that comes to the victor. In the glorious days of Greece the victor was rewarded with a wreath of laurel. I believed it was possible to bring together for this event the leading long-distance runners of this country, without arousing their greed by advertising the real worth of the trophy, and the result has justified my judgment. Only those who have already entered or to-day announce their intention to enter and make proper application will be accepted. Already the leading amateurs of the United States, with one or two exceptions, are entered. There is no longer a chance that greed will bring others into the contest. May the victor prove worthy of the trophy, and may it inspire him to his best efforts through life." This final speech was greeted with even more applause than the first had aroused. The astonishing generosity of Mr. Ashley was commented upon quietly by little groups, and it was universally agreed that the winner of the contest might properly lay claim to the title of cross-country champion of America.

Two young men entered and advanced to view the trophy. One of them attracted attention right away. Among those who hastened to speak to him was Herbert Hollingsworth.

"Jove, Merry!" exclaimed Hodge softly; "did you catch that chap's name?"

"What chap?"

"The one who just came in with the fellow in the blue suit. Hollingsworth is talking to him now."

"No, I didn't catch his name."

"Hollingsworth called him Huntley."

Instantly Frank gave the fellow more attention. He saw a slender, graceful young man of twenty-four or five, who had rather long legs, and who, in spite of his grace and suppleness, had about him a suggestion of strength and reserve power. His chin denoted pugnacity, his mouth determination and his nose command. His eyes were the only questionable features he possessed. Although they were not shifty and they looked at one squarely, to Frank they somehow suggested a nature not over-scrupulous—one who would sacrifice friendship or anything else for selfish gain and glory.

Proctor now discovered the newcomer and made some haste to shake hands with him, after which, taking his arm, he led him over to Frank.

"I think you will be pleased to meet Mr. Merriwell, Mr. Huntley," said the president of the club. "Mr. Merriwell, this gentleman will be one of your dangerous rivals for the golden trophy. He is the champion long-distance man of the Bison A. A., Buffalo."

"I am in truth glad to know you, Mr. Huntley," nodded Merry, as he shook the hand of the man from Buffalo.

"The pleasure is mutual," assured Huntley. "Even before coming to America I heard a great deal of you. Your career attracted the attention of Oxford and Cambridge men. I believe you are the only all-round athlete who has also excelled in competing with the champions who have made a specialty of many different sports. Usually an all-round man is in truth a jack of all trades and master of none. So you have entered for the magnificent Ashley trophy?"

"Not yet; but I have announced my intention of entering."

"Before the trophy was displayed?"

Something in this question gave Merry a slight flush of annoyance, but he concealed it perfectly.

"As Proctor can affirm, my intention was announced before the trophy was shown. Your friend, Hollingsworth, who seems to have great confidence in you, bantered me into it."

A slight cloud fell on Huntley's face.

"Mr. Hollingsworth is a mere acquaintance," he hastened to explain. "I was not aware that he had so much confidence in me."

Back of this Frank seemed to read the speaker's thoughts, and he was satisfied that Huntley was inwardly cursing Hollingsworth.

"I was led to believe him a friend and to think he had great confidence in you through some talk he made."

"Well, whatever Mr. Hollingsworth's opinion of me, I am certain he would rejoice to see me defeated by one or more of the youngsters he has developed here. It would be a feather in his cap to bring out a champion, you know."

"It would, indeed; and I should be pleased to see a member of this club secure the trophy."

"What, and you in the race?"

"Yes."

"Oh, then, were you to find yourself matched against an Ashport man toward the finish, with it settled that one of you two must come in first, you would give the other fellow the race?"

"I have not said so, nor would I do anything of the sort."

"I thought not!" said Huntley, with the slightest curl to his lips.

"Whenever I enter any contest I do so with the full determination to win, if such a thing lies within my power. Were I confident an Ashport man would win I would not enter at all."

"Your generosity is really surprising!" cried the Buffalo man laughingly. "Under any circumstances, I'll guarantee you'll enter and do your best to secure the runner of gold. In spite of your past reputation, however, I think you will find it no simple matter to obtain the trophy."

"Were it a simple matter," said Frank, "it would not be worth trying for."

"That is handsomely said, Mr. Merriwell; but I hardly fancy you could be deterred from trying under any conditions."

Having said this, Huntley again expressed his satisfaction over the meeting with Frank and bowed himself away.

"You touched him, Frank," said Hodge. "He didn't like it when you mentioned his friendship for Hollingsworth and the confidence the latter had in him."

"No, he didn't like it at all," agreed Frank. "The fact that it did touch him increases my suspicions."

"Naturally."

"There is something going on beneath the surface."

"I think it."

"What is it?"

"I'd like to know."

"So would I," confessed Merry.

"We may find out."

Bart now took a fancy to watch Huntley closely, and he was rewarded, after a time, by seeing a slight signal pass between the representative of the Bison A. A. and the Ashport trainer.

Five or ten minutes later Huntley sauntered out of the club-house. He stood a few moments on the veranda, surveying the track. Finally he crossed the track and walked out onto the field, seemingly highly interested in looking over the fine grounds of the club.

Still watching, Hodge observed that Hollingsworth left the club by the door opposite the track, and passed round to the bath-house, where he met the trackmaster, with whom he conversed for a few moments. Finally the trainer and the trackmaster started along the oval track, the former indicating by his gestures that he was criticising something that did not suit his fancy.

By this time Huntley was far down at the lower end of the field. He crossed the track down there and disappeared amid some trees.

At the western side of the baseball diamond and just inside the track were seats for spectators and a small covered grand stand for ladies.

Hollingsworth and the trackmaster paused just before reaching the stand. The trainer appeared to be pointing out something near that point which caused him dissatisfaction.

Hodge caught a glimpse of a man amid the trees, beyond the track, far down at the southwestern extremity of the field. The man was sauntering northward.

"Behind the grand stand!" decided Bart. "That's where they are going to meet!"

He was palpitating with eagerness, but for the time he seemed baffled and unable to make a move.

Finally Hollingsworth and the trackmaster parted, the latter turning back, while the Englishman sauntered on slowly, his head down. Twice he looked round toward the clubhouse, as if fancying he might be watched. Finally he disappeared behind the stand.

In a twinkling Hodge was outside the house and trotting away briskly along the track. He was taking chances. If seen, he hoped he might be thought a runner seeking to sweat off a few pounds or an enthusiast who had been spurred to try the track through seeing others at it.

As he ran, he watched for the men amid the trees, and also kept his eyes open for Hollingsworth. In case the latter reappeared beyond the stand, Hodge felt that it would be useless to make any further attempt to follow him.

At first Bart hugged the outside of the track. When he approached the turn at the shoulder of the oval, he crossed and pressed close to the curb.

He had now brought the stand and seats between him and the distant trees into which Huntley had sauntered. None too soon, for the Buffalo man reappeared, vaulted the outside fence and came walking up the track.

Hodge could not go much farther without appearing in full view of Hollingsworth, if the latter lingered behind the stand. Therefore he sprang over the inside fence and kept toward the stand in a straight line, running lightly on the turf.

Bart reached the stand, slipped past the corner, climbed into it without seeking the regular entrance, and walked softly toward the southern end. There, hidden from any one at the south by the boarding at that end and equally well protected toward the west, he mounted without noise over the seats until he reached the highest one at the back. He might have looked over the boarding in search of Hollingsworth, but he decided not to run the risk of being seen. Squatting there in the upper corner, he peered through a crack and saw Huntley rapidly approaching.

Bart knew his actions must seem suspicious to any one at the clubhouse who happened to observe them; but he minded that not at all, being determined to learn, if possible, if there existed a secret understanding of any sort between Hollingsworth and Huntley.

The Buffalo man hastened his steps. Finally he was so near that Bart could no longer watch him through the crack, being too high for that. A moment later he heard Hollingsworth speak and knew the fellow was behind the stand and almost directly below.

"What's the matter, Arthur?" asked the Ashport trainer.

"You've been talking too much," retorted Huntley, and there was suppressed anger in his voice.

"Talking?" exclaimed Hollingsworth.

"I said so!"

"'Ow—'ow 'ave I been talking?" cried the trainer, growing excited and beginning to misuse the eighth letter of the alphabet. "Hexplain what you mean!"

"You've been talking to Merriwell."

"What if I 'ave? He didn't get much satisfaction hout of it."

"He got enough to discover that we are friendly."

"'Ow did he? 'ow did he?"

"I don't know, but he did. Besides that, you were fool enough to say you had confidence in me."

"Never said hanything of the kind! Who told you all this?"

"Merriwell himself called you my friend and said you expressed great confidence in me."

"He 'ad no right to say it! I only said an Englishman might win the race."

"And I'm the only Englishman entered! That was a wise remark!"

Huntley's sarcasm was cutting.

"I didn't stop to think he might make hanything of it," said Hollingsworth, with some humbleness. "'Owever, it can't do no 'urt."

"It can do any amount of harm. I fancy this Merriwell is a shrewd fellow. If he should learn that I have been staying in the country within ten miles of Ashford for the past two weeks, he might get an inclination to investigate and so discover that during that time I have every day been over the course we are to run."

"Heven then he could not prove hanything damaging, Harthur. 'Ow could he say you found hout the course through me? Why, sir, no one 'ere 'as any notion I know the course, which Mr. Hashley will give hout to-morrow."

"You never can tell how things will leak out if some one goes nosing after the facts. I don't want it even suspected that I obtained an advantage by running the course day after day and making a study of the country so that I could cover it with the greatest speed, avoiding all the bad places and making a number of short cuts, like the one through Dead Timber Jungle. I cut off more than half a mile right there. Then I know a perfect path over Ragged Hill, and I'll wager more than two-thirds of the runners will skirt the hill. I'll gain on them there."

"If the truth hever came hout it would 'urt me more than it would you. They would learn 'ow I bribed the man hemployed by Mr. Hashley to lay hout the course and hinduced him to give me a map of it."

"It would be disastrous for us both. I want that trophy, but I don't want any one to suspect I obtained the slightest advantage over the rest of the contestants, who will see a map of the course for the first time to-morrow."

As may be readily understood, this conversation was proving highly interesting to the young man in the grand stand, who could distinctly hear every word. His eyes flashed as he whispered to himself:

"So you have it nicely fixed, my fine rascals! I rather think you'll make a fizzle of your crooked game after all."

Bart was now well pleased over the result of his efforts. It was quite in opposition to his natural behavior to thus play the eavesdropper; but what he heard in this manner fully justified the ruse and warded off any qualms of conscience that otherwise might have attacked him.

He continued to listen, for, believing themselves safe from prying eyes or listening ears, the schemers pursued their conversation.

"You will get the trophy, sir," declared Hollingsworth, growing calmer and once more restoring the eighth letter of the alphabet to its rightful position. "No man from the outside is better than you, and they will not have the advantage of your knowledge. As for the Ashport men, they might do very well on this track; but there's only one in the lot who will make a great showing cross country."

"You mean Prince, of course?"

"No, I don't mean Prince, sir."

"I thought you regarded him as the star of your runners."

"He is the star in many ways; but there is another I think you have to fear more than Prince."

"Who is it?"

"Bramwell."

"Where has he ever made a record?"

"He has no record."

"But you think——"

"He's a better man than any one imagines—that is, any one except this Merriwell chap. Hang him! He watched the men from the observatory to-day, and he picked Bramwell out as the best in the lot for cross country, although Prince was there, besides Clyde and Sheldon, both of whom look more like runners."

"How did he happen to select Bramwell?"

"I can't imagine."

"Why do you think Bramwell the most dangerous?"

"Because he is a perfect bulldog, sir—he sets his jaws and never lets go."

"An excellent quality in a cross-country man."

"It is Bramwell who might press you hard, sir, if he had confidence in himself, and had been trained in much cross-country running. I have not given him the training, and I've taken pains not to let him know he's half as good as he really is."

"Oh, I think you overestimate him, Hollingsworth. Besides, the men I fear are Pope, Neil, Lyons, and—Merriwell. There is where you made another blunder."

"Where, sir?"

"In hounding Merriwell to get into the match. Why did you do it?"

"I didn't think he would enter."

"He's going to enter, and he's the man I fear above all others."

"Which shows you have real horse sense," muttered the unseen listener in the stand, smiling grimly.

"Look 'ere," said Hollingsworth, growing excited again, "I looked at it this way, sir: If you defeat Merriwell it will be a great feather in your cap."

"If!" said Huntley significantly.

"You ought to do it with the advantage you 'ave. With 'im in the match, you can well claim the championship of Hamerica when you win."

"I tell you, Hollingsworth, you made a blunder when you forced him into it. No man in America understands the requirements of the work as well as he, and I have a feeling that he will be the one to defeat me. I would give a hundred dollars—clean, cold cash— to keep him from entering."

"Perhaps 'e may be kept hout of it."

"How?"

"Every man who henters must be a member of the Amateur Athletic Union of America."

"Of course."

"He must show his certificate of membership before starting in the race."

"That's the rule."

"If Merriwell didn't 'ave his certificate he couldn't compete."

"No."

"There may be some way to get 'old of it and destroy it."

"I see no way of doing that."

"Will you give me a 'undred dollars if I find a way?"

Apparently Huntley was surprised by this question, for he remained silent some moments, while the eavesdropper in the stand hushed his breathing and strained his ear in order not to miss a word.

Finally the rascal from Buffalo vehemently but guardedly exclaimed:

"Yes, by the Lord Harry, I'll give you a hundred dollars if you will find a way to do that trick—and do it!"

"It's good as done, sir!" declared Hollingsworth. "'Ave the money ready when I call for it."

"But how do you propose to perform the trick?"

Hollingsworth laughed craftily.

"I know the bell boys at the Hashport 'Ouse, where Merriwell

133

and his party are stopping."

"What of that?"

"They 'ave passkeys to all the rooms. They're not supposed to 'ave them, but that makes no difference."

"Go on."

"If I pay one of those boys, I can keep informed on all of Merriwell's acts. Let him enter for the race. Between now and the day of the run he will go over the course. On that day I'll get my bell boy to admit me to his room. Somewhere among his effects I will find his certificate. I'll destroy it."

Hollingsworth was calm again—calm with confidence in his own villainy.

"The plan is both desperate and dangerous," said Huntley.

"I'll take all the chances, Arthur. I never forget a friend and a countryman. Rely on me."

"I hope you may succeed, but I assure you that I have my doubts. I shall try to find a method of making sure Merriwell does not defeat me if you fail to keep him from running. In the meantime, go ahead and do your best."

"That I will, sir."

Although Hollingsworth claimed Huntley as a friend, it was plain from his manner of speech that he recognized the man as one of higher caste than himself.

"Yes, go ahead and do your worst!" mentally exclaimed Bart Hodge. "This plot will fizzle. I wish I knew what other method Huntley will seek as a last resort."

But this he was not to learn, as the rascals how became fearful that they might be seen together, and decided to separate, which they soon did.

CHAPTER XXI

TOM BRAMWELL.

Frank Merriwell and Bart Hodge were walking back to their hotel in town after the visit to the club, when the latter related to Merry all that he had heard while in the grand stand.

"What do you think of it?" cried Hodge, as he finished.

"I think you have unearthed some crooked work that ought to put an end to the career of Arthur Huntley as an amateur athlete and Herbert Hollingsworth as a reputable and honest trainer."

"Just what I think, Frank. We'll expose the plot. Huntley will be barred and Hollingsworth kicked out of his position in disgrace."

Merry meditated a little as he walked, his head slightly bowed. After a few moments he slowly shook his head.

"It won't do," he declared.

"What won't?"

"Your plan."

"I'd like to know why not!"

"I'll tell you. In the first place, the proof is not sufficient."

"Why, Merry, I heard their plot!"

"No question about that, but you have no one to back you up. You are the only person who overheard it."

"That's true," admitted Bart reluctantly; "but then——"

"If you were to accuse them, both men would deny it and demand corroborative evidence, which you could not produce. It would be two against one, and their word would be just as effective as yours under such circumstances. Merely on your statement of the truth you could not have Huntley barred."

Hodge saw the force of this, but he rebelled against it.

"It isn't right, Frank!" he cried. "It's wrong! It's outrageous!"

"It may be wrong, but that makes no difference."

"What can we do?"

"Try to obtain evidence that will accomplish the result."

"I doubt if we can do it in time."

"So do I," Frank confessed.

"Well, then——"

"The plot must be frustrated. Huntley must be defeated in his ambition to secure the trophy."

"You can do that," asserted Bart eagerly and confidently.

"I can try."

"But after that—is he to continue to be an amateur athlete in good standing?"

"Not if we can secure the needed evidence to expose his rascality. What was it you overheard about a jungle in some dead timber and a path over a hill?"

"Why, Huntley said he had found a number of short cuts over the course, one of which was through Dead Timber Jungle and the other over Ragged Hill."

"To-morrow, when the course is given out, we'll go over it and look for these short cuts. True, we may not find them in such short time, but we'll do our best. Plainly, unless we do find them, Huntley will have a decided advantage."

"No doubt of it."

"Then it is up to us, and may luck be with us."

"But how about their dastardly scheme to destroy your certificate of membership in the Amateur Athletic Union of the United States?"

"Leave that matter to me," smiled Frank. "Don't worry about it in the least."

"You mean to place the certificate where it cannot be found? Put it into the safe at the hotel, Merry."

"I will take care of it, all right," was the assurance.

Early the following day a map of the course the runners were to follow was placed on exhibition at the clubhouse. This map was eagerly studied by the contestants who had entered, and it was seen that the course would be a difficult one to traverse, as it led through many wild and rugged sections of the Ashley estate. At five different points along the course watchers were to be stationed to observe and record the passing of the runners. In this manner dishonesty on the part of the contestants in the way of failure to cover the entire distance was to be prevented.

Frank and Bart were among the first to examine the map, which was hung on a wall in the reading room of the clubhouse. Merry went over it rapidly, copying it on a sheet of paper, and questioning a man who had been concerned in laying out the course, this man being present for the purpose of answering such questions and giving the runners all needed information in regard to the country.

"There is the piece of woods known as Dead Timbers, Frank," said Hodge, in a low tone, indicating the spot on the map.

"I've taken note of it," nodded Merriwell.

"And here is Ragged Hill."

"I have that indicated on my copy of the map."

From the main clubhouse the old Fardale rivals and chums proceeded to the smaller house, where the dressing rooms were. Already Merry had been given a locker in one of the dressing rooms, and in this locker he had his running clothes, together with an outfit for Hodge.

While they were dressing for the purpose of taking a run over the course, one of the Ashport men came in and busied himself in like manner.

Frank looked up and observed the fellow.

"Hello, Bramwell," he said. "Going out to look the course over to see what we're up against, are you?"

"That's the idea," laughed Bramwell. "Four fellows have started already. I see you're going, too."

"Yes. My friend Hodge is coming with me. Won't you join us?"

"Sure. I know the country hereabouts pretty well, and I may be able to help you in following the course."

"Thank you," said Frank. "If you can give me any assistance that way I shall try to repay the favor in some manner."

"Oh! that's all right," assured the Ashport man. "Every starter must know the course. After that if he can find any means of covering it easier or quicker than the rest, that's his privilege."

"Well, I reckon some of them will find a few short cuts," muttered Hodge.

"One has already, that's sure," said Frank, in a low tone.

Bramwell cast a quick glance toward them, having failed to catch their words, although he heard them say something.

Merry finished dressing and walked over to the Ashport man.

"Who do you consider the best runner in your set, Bramwell?" he inquired.

"Why, Prince, of course," was the prompt answer. "We hope he'll be able to take the trophy."

"Has Hollingsworth ever told you that you could beat Prince in a cross-country run?"

"Well, hardly!" was the laughing answer. "Why should he?"

"Because you ought to do it, and I believe you can."

Bramwell looked surprised.

"Quit your kidding!" he exclaimed. "I'm going into this thing because I like the sport."

"That's one good reason why you stand a fine chance to win. You like it. Prince likes the glory, but he does not like the work. I want to tell you something in confidence: Hollingsworth really believes you stand a better show of winning than any other Ashport runner."

Bramwell showed his incredulity, which seemed to turn into resentment in a moment.

"Say!" he cried, "do I look soft? What do you take me for? I offered to show you the course in good faith, but if you're going to give me this sort of hot air——"

"If you knew me better," said Frank, in a convincing manner, "you would not accuse me of dealing in hot air. If we start out together to-day I'm going to tell you a few things that will interest you and may spur you on to victory."

"Why should you do that? You're out for the trophy, aren't you?"

"I am; still I give you my word of honor, Bramwell, if I do not win I hope most sincerely that you will be the man to do so."

Another person than Frank Merriwell might not have convinced Tom Bramwell that he was sincere in such a statement; but there was about Merry an indefinable something that always bespoke his absolute honesty and convinced the doubter and skeptic. Looking into Frank's eyes, Bramwell was convinced.

"I thank you!" he exclaimed, with a flush of pleasure. "I am sure I don't know why you feel that way toward me, but I appreciate it."

CHAPTER XXII

WATCHING HIS CHANCE.

erbert Hollingsworth was at the clubhouse when the map was suspended on the wall. He saw Merriwell arrive and begin to look the map over with the others.

"He'll go out this morning," decided the trainer. "It will give me the opportunity I am looking for. I must not miss it."

After that he pretended to take no interest whatever in Frank's movements, but he noted that Merry left the clubhouse for the small one adjoining and rightly decided that he had resolved to go over the course at once. A few minutes later he encountered Carl Prince and Clifford Clyde.

"Looking for you, Hollingsworth," said Prince. "We're going to start out to explore the course."

"Are you?" asked the trainer.

"Why, of course!" exclaimed Clyde. "That was understood. You agreed to go with us."

"I believe I did," admitted the Englishman.

"You made us promise to be on hand so you could. Sheldon is here somewhere, and I saw Bramwell not ten minutes ago."

"Unfortunately," said Hollingsworth, "I can't start so early in the day."

"How is that?"

"I have some important business to which I must give my attention."

"Well, that's fine!" cried Clyde sarcastically. "Is there anything more important just now than seeing that we are properly prepared for this race?"

"I'm going to attend to business in connection with the race."

"What sort of business?"

"Business that will be of great benefit to us. Never mind what it is; but I give you my word it cannot be slighted or put off. Do you know if Merriwell is going out this morning?"

"Think he's dressing now," answered Prince.

"If you wait until afternoon," said Hollingsworth, "I'll be able to go over the course with you."

"Of course, if you say we are to wait——"

"It isn't necessary. Perhaps you had better go on without me. Remember the instructions I have given you, Clyde. Take the rises as fast as you can without overdoing. Shorten your stride coming down the hills and keep your feet well under you. Don't overstride if you intend to keep in the race when it's pulled off. Get the proper gait; make it even and steady, so your heart, lungs, arms, legs, and your whole body move together correctly. You're inclined to be irregular in your gait. It's the long, steady pull that counts. Keep pounding away."

"Haven't you anything to say to me?" asked Prince.

"Not a word. You know your book."

Prince looked satisfied. He knew he was generally regarded as the champion runner of the club. He was a fellow who lived on his reputation and past record. Although he pretended modesty, he was as proud as a peacock over his Georgetown days and accomplishments.

Clyde and Prince started off to dress. They met Merriwell, Hodge, and Bramwell coming from the dressing rooms.

"Hello, Bram!" exclaimed Clyde, in some surprise. "You seem to be in a rush."

"No rush at all," was the assertion. "Is Hollingsworth going out with us?"

"Not this morning."

"Why not? He said——"

"I know, but he has business he must look after this forenoon. It's very important, and he says it will be of benefit to us."

Frank and Bart exchanged glances, but said nothing.

"Well, if he isn't going out with us," said Bramwell, "I think I'll start at once."

Hollingsworth stood in a window of the clubhouse and smiled grimly as he saw Merriwell and his two companions set off along the road that led toward the wild country to the west.

"Go!" he mentally cried. "If things come my way this morning I'll make a hundred dollars and fix you so you'll take no part in the run."

He watched until Merriwell, Hodge, and Bramwell vanished, and then he sought Paul Proctor.

"I have to go into town, Mr. Proctor," he said. "I'll be back soon as possible."

"Why, I supposed you were going out with our boys this morning," said Paul, his face betraying displeasure. "How is it that you are not?"

"Other business, sir. They don't need me. I told them I would go out after noon."

"But you claim that morning is the time for the best work. I am afraid——"

"Now I know what you're going to say, sir; but you are wrong. They don't need me this morning. I've given them complete instructions. It's all right, sir, I assure you. Those boys are going to make some people open their eyes. They're in fine form."

Proctor seemed anything but satisfied, although Hollingsworth added a great deal more.

A few minutes later the treacherous trainer set off toward the village, making considerable haste.

At the Ashport House, Hollingsworth lingered about until he found an opportunity to call one of the bell boys aside by means of a signal.

"Charley," said the Englishman, "do you want to earn a fiver?"

"What doin'?" asked the boy, with a mingling of doubt and eagerness.

"Something easy."

"What is it?"

"Frank Merriwell is stopping here?"

"Sure."

"Know his room?"

"Number forty-three."

"Any one room with him?"

"Chap named Hodge. Got it in for him. He gave me a call last night because I forgot to bring up a pitcher of ice water he'd called for."

"Both Merriwell and Hodge are out?"

"Yep. They've gone over to the club."

"I want to get into their room," whispered Hollingsworth.

The boy looked alarmed.

"You can't do it."

"Now hold on, Charley. You have a passkey."

"But I can't let no one into a room."

"It's a fiver for you."

"I'd be fired."

"Nobody need know it."

"It's too risky."

"I'm taking more risk than you."

"You want to swipe something, I know! Boy fired last week for swipin'. He came near goin' to the jug. Stole a ring out of a room. Feller who owned the ring let him off when he coughed it up, but he got chucked. Boss says he's going to have the next boy who swipes anything pinched."

"I'm no thief, Charley. You ought to know that."

"Watcher want, then?"

"I want to see something Merriwell has in his room. You know he's a great runner."

"You bet! They say he's goin' to come mighty near winning the cross-country race."

"I'm afraid he is. He has a secret preparation he takes every time he runs, and it makes him strong and swift. I want to find out what it is. I heard him tell another fellow that it was prepared from a prescription he has in his room. If I can get a look at that prescription long enough to remember it or copy it, I'll be able to use the stuff on my runners. No one will ever know it. I'll give you five dollars to let me have the passkey that will admit me to Merriwell's room."

"Is this straight goods?"

"Certainly."

"You may be seen getting into the room or coming out."

"I'm too blooming clever for that, Charley; but if I am seen, how can any one blame you?"

"They'll ask where you got the key."

"I'd never tell in a thousand years."

"Not even if you was arrested?"

"No."

"You might be tried and sent to prison."

"But I'd never blow, Charley. Give me the key before some one comes and sees us together."

Still the boy hesitated.

"Swear you won't squeal, no matter what happens."

"I swear it."

"Give me the fiver."

Hollingsworth produced a five-dollar bill.

"Give me the key."

Key and bill changed hands.

"Room forty-three, you said?" whispered Hollingsworth.

"That's right. Be mighty careful. Look out for any of Merriwell's crowd. They have rooms on that floor, and one or two of 'em are in."

"I'll look out."

"The housekeeper may be snoopin' round, too. Look out for her."

"All right."

"And gimme that key before you leave, if you can git a chance."

Hollingsworth lingered about the office a while, finally finding an opportunity to slip upstairs when he was not observed. He found Room No. 43 without trouble, and fortune seemed to favor him, for no one was in the corridor. He slipped the key into the lock and quickly opened the door. Having stepped into the room, he removed the key, transferred it to the other side of the lock, closed the door softly and turned the key.

"There!" he muttered, with a breath of relief; "that was easy enough. Now if I can find that certificate!"

Five minutes later, opening a long, leather pocketbook he had taken from Merry's suit case, he removed some papers, and almost the first one examined caused him to utter an exclamation of delight.

"Here it is!" he cried.

It was a certificate of the Amateur Athletic Union of the United States, properly filled out, dated and signed, attesting that Frank Merriwell was for the year of date an accepted and registered member of said union.

Hollingsworth's eyes glittered and he laughed softly.

"'Ow heasy it would be to destroy it!" he muttered, his excitement and triumph causing him to again abuse that much-tortured eighth letter. "But I 'ave a better plan—a much better plan! Oh! it makes me laugh jolly 'ard to think of it! I know I'll roar my blooming 'ead off if 'e brings it with 'im to show the committee, without hever taking a look at it 'imself!"

In his delight the rascal burst into such laughter that he was startled, and suddenly clapped a hand over his mouth, while he stood there listening, fearing he had been heard outside the room.

After a little, as there seemed no probability that the sound of his evil merriment had reached other ears than his own, he slipped softly across the floor to a desk that stood at one side. Placing a chair in front of the desk, he sat down and spread out the certificate.

For a moment or two he paused to glance over it before continuing his dastardly operations. From his pocket he quickly brought forth a small vial of colorless liquid, together with a camel's hair brush. Uncorking the vial, he dipped the tiny brush into the liquid, and began at once with this to follow the tracing of the pen upon the document.

As the moisture disappeared from the brush, he re-dipped it at intervals into the liquid. Almost as swiftly as he worked the writing thus touched by the moist brush faded and disappeared from the paper. He was using a powerful ink-eradicating fluid.

Ten minutes of this work was sufficient to remove from the certificate every trace of writing, leaving blank the places where it had been. At the end he used a blotter upon it to take up the moisture that had not dried out.

Then he picked up the ruined certificate and surveyed it in triumph.

"That settles the case of Mr. Frank Merriwell!" he declared. "'E'll take no part in the run for the Hashley Trophy, for 'e'll 'ave no certificate to show when it is called for by the committee. It has cost me five dollars to earn a 'undred."

Having finished his work and gloated over it a few moments, to the intense satisfaction of his miserable soul, he refolded the ruined certificate, replaced it among the other papers and restored the whole package to the pocketbook. The pocketbook he replaced in Frank's suit case, which he closed as he had found it.

"Now to get out of here," he whispered, as he hastened to the door, at which he paused to listen.

Hearing no alarming sound outside, he quickly turned the key and opened the door, stepping out briskly. His satisfaction was complete when he observed no person in the corridor.

Again locking the door, he hastened downstairs.

Three men were in the office, and their words attracted the attention of Hollingsworth as he looked around for the bell boy, to whom he wished to restore the key.

"It's a cinch that Frank Merriwell will win," said a slender man in black. "He should have been barred from the race."

"How is it possible to bar him?" inquired a stout man.

"On the plea of professionalism."

"But he is not a professional, you know," said the third man, who looked like a Spaniard and spoke with a slight foreign accent.

"If he isn't he should be," declared the slender man.

"I don't see why."

"He's too good."

"Oh, not at this game."

"Yes, at this game."

"What makes you think so?" asked the Spaniard.

"He wins at almost anything he undertakes."

144

"I've never heard that he is regarded as an especial wonder as a runner," grunted the stout man.

"Never mind what you have heard; he has a reputation that frightens people from risking any money on other contestants when he takes part. I came here to back Huntley, but I'm not risking my good money against Merriwell."

"You doped Huntley to win?" asked the man in black, smiling. "Why, man, if Merriwell wasn't entered I'd take the field and give you big odds. I'd almost go you even, if necessary, that Pope would cut the mustard."

Hollingsworth was keenly interested, and he did not hesitate to "butt in."

"Gentlemen," he said, "Merriwell is much over-rated. I don't believe he could win if he ran, but he will not run."

The trio turned and stared hard at him.

"Hello!" grunted the stout man. "I believe it's the fellow who was pointed out to me as the trainer of the Ashport squad."

"I am Herbert Hollingsworth," stated the Englishman, speaking slowly and taking care not to lose that troublesome initial letter from his name.

"What makes you think Merriwell will not run?" inquired the slim man.

Hollingsworth hesitated a trifle, and then said:

"You were just saying he should be barred from the race, sir."

"Yes; but——"

"If I am correctly informed he will be barred."

Naturally these words created a slight sensation.

"What information leads you to think such a thing?" was the quick demand of the Spaniard.

"I have it from a reliable source that he is not now a member of the Amateur Athletic Union, and the rules governing this cross-country run will exclude any one who is not a member."

"But he must be a member!" cried the man in black.

"Why so?"

"He is touring with his own team of athletes."

"But he has not taken part in any contest conducted under the rules of the A. A. U.," asserted Hollingsworth.

"Hasn't he? Are you sure?"

"I am positive."

"How can that be?" grunted the stout man.

"Why, he has simply been doing what might be called exhibition work. No record of any of his accomplishments on this trip has been made. Any one might get together an athletic team and go

146

about doing the same. Of course, he can secure baseball games, being Frank Merriwell, no matter if he should have a team made up of all professionals."

"If this is correct, it is quite surprising," said the Spaniard; but it was plain that he doubted.

Hollingsworth did not fancy having any one doubt his statement.

"Of course it is correct!" he declared, being stirred up slightly. "I am willing to bet a 'undred dollars that Merriwell does not start in the cross-country run."

It happened that Buck Badger and Bruce Browning, having returned from a stroll, entered the office just in time to hear this.

"Whatever is that you're saying?" demanded the Kansan, in surprise. "Did I hear you offering to bet that Frank Merriwell would not start in that race?"

"Hexactly," answered the trainer.

"Well, you're sure blowing off a lot of hot air, Mr. Man."

"If you think it is 'ot hair," spluttered Hollingsworth, "get hout your money."

"I haven't seen the color of yours yet," reminded Buck.

At this the Englishman plunged into his pocket, produced a leather pocketbook and slapped it against his left hand.

"There it is," he asserted.

"Still I can't see the money any," said Badger.

Hollingsworth opened the book and brought forth a package of bills.

"'Ere is my money," he declared. "Now put hup yours or shut hup!"

With a rumbling growl Bruce Browning went into his pocket; but the Kansan stopped him, saying:

"This is mine; I saw it first."

The hotel clerk had stepped from behind the desk, greatly interested by what was taking place. Badger made a motion toward him, observing:

"Put up your stuff, my bluffing friend. Mr. Curtis will hold it. You're still keeping your paws on the long green, ready to squeal when your bluff is called."

"Oh, ham I?" sneered Hollingsworth, as he hastily counted out a hundred, which took nearly the whole of his pile. "We'll see habout that. 'Ere it goes hup in his 'ands. Now, if you're not a blooming squawker yourself, let's see you cover it. I'm betting Frank Merriwell will be barred from the race."

Badger now hastily produced a roll of bills, from the outside of which he stripped two fifties.

"It's like finding money," he chuckled, as he handed the hundred to the clerk. "That's whatever!"

"It's like finding it for me," said Hollingsworth.

"Oh, I don't know!" laughed Buck.

It was true he did not know what had happened in Frank Merriwell's room while Merry was absent.

Hollingsworth left the hotel in a well-satisfied frame of mind. He could not refrain from chuckling aloud as he sauntered along the street.

"Well, this has been a good day for me," he muttered. "I've made two hundred dollars—or a hundred and ninety-five, taking out the fiver I had to give the boy. Oh, there'll be a rumpus when Merriwell and his blooming, insolent friend finds out what has happened. It's too late for him to get a duplicate certificate, even if he should find out without delay what has happened. It's a sure thing for me. I'm a clever one!"

He was so blown up with self-satisfaction that he nearly collided with Arthur Huntley without seeing him.

"What's the matter with you, Holl?" demanded the Buffalo man, grasping his arm. "Have you gone daft? You were grinning like a hyena and muttering to yourself. Came near butting me over. Have you been tippling?"

"No, but I'm blooming near choked for a drink, Arthur. Let's have one. I'll tell you something that will make you grin like a hyena, too."

"I don't like to be seen going into a saloon here on the main street. Step down this way."

On a side street they entered a saloon.

"What are you doing here in town?" asked Hollingsworth, expressing surprise for the first time. "I supposed you would be out pretending to get familiar with the course."

"I had some business, and I took this as the best time to do it when there would be no one to see me and get inquisitive."

They stood up to the bar and ordered whisky.

There was only one bartender in the place, and, after serving them, he gave them no further attention, which permitted them to talk in low tones without fearing that they would be overheard.

"I'm going to take no chances with this man Merriwell," said Huntley. "I propose to make sure he'll not win that trophy. I want it, and I'm going to have it."

"Don't be afraid of Merriwell," laughed Hollingsworth, with a significance that Huntley did not catch. "He won't beat anything."

"You don't seem to know what the fellow can do. He's a wonder, and he wins at anything he tries if given a fair show."

"But how can he have a fair show with you when you know a short cut through Dead Timber Jungle and another over Ragged Hill? Seems to me you're worrying too much about him."

"I tell you that you don't know him. He's out on the course now, and I'll wager he's looking for short cuts. It's likely he'll find the way over Ragged Hill, though he may not strike the one through the jungle. If he should discover both those cuts—well, unless something else stopped him, he'd surely carry off that trophy. I tell you I don't intend to take any chances. He'll never win. In order to make sure of that I decided not to cover the course to-day and came here. I've arranged it."

"How?" asked Hollingsworth.

Huntley glanced toward the barkeeper, and then whispered:

"I've engaged two ruffians to waylay and sandbag him."

The trainer whistled softly.

"Oh, you have?"

"Yes. I found the men for it. Twenty-five a piece I had to pay them."

"And wasted your money."

"No; they'll do it. The only thing is to make sure they'll get him at some point where he'll be sure to pass. And they must get him alone, too. That's the difficulty. I'm going to follow him close when he goes over the course to-morrow."

"You've wasted your money," repeated Hollingsworth.

"Not if they do the job."

"They won't."

"Why not?"

"They won't have the chance."

"I don't understand why."

"Because he won't race."

Huntley looked at the trainer intently.

"I don't suppose——" he began, then stopped and gazed still more fixedly at Hollingsworth.

"What are you doing here in town?" he suddenly asked. "You ought to be out with your men, chasing them over the country. I don't understand it."

"I had some business to look after," grinned the trainer. "Drink up, sir. Here's success to you, and may you take pleasure displaying the Ashley Trophy when you have won it."

They drank; but Huntley now knew his companion had been up

to something, and his curiosity was great.

"What did you do here in town?" he repeated.

"I made one hundred and ninety-five dollars," was the answer.

"Did you?"

"Yes."

"In what manner?"

"To begin with, I made a hundred dollars off you."

Huntley clutched the arm of the trainer.

"You—you didn't get hold of Merriwell's certificate and destroy it?" he hissed.

"No, I didn't destroy it."

"But you got hold of it?"

"Yes."

"Are you telling me the truth?"

"Why should I lie?"

"Then you have it with you?"

"No."

"Where is it?"

"In Merriwell's room, at the hotel."

"You—you—what did you do?"

"I made it a worthless piece of paper."

"How?"

Hollingsworth now related the whole story briefly, explaining how he had obtained admission to Frank's room, found the certificate, and eradicated the writing from it.

"Hand over the hundred dollars you promised," he chuckled.

"You shall have it," declared Huntley; "but I must be sure the work was well done. If Merriwell fails to produce his certificate——"

"I hope you don't doubt my word, sir?"

"No, not at all; but I'm going to be sure. I'll take no chances."

This did not wholly please Hollingsworth.

"I had to put up a hundred against the money of that cowboy chap," he said, "and that nearly cleaned me out. I thought you would pay me as soon as I told you what I had done. I'm your friend, Arthur, and I ran a great risk for you in getting into Merriwell's room. If I'd been caught——"

"The hundred dollars I offered was some inducement, I take it," said Huntley. "Of course I know you are my friend, Holl, and I appreciate it; but I notice that money always makes you much more willing to do a friendly turn."

"You wrong me, sir—indeed, you do!" protested the rascally trainer. "However, it is all right. Only I expect you to have the honor to pay me, even if something happens that you do not win after Merriwell is barred."

"Don't let that worry you. We'll have another drink."

"It's a shame you was in such a great hurry about engaging them two sandbaggers," muttered Hollingsworth, as they stood with their glasses lifted. "Too bad they got money they never can earn."

"I'll not regret it if I win that trophy. Better take too many precautions than not enough."

"I suppose that's right; but just think of fifty good American dollars spent for nothing!"

This seemed to worry the trainer far more than it did Huntley, who, in the slang of the day, which he had acquired in Buffalo, advised him to forget it.

In truth, Huntley, rascal though he was, was ashamed of Hollingsworth, whom he was inclined to use simply as a tool. The trainer's protestations of friendship annoyed him.

Between them, however, there was little choice. At heart one was quite as bad as the other.

CHAPTER XXIII

THE CERTIFICATE.

The day dawned. The sun rose round and red in the eastern sky, turning soon to a ball of gold that rapidly diminished in size until it appeared normal. Birds sang amid dewy thickets, where cool brooks babbled in the soft shadows. There seemed no hint of treachery, plot, or wickedness in all the "so glorious, high-domed, blossoming world."

It was the day of the great cross-country race for the Ashley Trophy, and at an early hour the human tide of the country roundabout set toward the grounds of the Ashport A. A. People on foot and in conveyances of many sorts came pouring in. It was a surprising gathering, considering the nature of the contest and the fact that such affairs seldom attract and interest people in general.

The watchers were posted at five given points along the course, the judges were arranging preliminaries, the starter was ready to do his part.

A number of deputies were kept busy clearing the road down which the runners would dash from the starting point, and along which it was understood they would return to the finish. The spectators were good-natured. They lined up all along both sides of the road to the distance of more than half a mile from the clubhouse. There were old folks and young, many from the country, and not a few from cities near and far. There were groups of collegians and schoolboys. There were pretty girls in summer attire, many with their elders and some in laughing clusters. People stood up in the country wagons and on the tops of tallyhos and coaches.

"Pope, Pope, he's our hope!" chanted a dozen young men who had obtained a fine position on a high ledge.

"Clyde, Clyde, Clyde of Yale!" flung back a group of younger chaps, several of whom wore knots of blue ribbon.

"What's the matter with Huntley?" yelled a ruddy-faced man; and the answer came from fifty throats. "He's all right!" "Who's all right?" was the question that followed. Once more the answer was prompt: "Why, Huntley! Huntley! Huntley!"

"Prince! Prince! Rah! rah! rah!" barked the Ashportites.

Near the clubhouse were ten young fellows comprising Frank Merriwell's athletic team. Of a sudden they gave a yell of their own:

How is Merriwell?
Oh, he's very well!
Merry! Merry!
He's the huckleberry!

This created a laugh, and suddenly the cheer for Merriwell was taken up all along the two lines following the shoulders of the road. The cheering for others had broken out in spots. This cheer for the best-known amateur athlete in America began at the clubhouse and ran away into the distance, growing in volume, until it seemed that every man, woman, boy, girl, and child was shouting.

In the dressing rooms the contestants were making final preparations. Frank was there. He and Tom Bramwell spoke a few low words together.

"Don't miss the splintered pine, Bramwell," said Frank. "It marks the spot where we cut into the Dead Timbers. You know how easy it can be missed."

"I know," nodded Bramwell. "I'm going to stick by you that far—if I can."

"If you can! Don't get an idea that you can't do it. After we pass Ragged Hill will come the grand pull to the finish."

Arthur Huntley, ready for the start, came through the room from another.

"Oh! make sure your shoes are all right, Mr. Merriwell!" he mentally exclaimed. "Lots of good it will do you! I've taken no chances on you to-day. I know you've found the cut over Ragged Hill, and my two sandbaggers wait for you at the break in the wall. I don't trust Hollingsworth, for all of his certificate story. You may start, but you'll never finish."

A whistle sounded. A voice called the runners to come forth.

The hour had arrived!

Herbert Hollingsworth was waiting. The judges were assembled in the clubhouse. As the runners passed through, Merriwell was spoken to by an official.

"Mr. Merriwell, you are the only one who has failed to show a certificate of registration in the A. A. U., according to the requirements. We have been informed this morning that you are not registered."

"The statement is false," retorted Frank quietly. "Who made it?"

"Never mind that. If you have your certificate it will settle the point."

"I have it, but not with me. Will you take my word for it and permit me to show the certificate after the contest?"

"Impossible, for you are challenged."

"Then I demand to have the challenger face me."

There was a moment of hesitation, and then Herbert Hollingsworth stood out.

"I am the challenger!" he cried. "You'll 'ave to show your certificate or be barred!"

Merry looked him over with an expression of contempt and withering scorn on his handsome face.

"You're a very clever rascal, Hollingsworth," he said; "but the cleverest rascals sometimes overreach themselves."

"I hobject to such language!" snarled the trainer.

"Oh, I haven't begun to tell you what I think of you!" said Frank. "When the race is over, if you remain, I will, in your presence, tell the judges and the officials of this club all about you and your rascally tricks. I know you were in my room at the Ashport House day before yesterday. You——"

"Lies habout me won't 'elp you!" sneered Hollingsworth. "You'll 'ave to show your certificate. If you can't do that, you can henjoy the pleasure of being a spectator."

"Enough of this!" commanded Robert Ashley, in high disapproval. "Mr. Merriwell, like the others, must show his certificate."

"Which he can't do," asserted the trainer.

Frank turned and called:

"Bart! Bart Hodge!"

It seemed that Hodge had been waiting for this.

"Coming, Frank," he answered, and pushed into the room.

Merry held out his hand.

From an inner pocket, Hodge produced a folded paper, which he delivered to his friend.

"Here, gentlemen, is my certificate," said Frank, as he passed it to the judges.

The paper was opened and scanned. Herbert Hollingsworth, his face gone pale and wearing an expression of astonishment and perplexity, pressed forward and stared at it. He seemed to doubt

163

the evidence of his eyes.

"The certificate is correct," decided one of the judges. "Mr. Merriwell is eligible, being a regularly enrolled member of the A. A. U."

"I thought it remarkable if he were not," said Mr. Ashley.

Hollingsworth was dazed.

Frank turned on him, speaking in a low tone, his voice indicating suppressed anger:

"I'll see you, sneak, and square the account after the race!"

Hollingsworth said not a word.

Frank passed on from the clubhouse to join the other runners at the starting point.

CHAPTER XXIV

WHAT BART HODGE DID.

hey're off!"

"There they go!"

"Rah! rah! rah! Huntley!"

"Rah! rah! rah! Merriwell!"

The cross-country run had started. Twenty-four lithe-limbed, clear-eyed young fellows went flashing along the road, amid two lines of shouting people, who were waving hats, handkerchiefs, hands, and colors.

They all started swiftly, having a fine stretch of road for some distance, and being determined to make the most of it. They were fairly well bunched when they came to the point where the road turned to the north and left them to keep on over hills, valleys, and fields, through woods and thickets, each selecting a course for himself.

Mr. Ashley, Paul Proctor, the judges and a certain number of especially favored ones, had mounted to the observatory on the top of the clubhouse.

Bart Hodge was one of those favored by an invitation, but he lingered behind. He observed Herbert Hollingsworth, head down, sneaking away toward the trackmaster's house, where were located the baths and dressing rooms.

Bart followed.

In one of the rooms he found the trainer, sitting on a locker and looking vastly dejected.

Hollingsworth looked up and saw Hodge. Immediately he sprang to his feet.

Bart came forward with his lips pressed together, his face clouded and his eyes flashing. His manner and appearance were suggestive of a thunderstorm.

"What—what do you want?" faltered the treacherous trainer.

Bart paused three feet away.

"I want to tell you that you are the meanest and most contemptible cur I've encountered in a long time," answered Merriwell's friend. "You're a crawling, slimy, disgusting snake. I think that is plain enough for you."

"'Ow dare you talk to me that way!" gasped the rascal.

"How dare I? Why, I can't find words to express the contempt I feel for you! I can't think of epithets nasty enough to fit you properly!"

Although Hollingsworth was infuriated, something about Hodge held him in check.

"I suppose you're whining because I challenged your friend," he said. "Didn't I 'ave a right to do that?"

"You had a right to challenge him; but you know that is not what I mean."

"I don't know what helse you can mean."

"Oh, yes you do know."

"You lie! 'Ow can I know?"

"Because I know what you tried to do. I know how you happened to challenge Frank."

"I challenged 'im because 'e 'adn't shown his certificate."

"And because you believed you had ruined that certificate."

Now Hollingsworth had been wondering greatly over Merriwell's ability to produce the certificate, for he was absolutely certain he had obliterated from the document every trace of writing. The restoration of the paper to its former condition—for Hollingsworth fancied it had been somehow restored—was something in the order of magic and the doings of the black art.

"'Ow could I ruin it?" muttered he huskily.

"You sneaked into his room when he was away and obliterated the writing upon it."

Hollingsworth started. Then the writing had been obliterated, for Hodge said so.

"It's a forgery!" cried the trainer, of a sudden. "Merriwell retraced the writing! 'E forged it! Proof of that will keep 'im from getting the trophy, heven if 'e wins!"

"Which language from you is the same as a confession that you did sneak into Frank's room and tamper with the document."

"Prove it! I deny it! But it's forged! 'E'll 'ave no right to the trophy if he wins!"

"You poor fool!" sneered Bart. "You thought you were clever, but you were easily deceived. The certificate you found was left for you to find. It was last year's certificate."

"No!" contradicted Hollingsworth. "I took special pains to look at the date. It was this year."

"You unblushingly confess your villainy! Well, let me tell you how you were fooled still further. Expecting you to do just what you did, Merriwell had altered the date on his certificate of last year. His last certificate he placed in the safe at the hotel, where it remained until he called for it to-day."

The outwitted scoundrel saw his last hope vanish. He realized he was baffled and done for.

"Take off your coat!" Hodge suddenly cried, stripping off his own and flinging it upon a locker.

"What are you going to do?" gasped Hollingsworth.

"I'm going to give you the soundest thrashing you ever received," was Bart's answer.

He did.

157

CHAPTER XXV

THROUGH DEAD TIMBER JUNGLE.

here they go along the edge of the Dead Timbers," said Mr. Ashley, watching the runners through a glass. "I've counted them all but three. Three seem missing entirely."

"That's so," agreed Paul Proctor, who likewise had a pair of strong field glasses. "They strung out now, but three of them have never issued from the cedars down in the hollow."

"Can you see anything of Merriwell?" anxiously asked Hodge, who had just mounted the steps to the observatory.

He bore not a mark of his encounter with Hollingsworth, although his face was somewhat flushed and he seemed to be perspiring freely. He had field glasses of his own, and these he quickly trained on the distant moving specks which were creeping up along the edge of the far-away, dark timberland.

"I haven't been looking for him particularly," acknowledged Proctor. "I think one of our boys is missing, although I cannot tell which one. I wonder what happened in the cedars."

Something had happened to Frank Merriwell before he plunged into the cedars. Leaping a bit of thick brush, he thrust his left foot into the hole of some sort of burrowing animal and went down, giving his ankle a fearful wrench. For a moment he fancied he had broken the bone.

"Hurt?" cried Tom Bramwell, as he passed.

"No," answered Frank, rising quickly.

When he tried to step on that foot, however, he nearly went down, and an excruciating pain shot from his ankle to his hip. This cutting pain threatened to rob him of strength and put him out of the race at once.

But he found the ankle was not broken. It was a wrench or a sprain. He knew sprains were sometimes more obstinate than breaks in the recovery, yet he had no thought of letting that stop him.

So he ran on in the rear of several of the contestants, the whole pack being stretched out and more or less scattered. He could not run fast, and it was only by setting his teeth and forcing himself forward that he got on at all.

More than that, every moment his ankle seemed to get worse. He had thought the pain might cease after a little, but each time his foot met the ground it jabbed him afresh.

Not one fellow in a thousand would have continued in the running. But Frank Merriwell was one in ten thousand. He had the fortitude to endure pain stoically. Not a sound came from his lips. His jaws were set and his eyes filled with unconquerable fire. He forced himself to greater speed and plunged into the cedars whither Bramwell had disappeared.

Instead of keeping straight through the cedars Frank bore to the right. He fought his way into a tangled thicket, where branches whipped him stingingly in the face, and at last came staggeringly through. Close at hand was the border of the Dead Timbers, a wild and seemingly impassable tract of forest, swept and blackened by fire, overtaken some time by a tornado, with tall trunks twisted and tangled in chaotic confusion.

Merry looked for the shattered pine and found it where he looked. It was his guide post. There he plunged into what seemed the most impassable portion of the jungle. He fell on his hands and knees to creep some distance along a hidden path, but soon arose, with the fearful pain stinging him to weakness at each step.

He wondered if Bramwell was far in advance. Together, aided by the hint overheard by Bart Hodge and conveyed to Frank, they had searched for the secret passage and found it. By means of it they could cut off much of the distance, those who knew nothing about it being compelled to follow round the edge of the timbers.

Soon the path became more open. On either side the dead branches had been cut away. Huntley had prepared it so he could run with speed through this portion of the secret cut-off.

Finally Merry arrived at a part of the forest where the trees had been caught and twisted and scattered in such a tangle that passage seemed impossible. There he found a long tree trunk that extended upward slopingly over the tangled mass; and, balancing himself, he used it as a bridge, mounting along it until he was at least twenty feet above the ground, with a dark jungle below, from which, should he fall, it might be almost impossible to force an egress.

Up there he found yet another dead tree upon which he ventured.

Suddenly he halted.

From beneath his very feet came a call for help!

Frank was astonished. He looked downward, clutching an upthrust limb to steady himself, but could see no one.

"Oh, Merriwell!" came the call.

"Hello!" he answered. "Who's down there?"

"It is I—Bramwell."

"Bramwell? What are you doing down there?"

"I'm stuck and I can't get out. I've climbed part of the way out, but I can get no higher. Go on and finish the run, but come back for me afterward, for I think I'll have to stay here."

And now, peering into the gloom, Merry caught a glimpse of the gray face of Bramwell upturned some distance below. Evidently the fellow had fallen from the tree trunk in trying to cross.

"I'll get you out now," said Frank.

"Don't you do it—don't stop for it!" exclaimed the fellow below. "If you do Huntley will win the race."

"If I don't he may win just the same. I've sprained my ankle. You're the man to beat him in case I give out entirely."

Frank was acting even as he spoke. At a distance he saw a long, dead limb that had been almost twisted off at the base. It did not take him long to reach the limb, break it wholly clear, return with it and thrust one end down until Bramwell could grasp it. There were other branches and limbs and tangled masses by which the fellow could assist himself, and slowly, little by little, Merry drew him up. Although it was not done swiftly, little time was wasted, and soon Frank was able to give the other a hand and assist him to the tree trunk. Together they passed over the jungle and reached that part of the path beyond.

"Oh, if we can beat Huntley after this!" exclaimed Bramwell. "I did not fall down there, Merriwell. He met me on that tree trunk and struck me off with a heavy stick. I did not see him until I was right upon him, so busy was I watching where I placed my feet. Evidently he had discovered I was following him closely and knew of the path."

"He is in the same class with Hollingsworth," said Frank. "They make a fine pair! I've sprained my ankle, Bramwell."

"Did it when you fell?"

"Yes."

"But it isn't badly injured?"

"Bad enough. I'm afraid it will put me out of the running before

I can cover the distance. You take the lead and do your prettiest.
If you can beat Huntley, by all means beat him."

"I will!" fiercely cried Bramwell. "He shall never have that trophy if I can help it! But he has a start."

"You should cut his lead down. He'll think you are disposed of,
and he may take it easy as soon as he fancies he is reasonably sure
of winning."

Bramwell took the lead, as Merry had suggested, but Frank kept
at his heels. Together they came out from the Dead Timbers and
pressed on.

With the endurance of a man of iron, Merry seemed to pay no
heed to the pain and his now badly swollen ankle. He talked to
his companion, giving him advice and instructions as they ran.
Where the ground was rough and uneven he warned Bramwell
to run loosely, in order not to jar and shock himself as he would
were his muscles taut. He corrected Bramwell's too long stride
in descending steeps and urged him to a steady, strong gait in
mounting ordinary slopes.

"Why," said the Ashport man, "with you for a coach we might,
all of us, have learned much more about cross-country running
than we now know."

Together they passed the first point where watchers noted their
numbers and recorded them. From a height they looked back and
discovered the most of the runners behind them.

One man, however, was in advance.

CHAPTER XXVI

THE WINNER OF THE TROPHY.

No one save Merriwell himself ever knew how much he endured and how keenly he suffered during that cross-country run. Considering what he accomplished no one could have appreciated his unconquerable determination not to give up and drop out.

Toward the end, when all the greater difficulties were passed, he and Bramwell still clinging together, they came to Ragged Hill. They knew that not more than one man was ahead of them, and that man they had seen disappearing over the crest of the hill as they mounted its lower slopes.

Once or twice before this Bramwell had urged Frank to take the lead. This he now did once more.

"You are the man to beat Huntley," he declared. "I fear I can't do it."

"You have too many fears," said Frank. "Huntley hasn't seen us. From the top of the hill he surveyed the country behind him. He must have seen most of the runners who are near, and he must feel that he has time to burn. He is full of confidence now."

"You're the one to take the confidence out of him."

Frank waited for no further urging. He took the lead and set such a pace in mounting to the crest of the hill, following the difficult path they had discovered, that Bramwell dropped some distance in the rear.

The eastern side of the hill was partly cleared or had never borne timber. Down the declivity sped Merry. He cut hither and thither, choosing the best course.

Halfway down the hill was an old stone wall. In one particular spot the wall was lower than elsewhere, and behind it, just at that point, crouched two masked ruffians clutching sand bags.

One of them had peered over the wall and seen Frank coming

down the hill.

"This is the bloke, pal!" he growled. "Reddy ter soak him!"

"All right!" hissed the other.

On came the runner. Like a bird he sailed over the weakest part of the old wall, wholly unaware of the masked ruffians who were lying in wait for him at that point.

They rose as he came over, and both leaped at him.

He saw them before his feet again touched the ground. With his upflung arms he sought to protect his head. The moment his feet touched the earth he ducked.

They were on him. One struck him a blow that staggered him, although it did not land full and fair.

The other missed him entirely.

But Frank went down to one knee, and they followed him up.

"Lay him stiff, pal!" snarled one.

"Stiff an' cold!" panted the other.

Instead of seeking to rise, as they expected him to do, Frank shot out a foot and caught one of the men fairly in the pit of the stomach, doubling him up and hurling him backward.

Then he turned instantly on his back, with his feet toward the other, who sought to fling himself on Frank as he lay thus.

Both of Merry's legs shot up from the ground as the man came down upon him. They caught the legs of the ruffian across the shins. A surprising result followed. The man's feet went upward and he turned over in the air, falling on his back beyond Merry, with his head toward Frank's head.

By this time Merriwell was up and had the wretch by the throat. He held him thus with one hand, tearing off his mask with the other.

"I want to see your features, my fine bird!" he said. "A trip to the stone jug will cure you of your pranks, perhaps."

In the meantime, the other fellow had been flung back toward the weak point in the stone wall, and Bramwell, following Merry over, landed on the wretch with both feet and stretched him quivering on the ground.

"This one is cooked, Merriwell!" he cried.

"Go on, Bramwell—go on!" urged Merry. "Leave them to me! I'm out of the race now."

The Ashport man hesitated a moment. He saw that Frank was in a position to make the ruffians his captives. If he lingered to give aid there would be no chance of defeating Huntley.

Away he went.

Frank was on his feet now. He limped to the spot where the second man lay, stripped off his mask and looked at him.

"I'll know you both," he muttered, and shot away in pursuit of Bramwell.

The waiting crowd had grown weary when, from the observatory of the clubhouse, came a cry. Then followed the announcement that the first runner had appeared in sight.

Word ran down the line. The road was cleared again. People began to cheer and stand on tiptoes.

Bart Hodge, watching in the observatory, had found it difficult to repress an exclamation of bitterest disappointment when he turned his glass on the runner far away across the fields and discovered it was not Merry.

"It's Huntley!" he mentally groaned. "Where is Frank?"

"There's another!" shouted Paul Proctor. "Who is it? Who is it? It's one of our boys!"

"I believe it is," said Robert Ashley.

"It—it's Bramwell!" declared the astounded president of the club. "He's gaining on Huntley, too! Huntley is fagged! Bramwell seems fresh! It's going to be a hot finish!"

The excitement was growing, but it increased when a third runner appeared.

"There's Merriwell!" said Hodge, unable to keep still.

It was Frank, and Bart saw he was gaining on both Bramwell and Huntley. Still he detected something wrong in Merry's gait and began to suspect that an accident had befallen him.

"That's it—that's what's the trouble!" he muttered. "Otherwise he'd be leading now."

Huntley looked back and saw the two pursuers. He tried to spurt, but his knees seemed weak beneath him. However, he held on grimly.

Down at the far end of the people who lined the road cheering rose. They could see the runners.

"Come on, Merry—come on!" whispered Hodge. "You can do it yet!"

Huntley reached the road. His strength seemed renewed. The cheers of his friends braced him wonderfully. It was but half a mile to the finish, and he let himself out. But he was in distress, and occasionally he lifted his clenched hands and pressed them to his breast.

Bramwell continued to gain. He struck the road and came after Huntley in a manner that threatened to do the work in a hurry.

Then came Frank.

"Look at Merriwell!"

"He's running like a man in a hundred yards dash!"

"He's closing the gap!"

"He'll pass them both!"

The strain was too much for Huntley. Within sight of the finish he began to reel.

Bramwell shot past, and a wild yell went up from the Ashportites.

But Merriwell was gaining, gaining, gaining! Could he pass Bramwell? He was doing his best.

The tape was stretched; the judges were waiting.

Bramwell heard thudding feet close behind him. Something seemed bursting in his breast. It was his heart. Let it burst! He heard a dull roar, which was the cheering of the excited throng. But he could not see. Twenty yards from the tape he went blind for the time. He kept on his feet, however.

To the crowd in general it seemed that the two runners breasted the tape at the same moment.

But, looking down from the observatory, Bart Hodge uttered a groan, for he saw that Bramwell reached it a second in advance.

The Ashport man had won.

That night, in the Ashport Opera House, before a great gathering of enthusiastic people, the trophy was presented to Bramwell by Mr. Ashley.

Then Tom Bramwell spoke up and told how he came to win. He told how Merriwell had discovered the short cut through Dead Timber Jungle, and how Frank had rescued him from the trap into which he had been cast by Huntley. He also told how Merry had covered more than three-fourths of the distance with a sprained ankle, and how, at that very moment, he was in bed under the care of a doctor. Then he proposed cheers for Frank, which were given with such a will that the windows of the building rattled.

Herbert Hollingsworth was not there, for he had not waited to witness the finish of the race. Fearing Merriwell's wrath, he fled from Ashport.

Nor did Arthur Huntley linger. With Phil Proctor's assurance that charges would be preferred against him, he decided it best to get out quickly—and did so.

As for the two ruffians who had tried to sandbag Merriwell, they followed the example of their employer and vanished.

CHAPTER XXVII

NOT IN FORM.

The next stopping place of the Merries on their eastern journey was Elkton, Ohio, a red-hot baseball town, its team being one of the four-cornered Central League.

Elkton's misfortune was its lack of first-class amateur baseball players. Although there were many players in town, it happened that the place had not produced a single star in many seasons.

For this reason, according to the agreement entered into by the managers of the different teams in the Central League, Elkton was greatly handicapped.

By this agreement, no team was to have on its list more than three salaried players, or professionals. In order to make the games fast and attract spectators who would not be satisfied with ordinary amateur baseball, the by-laws of the league permitted each manager to engage three professionals. For the most part the teams had secured expert pitchers and catchers.

The early part of the season had proved discouraging for Elkton, as her weak local men were unable to bat effectively against the fine pitching of the clever "slab artists" of the other clubs. As a result, Elkton had fallen to the foot of the list and seemed destined to remain there.

The pride of the Elkton followers of the game was aroused. The association held a meeting, at which it was made plain that one of two courses must be pursued. Either the local team must be disbanded and Elkton must retire from the league in disgrace, or, at any cost, something must be done to make the Elks as strong as the strongest of their rivals.

Elkton could not bear the thought of confessing itself too weak to cope with the other towns on the diamond. After a deal of heated argument and discussion a proposition was made to secure a new team throughout—a team that could "wallop" anything in the State, barring only the big league teams of Cincinnati, Cleveland, and Toledo. It was even proposed to have an aggregation that could "trim" Toledo.

It would take money to do this, and, at the height of the patriotic fever developed in the meeting, one of the directors announced that he would start a subscription paper with one hundred dollars. He backed up his talk by hastily drawing up the paper and attaching his name thereto, pledging himself to pay one hundred dollars for the support of such a team, providing one thousand dollars was raised.

Within ten minutes seven hundred and fifty dollars had been subscribed.

Then, somewhat cooled, the enthusiasts paused and began to consider another difficulty.

It was plain the required amount would be pledged; but money could not overcome the clause in the by-laws of the league whereby each team was restricted to not more than three salaried players.

There was further discussion and argument, which was settled at length by the suggestion that the players required be engaged by different men of business in Elkton, not to play baseball, but to act as grocery clerks and in other capacities. Of course, these men would not be required to work like other clerks; but they could appear at the business houses of their employers and seem to busy themselves for an hour or so each day, and these so-called employers should pay them their salaries. Their real business would be to play baseball and defeat the now crowing rivals of the spirited little town.

This was the plan Elkton attempted to carry out. The manager of the team scarcely hesitated at any expense in securing players, and in a wonderfully brief space of time he brought together a team that was really formidable and one that far outclassed any other organization in the league.

Then arose further trouble.

The league association held a meeting, at which the managers of the various teams were commanded to appear. At this meeting it was asserted that Elkton had transgressed the by-laws, and it was voted to suspend the Elks until the team should be placed in organized form to comply with the requirement concerning salaried players.

Elkton stood her ground, contending that if her business men were patriotic enough to employ baseball players as clerks and let them off from their labors to play baseball the by-laws of the league were not transgressed.

The matter was hanging fire. The Central League was puttering along with three teams. Elkton believed the other places would succumb in time. And so, in order to keep things moving and get her team into the best form possible, Elkton arranged games with independent teams.

And it happened that this was the situation just when the Merries struck the town. Frank and his team had not been an hour in the town when their presence became known to the manager of the Elks, and a representative at once called on Frank and challenged him to a game. The challenge was promptly accepted, and the citizens of Elkton and the surrounding country turned out in large numbers to witness the work of the reorganized Elks against what was known to be the strongest independent team in the country.

At first the spectators had been disappointed as the visitors seemed to have everything their own way, but at the end of seven hard-hitting innings the Elks tied the score at nine to nine.

Dade Morgan was pale and dejected as he took a seat beside Frank on the bench.

"You must go in and pitch the game out, Merry," he said. "My arm is gone. I've pitched it clean off trying to hold them down. They'll bat me all over the lot if I stay in. It will be a shame to lose this game after holding them down to one run for five innings. If they take the lead we're ruined. That man Wolfers, who replaced Cutts in the fifth, is a wonder. We haven't been able to get a hit off him."

"He's a good pitcher," agreed Frank. "I've been watching him. He has all kinds of kinks and speed, and his head is full of brains. But you know why I don't want to pitch to-day, Dade. My ankle is almost well. If I pitch, I'm sure to hurt it. Next week, according to promise, I'm due back at Ashport to take part in the all-round championship contest. I can't compete in that with a lame ankle."

"You're right," admitted Morgan. "I'll finish the game if you say so; but I'm confident I'll never pitch again if I do. It will ruin my arm. You know I'm not a quitter, and I——"

"No one knows you're not a quitter better than I do," said Frank promptly. "If you feel that way about your arm, I wouldn't have you stay in the box for anything in the world."

"Besides," said Dade, "the game is tied, and you can hold those sluggers down. They are the fiercest batters we've encountered this season."

"Sluggers is the correct name for them," nodded Merriwell. "No wonder the Central League of Ohio is fighting against taking in the reconstructed Elkton aggregation. Every man on this team is a professional with a reputation."

Frank pulled off his sweater.

"What are you going to do?" eagerly asked the other players. "Are you going in?"

"Sure," he nodded. "You bat this inning, Dade, if your turn comes."

Instantly the whole team seemed to brighten up. They had been dejected by the manner in which the Elks of Elkton had climbed up on them and tied the score; but with Merry in the box it seemed that they would have little trouble in stopping the tally-getting career of their opponents.

Dick Starbright, who had taken his place at bat, smiled joyously on observing that Merry was preparing to warm up.

Hodge being the batter who followed Starbright, Frank asked Badger to do the catching.

"One to the stable!" bellowed a delighted Elktonite, as Frank started to warm up.

"We'll send this one after him!" shouted another.

"He'll be fruit for our boys!" whooped a third.

"You'll find it some different, gents," muttered Buck Badger, as he tossed the big catcher's mitt at his feet for a base in order to let Merry find control by throwing over it. "This game is ours now. That's whatever!"

Wolfers grinned viciously. There was something about his appearance, as well as his name, that suggested a wolf. He was pleased to see Merriwell preparing to enter the box, for he had absolute confidence in himself. But he discovered a sudden and surprising change in the manner of the batters. Starbright went after the ball with resolution, making foul after foul.

"Oh, you would, would ye!" muttered the Elkton pitcher. "Well, why don't ye!"

"Tut-tut-taking a bub-bub-bite out of it every time, Dick!" cried Joe Gamp. "You'll land on the trade-mark in a minute."

"Yah!" nodded Dunnerwurst; "der trade-mark vill land on you in a minute, py Shimminy! Id vill knock you a mile."

"Strike him out, Wolfers!" implored the spectators. "He's easy. Strike the big fellow out!"

Wolfers was working hard, and he finally succeeded in fooling the yellow-haired chap to his satisfaction, for Dick missed the third strike and was declared out.

"How easy!" laughed a man on the bleachers. "That's the kind of a pitcher to have!"

"That's the kind they raise up in Wisconsin," said another man. It was Bart's turn to strike.

"Got to get a hit," thought Hodge, as he chose a bat of medium weight.

"He's using the spit ball, Bart," said Starbright. "The things are slippery, and you have to hit them square on the nose."

Bart nodded. It was the first time for the season that the Merries had encountered a pitcher who was master of the new "spit ball." Wolfers seemed to have it down fine, his control being something beautiful to witness.

As Merry had observed, the Elkton twirler had a head full of brains. Although master of the spit ball, he did not use it constantly. He worked different batters in a variety of ways. His curves were fine, but he had something better than curves, which was control. He seemed able to put the ball exactly where he desired. He studied the batters. While sitting on the bench, he had watched closely to discover the weak spots of every man. If he found a player inclined to strike over a low ball, he kept the ball low on him all the time. If he found a man who was inclined to step toward the plate when striking, he kept the ball close to that man, thus making it almost certain that he would hit it close to his fingers if he hit it at all. On the other hand, if a hitter pulled away from the plate, he used an outcurve, keeping the ball over the outside corner or beyond it. If such a batter hit it, the end of the bat was almost certain to be the point of contact, and there is seldom much force in a hit made in such a manner.

In Wolfers, Merriwell fancied he discerned "big league material." He believed the man would be "discovered" by some manager and "reserved" before the season closed.

Hodge was grimly determined, but determination did not count for much in the face of Wolfers' pitching. Bart did his best to "work" the man from Wisconsin, but was finally "worked" himself, being led into putting up a weak pop fly to Rush, the Elkton shortstop.

"Oh, we've got ye!" howled one of the local rooters. "You may as well give up."

"We're not the kuk-kuk-kind that gives up," growled Gamp, as he strode out with his bat on his shoulder.

In the meantime, Merry was working his arm out slowly, taking care not to twist his weak left ankle.

It was no easy matter to pitch without putting a big strain on that ankle. He could not throw himself back and balance on one foot, for when he came down it jarred his ankle, and, therefore, he was unable to put the force of his body into his delivery.

Merry had long ago learned to make his body and back muscles do much of the work in throwing a swift ball. This was done with the body swing, as it is called. He actually made his body do at least two-thirds of the work, thus sparing his arm.

Young and inexperienced pitchers seldom use this body swing properly, and, therefore, they strain their arms unnecessarily. Sometimes they stand on both feet and throw with all the force of their biceps in order to get speed. In this manner they bring a fearful strain on their arms, and many a promising chap has ruined his wing just as he was beginning to develop into a real pitcher.

Merry had discovered the secret of the body swing in his college days, and for this reason he had withstood the strain of much pitching and steadily grown better from year to year.

When ready to deliver the ball, he swung his body backward as his arm was drawn up. On securing the proper poise, he came forward with the full weight and force of his body, at the same time making the delivery. Often his arm did little except to guide the ball, speed being secured by the great force of the back and shoulder muscles.

Frank was not a "wind-up" pitcher. He resorted to no windmill movements, yet he used the force of his back and shoulder muscles in almost every delivery. In doing so, he threw himself forward with force onto his left foot, and he now discovered that this would be impossible without great risk in regard to his ankle. He was compelled to stand up straight and pitch without the swing. As this was not his usual custom, he quickly discovered it interfered with his control. He could not, as he usually did, put a ball where he desired.

This surprised and annoyed Merry, for it was his custom when runners were on bases to cut out much of the body swing. Often he would snap the ball to the plate before the runner was aware that he meant to deliver it, thus preventing the man from getting a start to steal.

In a very short time he realized that he was in poor condition to do effective work against good hitters; but Morgan had said that it would ruin his arm to pitch any more, and so Frank was determined to go in and do his best.

Wolfers worked Gamp as he had worked Starbright and Hodge, finally striking the lanky chap out.

"Now," cried a spectator, "we'll see them hammer the head off the great and only Merriwell."

CHAPTER XXVIII

NO CONTROL.

Dodge knew Merry's ankle was in poor condition, but he was not aware of Frank's trouble in securing control of the ball. Therefore he was satisfied when he donned the body protector and mask that there would be a great and immediate change in the run of the game. He doubted not that Merriwell would check the run getting of the enemy.

Cronin, the lank and lively third baseman of the Elks, was the first batter to face Frank.

Merry knew Cronin was a great sacrifice hitter, his position being second on the batting list.

Still the man had shown that he could hit out beautifully when occasion demanded, and, with no one ahead of him on the bags, he would be sure to try for a hit or a pass.

This man's only weakness was a high ball, close to the shoulder; and sometimes he could hit those safely.

Frank's first ball was handsomely placed and cleanly missed.

"Str-r-r-rike—kah!" called the umpire.

"Hit id vere id missed you!" yelled Dunnerwurst, from the field.

"That's the place, Merry," laughed Hodge, all the clouds gone from his face. "It's so easy!"

"Verily it is a thing of great delight," murmured Jack Ready.

"How can he hit them when he can't see them?" rumbled Bruce Browning.

Dade Morgan, sitting on the bench, his left hand clasping his right arm above the elbow, smiled and nodded with satisfaction.

"Merry will save the game," he muttered to himself.

"He's a snap, Billy," called Rush, the Elkton shortstop. "Let those whisker trimmers go."

Cronin nodded and winked. He was satisfied that he would have no trouble in getting what he wanted off Frank.

As for Merry, he was agreeably surprised by his success in placing the first ball.

"If I can only keep that up!" he thought.

His next ball was lower, but still close.

Cronin let it pass.

"Ba-a-a-all—ah!" came from the umpire.

"He's got to put it over, Billy," chirped Rush.

Hodge snapped the ball back to Frank, who instantly returned it.

Cronin was caught napping and did not try to hit.

It cut the plate in halves.

"Str-r-r-ike—kah two!"

"Come, come, Mr. Batter!" yelled one of the spectators; "smoke up! You're in a trance."

"It surely is a thing of exceeding great delight," again murmured Ready.

Cronin was somewhat disgusted. He was not, as a rule, the sort of chap to be caught in such a manner, and it made him sore. His face flushed and his eyes glinted. He gripped his bat and stood ready for anything.

Frank tried an outcurve, causing it to sweep outside the plate.

Cronin grinned derisively and let it pass.

"Ba-a-a-all—ah!"

"Even with him, Merry," said Hodge. "Put the next one right over. Let him hit it a mile—if he can."

At the same time he called for a drop.

Frank had abandoned the practice of shaking his head when about to pitch a ball different from the one called for. Instead, he assumed a position that plainly told Hodge he would use a rise or a very high ball.

It proved too high, and Cronin did not move his bat.

"Ba-a-a-all—ah three!" announced the umpire.

"Got him in a hole, Billy!" chuckled Rush. "Now he's got to put 'er over."

Merry had no intention of putting the next one straight over. It was his object to keep it shoulder high and on the inside corner. This time, however, he did not gauge it accurately, and, to his dismay, he did put it over the middle of the pan and a trifle lower than the batter's shoulder.

"Just what the doctor ordered!" cried Rush, as Cronin hit the ball.

It was a clean drive to left field, and, by swift running, Cronin succeeded in reaching second before the ball could be fielded in.

"Why, how easy he is!" laughed Rush. "Put it over the fence, Sparks."

Sparks, the centre fielder of the Elks, was the next batter.

Although Merry was greatly displeased with himself, he did not betray it. He knew it was the easiest thing in the world for a disappointed pitcher to take the spirit out of an entire team.

Hodge was cheerful.

"Accidents will happen, Merry," he said. "Never mind that."

Apparently Frank did not mind.

"I'll have to try the double shoot for a strike-out ball," he mentally decided.

Sparks expected to find Frank easy.

"It's a shame to do it," he declared. "I'm afraid you'll loss your reputation to-day, my boy."

"Don't let that worry you," said Frank, with perfect good nature.

"Oh, I'm not worrying. Still I'm sorry for you. It can't be helped, you know. We can't afford to let you youngsters have this game. The whole Central League would laugh at us."

The Elks had discovered that Hodge was a beautiful thrower to the bags, and it was not difficult to hold Cronin close to second, although he took sufficient lead to go to third on a sacrifice or any sort of a scratch hit.

Cronin was a fast runner, and Frank knew he might score on a clean single.

Merry worked carefully. Finally, with two strikes and three balls called, he ventured to try the double shoot.

Sparks was fooled handsomely and missed.

"Str-r-r-rike—kah! You're out!" said the umpire.

"Now you're doing it, Merry!" nodded Hodge.

But Frank had hurt his ankle with that final delivery, and he limped about the pitching plate a few moments.

"Can't use the double shoot unless I'm willing to go onto the shelf," he decided. "It's out of the question."

He felt now that it was necessary for him to win the game without resorting to his most effective curve.

"Try it on me," invited Rush, the talkative, as he danced out to the plate.

"I'd like to," thought Frank. "You're one fellow I'd enjoy striking out."

"Get after him, Rushie!" urged an Elktonite. "You say he's easy. Now prove it."

Rush made no retort to this, but he hit the second ball pitched. The ball was driven straight at Badger, who was playing at short.

Buck felt sure of it, and Cronin did not try to take third, although

174

he was ready to move to draw a return throw if the stocky young Kansan whistled the sphere over to first.

Just before the ball reached Badger it struck a small pebble and was deflected. Buck managed to cuff it with his glove, but did not get hold of it. It rolled toward second. Badger went after it, Cronin being forced back to the bag.

Merry took in everything quickly, seeing that it would be dangerous for the Kansan to attempt a throw to first. It was extremely doubtful if Rush, a fast runner, could be caught, and a bad throw would let Cronin reach third, to say nothing of the possibility that it might permit him to score.

Therefore Frank shouted for Buck to hold the ball.

"Well! well! well!" laughed Rush, as he crossed the initial sack. "This is too much!"

"It is," agreed Browning. "You should have been out."

Badger was dismayed, but he did not receive a calldown from Frank. Nevertheless, Merry regretted that he had not placed Morgan at short after taking him out of the box. Buck was playing out of his regular position, while Morgan could cover shortstop's territory in a most beautiful manner.

It was too late now, however; Morgan had been retired. Badger was the only man for the position, Stretcher having left the team at Ashport to return to his home in Missouri.

Jack Lawrence, the manager of the Elks, was pleased by the prospect of victory. On hearing that the Elks would play with the Merries, the managers of other teams in the league had given Lawrence the laugh, all of them saying his great aggregation would be downed by the visitors. Lawrence was anxious to win the game.

Glade, the right fielder of the Elks, was the next man to hit. That is, he was the next man in order on the batting list. He did not try to hit, for it was not necessary. Merriwell's control was poor, and he could not find the plate. Two balls were called. Then came a strike, although, if anything, the umpire favored Frank.

"He can't find the pan again," yelled a coacher.

It seemed that he was right, for the next one pitched was a ball— and the next.

Glade was sent to first.

The bags were filled, with only one out.

Well might the Elks and the Elkton crowd be confident and jubilant.

Things were coming their way.

The local team had played an uphill game, and victory seemed in sight.

Frank was in a tight box.

Tinker, the next batter, was no slouch with the stick. He had a reputation for making hits when they were badly needed.

Behind the wires of his mask, the face of Bart Hodge looked grim and a trifle worried.

Hodge knew now that Merry was in anything but good form. He realized that the game might go against them, and no one disliked to lose a game more than did Bart, the bulldog. Especially hard was it to lose after seeming to have victory within reach.

But Hodge did not have a thought of giving up.

"Line it out, Tink!" urged Rush. "We've quit fooling. Give us some runs."

Tinker looked harmless enough. He was an awkward chap with a half-foolish face. Apparently he did not waste much of his time in thinking real thoughts.

Merry knew the fellow was not nearly as foolish as he appeared. So Frank worked carefully with the batter, using a change of pace, but making no further effort to throw the double shoot.

Finally Tinker put up a foul.

Hodge went after it, although the spectators yelled derisively, thinking he could not touch it.

In some manner the catcher stretched himself amazingly and got the ball on the end of his big mitt as it was falling to the ground.

It bounded off.

On the dead run, Bart caught it a second time.

And held it.

After a moment of silence, the spectators applauded. The people of Elkton were generous enough to recognize a good play, whether made by one of their own team or by an opponent.

"Hard luck, Tink!" cried Rush. "That catcher ought to be decorated with horseshoes."

"Clever, Bart," smiled Merry approvingly.

"Only one more man this inning, Frank," said Bart.

Could Merriwell "get" the next batter?

The situation was one to work up the spectators, who felt that it would be shameful to have their new team, on which they had spent so much money, defeated by the visitors.

"A pall nefer couldt catch dot Part Hodge!" shouted Hans Dunnerwurst joyously.

Sitting on the bench, Wolfers growled a little to the manager of the team.

"What's the matter?" he said. "Why don't they hit some? I can't win the game if they don't hit. I'll hold those kids down all right, but the rest of the team must bat a little."

"A hit right now will win the game," asserted Lawrence.

"But Tink was the man to make the hit. If he had lifted a long one to the field it would have been something. Cronin could have scored on it, even if it had been caught."

"Cross will have to turn the trick."

"He ought to," nodded Wolfers. "That pitcher is pie. He's pie, I say. Don't see how he ever got such a reputation."

"He has a lame ankle to-day."

"Don't you think it! That's a bluff. He was afraid to pitch against us, and so he put up that squeal about a lame ankle."

"But the rest of his players say his ankle is lame."

"He gets round on it all right, don't he?"

"He limps."

"Well, a lame ankle isn't much beside a lame wing. Hey, there, Lem, what are you doing?"

Cross had reached for a wide one. He shook his head and settled his feet into position.

"He's trying for the fence," said Wolfers. "Better stop him."

Instantly Lawrence rapped on the bench in a manner that caused Cross to give him a look. The manager signaled for the batter to attempt to single.

"Oh, it's easy!" growled Cross.

Lawrence persisted.

A moment later the batter hit a ball that struck the ground and rolled slowly toward Frank.

Merry sprang forward, but as he sought to pick the ball up his weak ankle seemed to melt beneath him, and he went down onto one knee. He secured the ball, however, and snapped it instantly to Hodge, who was standing on the plate.

Bart promptly whistled the ball to Browning, although it was not necessary, Cronin having been forced.

The local team had failed to secure a run in the eighth, after having everything in its favor.

The crowd was keenly disappointed.

Frank was relieved and his players were delighted.

Now came the ninth inning.

177

CHAPTER XXIX

FRANK'S TURN AT THE BAT.

"Frankie, you vos a pird!" said Hans Dunnerwurst, as he waddled in to the bench. "I nefer expectorated you couldt pitch a pall by your lame ankle much; but you dooded der trick mit a greadt deal of satisfactoriness. Yah!"

"I didn't do it, Hans," confessed Merry. "It was a case of good luck."

"Don'd let me toldt you dot!" exploded the Dutchman. "You don'd pelief me!"

Frank had limped to the bench.

"How is the ankle?" anxiously asked Morgan.

"Oh, I think I'll get through another inning with it."

"I'm sorry I was not able to stay in; but you see how much better you did."

"Which was luck, just as I told Hans."

"I can't see it that way. You made Cross roll that weak one to you."

"Perhaps it looked that way," said Merriwell; "but I want to whisper in your ear that I thought all the time that he was likely to lift out a two-bagger or something of the sort."

"You're too modest, Merry."

"It's not modesty, Dade; I'm simply telling you the truth. Let the rest of the boys think what they please."

"Let them get some runs this inning and we'll carry off this game," said Dade. "I feel it in my bones. All we need is one run. That will do the trick."

Browning was the first man up. The big fellow did not try for a long hit. He made an effort to drop the ball over the infield; but Rush covered ground swiftly and made a handsome catch.

"Too bad, Bruce," said Frank, as Browning returned to the bench. "With a poorer shortstop out there, you would have had a safe one."

"It's rotten!" growled the big fellow, in disgust. "We want this game! We can't lose it! We've got to have it! These fellows are too conceited. They call us kids! If we're kids, I wonder where they can find their men!"

"This game vill vin us," asserted Dunnerwurst. "Id can't lose us."

"Oh, go on!" blurted Bruce. "You'll find it's easy enough to lose this game. You think we can defeat anything, just because we've had good success thus far. I suppose you have an idea in your head that there are no teams in the country that can down us?"

"Oh, I don'd know apout dot!" admitted Hans. "Some uf der big league teams mighdt us down; but der Chicagos dit not dood id in California."

Rattleton was the next man to face Wolfers. The local pitcher grinned a bit, for Harry had not even touched the ball during the game.

Wolfers regarded Rattles with supreme contempt, which led him into carelessness, and the first thing he knew Harry cracked out a daisy cutter and capered down to the initial sack.

"Dot peen der kindt!" yelled Hans, seizing a bat. "Now we vin der game alretty! Der pall vill knock me vor a dree-pagger righdt avay soon. Holdt yourseluf readiness indo to come home, Harry."

"Oh, go ahead!" snapped Wolfers. "Stand up to the plate and let me strike you out. You talk too much with your face."

"You couldn'd struck me oudt a year indo!" retorted Hans. "Shust vatch und see me put der fence ofer der pall. I vill dood id! Yah!"

He swiped wildly at the first ball and missed by at least a foot.

Wolfers chuckled.

"Oh, yes, you'll put it over the fence!" he sneered. "It's easy for you to do that."

"Sure id vos easiness vor dot to do me," said Hans. "Nexdt dime I vill hit id vere you missed id dot dime."

The Elkton twirler kept Rattleton close to first.

Harry dared not try to steal unless he could secure a good lead, for Sprowl was a beautiful thrower to second.

After wasting one, Wolfers used the spit ball. It came from his hand with great speed and "broke" handsomely at exactly the proper point, taking a sharp jump.

Dunnerwurst tried to hit it.

Again he missed by at least a foot.

"Why don't you drive it over the fence?" laughed the Wonder

from Wisconsin.

"Sdop vetting der pall all ofer und I vill dood id," asserted Hans. "Uf der ball hit me, id vos such a slipperiness dot id vould der bat pop off a foul for. Yah!"

"Oh, I can toss you one and you can't hit it."

"I vish I thought id!"

"Well, here goes."

Wolfers actually tossed the Dutchman one.

Hans basted it full and fair on the trade-mark!

"Yow!" he whooped, as he dropped his bat and started for first. But he stopped short, for the ball had landed in the hands of Tinker, where it stuck.

Tinker snapped it to first to catch Rattleton.

Had the throw been accurate Harry would have been caught, but Cross was compelled to jump for it. He muffed it, giving Rattleton time to get back to the bag.

"Wouldn't dot jar you!" half sobbed Hans, as he turned toward the bench. "I had dot pall labeled dree pags vor."

"Oh, give up! give up!" laughed Wolfers. "You're beaten."

"It is my hour of glory," said Ready, as he picked out a slugger and sauntered toward the plate.

"You'll be a snap," said the Elkton pitcher.

"Don'd you pelief him!" cried Hans. "Der pall can hit you easy. You vill a three-pagger get."

"A safe hit wins this game," declared Jack. "Merry follows me, and he will promulgate the ball out of the lot."

"You'll get no safe hit off me," asserted Wolfers.

He was mistaken. Ready did not try to "kill" the ball. He took a short hold on his bat and drove a clean hit out between first and second.

Rattleton stretched his legs and raced to third, while Ready took first.

Wolfers was disturbed.

"Here's where de Merries win der game!" yelled a small boy. "Frank Merriwell is goin' ter hit, an' he always does de trick."

Instantly a dozen of his companions turned on him.

"What's der matter with you, Spud Bailey?" snarled a big chap, with red hair and plenty of freckles. "Wolfers will strike him out!"

"Bet you two hundred t'ousan' dollars he don't!" hotly retorted Spud. "Dey never strike dat boy out!"

"Bet your small change," advised Freckles. "How do you know so much?"

"I've read about Frank Merriwell. Wot's der matter with you!

You're a back number!"

"You'll think you're a back number arter you see wot Wolfers does ter him."

"Will I?"

"Yes, yer will!"

"Naw, I won't!"

"Yes, yer will!"

"Naw, I won't!"

By this time they had their fists clenched and their noses close together, while they were glaring into each other's eyes.

"Say," said Freckles, "arter ther game I'll give you all that's comin' ter ye!"

"You try it! I ain't skeered of you!"

"Stop that an' watch ther game," said another boy, butting between them. "A hit will do ther trick fer them fellers now."

"Wolfers won't let him hit," asserted Freckles.

"He can't help it," declared Spud. "Don't you never read no papers? Don't you know northing about Frank Merriwell? He's the greatest baseball player in the country."

"Guess ag'in," advised Freckles.

Frank fouled the first ball pitched.

"Wot'd I tell yer?" shouted Freckles.

"He bit a piece outer it," said Spud.

"He'll have ter do better'n dat."

"He will, all right, all right."

Needless to say that Merry's players were anxious. On third Rattleton crouched, ready to dash home on any sort of a hit. Ready played off first. He was tempted to go down before getting a signal from Frank. After that foul, Merry signaled. On the next ball pitched Jack scooted for second.

Sprowl made a fake motion as if he meant to throw to second, but snapped the ball to third.

Ready had slackened speed, intending to be caught between first and second if Sprowl threw to Tinker. Merry had signaled for Jack to work this trick in order to give Rattleton an opportunity to try to steal home.

The Elks declined to step into the trap.

Rattleton was compelled to plunge back to third.

"It's all right now," asserted Spud Bailey. "Frank Merriwell will drive in two runs, an' he may make a homer."

"You make me sick!" sneered Freckles. "I don't berlieve he ever got a hit in his life."

"You'll see! You'll see!"

Merry refused to bite at Wolfers' "teasers," but he missed one that was over the inside corner.

A moment later the third ball was called.

With two strikes and three balls declared, every one seemed to feel that the critical point of the game had been reached.

The next ball pitched might settle the contest.

Could Merriwell make a safe hit? That was the question.

"It wouldn't surprise me to see him lift it over the fence," muttered Bart Hodge.

Wolfers delivered the ball.

Frank struck!

And missed!

Plunk!—the ball landed in Sprowl's mitt.

"You're out!" yelled the umpire.

Frank had struck out!

His comrades on the bench seemed completely dazed.

Freckles gave Spud a jab in the stomach, whooping with delight:

"What'd I tell yer? Oh, you're a knowin' feller, you are! He done a lot, didn't he!"

Spud made some kind of retort, but the roaring of the delighted crowd drowned his words.

Wolfers was the hero of the moment as he swaggered in toward the local bench.

Hans Dunnerwurst could not believe the evidence of his eyes.

"A misdake has made you," he muttered, as he stared at the umpire. "Nefer in his life dit der pall strike him oudt."

"Into the field, boys," said Frank. "We must hold them down and get another inning. We still have a chance for this game."

"How could you strike out, Merry!" muttered Bart Hodge. "How could you!"

Frank saw that his companions were badly broken up over what had happened.

His reputation as a safe hitter at critical moments was such that a failure seemed impossible.

"Brace up, fellows!" he sharply commanded. "The score is still tied."

Morgan was angry.

"What's the matter with you fellows?" he sharply demanded. "You think a man ought to hit all the time. Keep in the game, and Merry will pull it off the coals."

The Elks were jubilant. They patted Wolfers on the back and complimented him on his cleverness.

"Get out!" he growled. "It was no trick at all. I can strike him out four times out of five. I know his weak spot."

"I've been told he has no weak spot," said Billy Cronin.

"That's rot! He has a weak spot, all right enough. I wish all the others on his team were just as easy."

"Well, you've made yourself solid in this town, anyhow," said George Rush. "The crowd was frightened. A hit just then might have fixed us."

"Well, you must jump in and get some runs now," said the manager. "We may as well wind the game up. The crowd is satisfied, and the town will back this team after to-day."

"If we ever get a chance at the other teams in this old league we'll trim them for fair," grinned Rush. "But I'm afraid we'll frighten them so they'll continue to hold us out."

"They can't do it," declared Lawrence. "The Central League can't run without us. A three-cornered league is rotten, and the other towns must have us. They'll come to time pretty soon. If we can get games enough, we'll lose no money while this thing is hanging fire. We'll make something on the game to-day. It might have hurt us if we'd lost, as I agreed that the winners should take two-thirds of the net receipts. Merriwell made the terms. He'll have to be satisfied with a third if we carry off the game."

"We'll carry it off," said Sprowl, as he selected a bat. "This inning ought to be enough."

"Aw, it'll be enough," nodded Wolfers. "Go ahead and get first, Chuck. I'll drive you round. That feller can't pitch any better than he can bat."

Wolfers had a very poor opinion of Merriwell's ability.

Sprowl hit the first ball pitched.

It skimmed along the ground about four feet inside the line to first base.

Browning sprang in front of it, but he did not touch it with his hands, and it went between his legs.

Sprowl turned toward second, but Dunnerwurst had secured the ball, and he dodged back to first.

"You're a mark, Merriwell," laughed Wolfers, as he walked out to hit. "How did you ever get a reputation as a pitcher, anyhow?"

Frank was a trifle "touched" by the fellow's insolence, although he did not betray it.

"Getting a reputation isn't as difficult as keeping it sometimes, you know," he said.

"Well, don't you care. You're up against the real thing to-day. You might beat dub teams; but it's different when you have to face the real hot stuff."

"If I'm able," thought Merry, "I'm going to strike you out."

He knew this would not be a simple matter in case Wolfers tried to sacrifice for the purpose of advancing Sprowl; but the conceit and insolence of the fellow made him long to accomplish the feat.

Frank summoned all his power of self-command. He had watched to learn the weak points of the man at bat, and now he commanded himself to be accurate and to do the things he wished.

As a result, he fooled the hitter with the first two balls pitched, Wolfers going after both of them and missing.

As Hodge snapped the ball back to him, Merry decided on the course he would pursue. He knew Wolfers would expect him to "waste" a ball in an attempt to fool him, this being the natural course when two strikes and no balls had been called. Instead of doing so, Frank summoned his speed and control and drove a straight one over the very heart of the plate.

When it was too late, Wolfers realized what Merry had done. He made a weak and tardy swing at the ball, which he did not touch.

"Str-r-r-rike—kah three!" cried the umpire. "You're out!"

Wolfers flung aside the bat and paused, his hands on his hips, staring at Merry.

"You're very clever!" he sneered.

"Thank you," said Merry.

"No thanks needed. Only an amateur would put a straight one over under such circumstances. It's always impossible to tell what a greenhorn will do."

Wolfers was sore. He did not like to acknowledge that he had been outwitted, although such was the case.

"Go sit down, Bob," laughed Kitson, as he walked out to strike. "You missed. Let it go at that."

Wolfers retired to the bench, feeling very sore.

Frank knew Kitson was reckoned as a clever base getter, for which reason he had been placed at the head of the list. Merry felt that it would be best to force the man to hit, if possible, and this he tried to do.

Now, however, all at once, he had lost control. The batter saw this and waited. As a result, he walked.

"It's all to the good!" yelled Rush, as he capered on the coaching line. "Get away off! Take a lead! Divorce yourselves from those sacks! Don't force Chuck, Kit. Remember he's ahead of you. How easy to win a game like this! It's a cinch! Move off, you snails! Get a long lead! Let him throw the ball. He'll throw it wild in a minute. He hasn't any control. He's off his feed to-day."

The spectators began to "root," hoping to rattle Frank.

Merry took his time. He knew he was in poor condition, yet he was fighting to win the game, if such a thing could be done. For once in his life, he lacked confidence; but this was caused by his lame ankle, which had seriously interfered with his control.

In endeavoring to fool Cronin he put one straight over. It happened that Cronin had not expected it and simply drove a foul down back of first base.

Hodge was shaking a little, for he saw that Merry was in no condition to pitch against good batters.

"Give me another like that," invited Cronin.

"Once is enough," smiled Merry. "Why didn't you take advantage of your opportunity?"

"Oh, well, give me anything. I'll hit anything you get over the pan."

In spite of this boast, Frank finally struck Cronin out with a ball close to his shoulder.

Hodge breathed easier.

"Merry will do it," he thought. "He never fails. It isn't in him to fail. But I fear he'll fix his ankle to-day so he'll take no part in the meet at Ashport."

Perhaps Bart was the only one who fully realized how much it was costing Frank to pitch that game.

Two men were out now, and two were on bases.

Sparks, the centre fielder of the Elks, advanced to the plate.

"Give it a ride, Sparkie!" implored Rush. "You can do it! You must do it!"

"Hit it! Beef it out!" roared the crowd.

Sparks was eager to comply, for he felt that the game depended on him. He was a fine hitter, although Merry had struck him out in the eighth.

Frank worked carefully, taking all the time permissible. Hodge talked to him soothingly.

"This chap is shaking, Frank," said Bart. "He remembered what you did to him before. He knows you can do it again. Watch him shake."

"Shake your grandmother!" growled Sparks.

"It would be shameful to shake an old lady like that," said Hodge. "I wouldn't think of it."

"Str-r-r-rike—kah two!" called the umpire, as Sparks missed a bender.

"Got him, Merry!" said Hodge confidently. "It's a ten-inning game."

"Who told you so much?" grinned Sparks.

"It's all settled," declared Bart. "Shut your eyes next time you swing. You'll do just as well."

He was trying to bother the batter by talking to him.

Frank attempted to fool Sparks with the next ball pitched. To his dismay, he realized the moment the ball left his hand that it was certain to curve over the plate.

Sparks was watching like a hawk. He saw the ball break and judged it correctly.

A moment later he hit it.

At the crack of ball and bat the spectators seemed to rise as one man. They saw the ball go sailing out on a line, rising higher gradually. It was a long, hard drive, not a rainbow fly.

Sprowl and Kitson capered along over the bags.

Gamp stretched his long legs in an effort to get under the ball. He covered ground with amazing strides.

"All to the mustard!" yelled Rush. "He couldn't touch it in a thousand years! The game is ours, boys! We had to have it!"

"Get dot pall under, Choe!" squawked Dunnerwurst. "Pick id oudt uf a cloudt! You can dood id!"

Frank was watching with no little anxiety. He knew Joe was a wonderful fielder, and he had seen him make some astonishing catches; but his judgment told him that the chances were decidedly against the long-legged chap.

Gamp knew it, too, and he was trying harder than he had ever tried before in all his life.

"I must get it!" he thought. "I will get it!"

Joe knew the game depended on his success. If he failed, the Elks would be the winners. His heart leaped into his throat. He seemed to find it necessary to set his teeth to keep it from leaping quite out of his mouth.

He saw the ball beginning to fall.

"I must get it! I will!" he repeated.

In his mind he saw what would follow failure. He saw the Elks triumphant, the crowd roaring with joy, his own friends dejected and downcast. He even saw himself walking in from the field, his head hanging, unable to look Frank in the face. He knew how Frank would take it; he knew he would be a good loser.

Across from right field came the wail of Dunnerwurst:

"Get dot pall under, Choe! You can dood id!"

He was doing his level best; it was not in him to do more. He realized at last that he was going to miss the ball by inches—if he missed it.

Oh, that he could cover a little more ground! Oh, that he had wings!

His comrades knew how madly he was trying. They scarcely breathed.

"Good old Joe!" whispered Rattleton. "He can't fail!"

But there are things beyond human accomplishment. It was possible for Gamp to fail.

He made a last great leap, his hands outstretched.

The ball barely touched the ends of his gloved fingers.

Three inches farther and he might have held it.

He did not catch it, and Elkton had won the game.

As soon as Joe could stop he looked after the ball a moment and then turned to walk in, refusing to chase and recover it.

Roar after roar came from the stand and the bleachers. The crowd was wild with delight. It was the sort of finish to fill them with unutterable joy. They waved their hats, hands, and handkerchiefs in the air. Men howled hoarsely; women added a shriller note to the volume of sound.

For the moment Sparks was the hero; but Wolfers was not forgotten. Down from the bleachers poured the spectators and out onto the field they streamed. They wanted to get near those two great heroes. They packed close about them. They even tried to lift and carry them, but neither man would have it.

"Stop your foolishness!" cried Wolfers sharply. "Didn't you ever see a game won before?"

"This certainly is a red-hot baseball town!" laughed Sparks.

"It will be red hot after this. The game went just right to please the bunch."

In all Elkton it seemed that just one inhabitant was downcast. Spud Bailey looked sick. He said not a word when Freckles jumped on him and punched him, crying jubilantly:

"Yah! yah! yah! What do you think about it now? Knew a lot, didn't ye! Your great Frank Merriwell got his dat time! He jest did!"

Frank Merriwell waited for Gamp. Joe had his eyes on the ground as he came up. Merry took his arm, and they walked in together.

"Dud-don't touch me!" said Gamp huskily. "I'm a lul-lobster!"

"You made a wonderful run for that ball, Joe," said Merry. "I didn't think you could get anywhere near it!"

"Th-three inches mum-mum-more and I'd ha-had it!" groaned the sorrowful fellow. "I lul-lost the gug-game!"

"Nothing of the sort!"

"Yes, I did!"

"I lost it myself. I couldn't control the ball, and I gave that batter one just where he wanted it."

"It's all right for you to sus-say that, Merry; but I didn't cuc-catch that fly."

"No fielder could have caught it, and not one in a thousand could have touched it."

Still Gamp blamed himself.

Hodge had flung aside the mask and body protector. He glared at Joe as the tall fellow came up.

"Why didn't you get your paws onto that ball?" he snarled.

"I ought to," said Joe.

"Of course you had! That would——"

"Stop, Bart!" commanded Frank promptly. "You know, as well as I, that Joe came amazingly near getting it."

"Well, why didn't he?"

"Because it was beyond human accomplishment. You have no right to speak to him that way. Better take it back."

Bart muttered something and began overhauling the bats to get hold of his own stick, which he religiously cared for at all times. The sting of defeat was hard to bear.

Merry was not satisfied.

"You know who lost the game, Bart," he said. "You know I am alone to blame. Don't try to put the blame onto any one else. Kick at me for my rotten pitching, if you like."

Hodge said nothing now. He had found his bat, but he glared at the stick as if that were somehow to blame for the misfortune that had befallen them.

Dunnerwurst seemed on the verge of tears, while Rattleton looked sad enough.

The loss of this particular game had depressed the whole team more than anything that had happened on the entire trip.

Finally Hodge turned to Gamp, who was pulling on his sweater.

"I beg your pardon, Joe," he said sincerely. "I was wrong. I know it. You were not to blame."

"Yes, I was!" persisted Gamp, willing and ready to shoulder the burden.

"Not a bit of it," asserted Bart. "It was fate. We had to lose the game. We were all to blame. We couldn't hit Wolfers! I'd like to try it again!" he savagely ended.

"We'd all like to try it again," said Browning.

"Can't we?" eagerly asked Rattleton.

"Let's!" grunted Badger.

"Get together, fellows," directed Frank. "We'll give Elkton a cheer."

"It's their place to cheer us first," objected Hodge.

"Never mind that. We'll get ahead of them. Open it up good and hearty. Let's show them that we can lose without crying baby. None of us fancies a baby."

He gathered them about him and led the cheer, which was hearty enough.

The Elks were taken by surprise. Some of them had started to leave the field. The manager realized he had been outdone in politeness, and he hastened after his players, hustling together those he could assemble. Then they cheered, but it lacked the vigor of the cheer from the Merries.

This little piece of business on the part of the visitors caught the fancy of the crowd. The spectators realized now that Frank and his comrades had made a game fight.

"You're all right, blue boys!" shouted a man. "You can play the game!"

"That's right," agreed another. "You're dandies, boys!"

Others followed their example. The crowd could afford to be generous. It was perfectly satisfied.

CHAPTER XXX

THE STING OF DEFEAT.

On their hotel at Elkton the boys had one room which was used exclusively as a "dressing room." In it was kept all the paraphernalia which they carried on the tour.

After the game they hurried silently to the hotel, few words passing on the way.

In the dressing room they were very quiet. Dade Morgan came over to Frank, speaking in a low tone.

"I'm sorry, Merry," he said simply.

"We can't win all the games," answered Frank.

"But this was a hard game to lose."

"Almost any game is a hard one to lose."

The defeated players sat around meditatively as they slowly stripped off their playing clothes. Connected with the room there was a bath with a shower. One after another they jumped under the shower, turned on the cold spray, drenched themselves thoroughly, jumped out, rubbed down until glowing, and then dressed.

"That was a great catch you made in the second inning, Hans," said Browning.

"Oh, I don'd know apout dot," retorted the Dutchman. "Id peen nottings peside der pall vot caught you ven Chack threw him so high der first innings indo."

"Say, Badg, you nipped Glade beautifully in the fourth," said Rattleton. "Hodge made a great throw. Glade thought he had the sack purloined."

"I noticed you were backing me up all right," said the Kansan.

"I saw you were going to cover the bag. I was playing too deep to cover it for the throw."

Starbright slapped Morgan on the shoulder.

"You had 'em guessing, my boy."

"Rot!" growled Dade. "I've got a crockery wing. It went back on me in a pinch. Still I might have stayed in the game. I'm afraid I squealed."

Then they all sat still some moments. Of a sudden Browning turned on Morgan.

"Why didn't you cover first when I went off after that foul in the third?" he rumbled, frowning. "We could have made a double play on it."

"Oh, go on!" retorted Dade. "It wasn't your ball. Why didn't you let Hodge have it and stick to the bag? Play your own position and you'll do better."

"You made a nice mess in muffing that short throw from Hodge in the seventh!" snarled Rattleton, glaring at Badger. "That let in a run. Why don't you do your neeping slights—I mean your sleeping nights?"

"Oh, you haven't anything to say!" fiercely retorted the Kansan. "You muffed the ball when I picked up Tinker's grounder and snapped it to you."

"How did I know you was going to snap it underhand that way? You had plenty of time."

With the exception of Merry, the whole team seemed growling and snarling all at once.

Underneath it all, however, Frank saw the real true spirit that longs for victory. They were not really malicious, but each man was to do his level best and to have every other man do the same.

"We lost the game, fellows, and it's no use to kick," said Merry. "I think every man did his best. I know I did. It was poor enough. We'll have to swallow defeat and go out for the next game we play."

"It would be different if we could get another crack at these fellows," muttered Ready, all his usual flippancy gone.

"We'd eat 'em!" roared Badger fiercely.

"You'd have quite a job with that man Wolfers on the pitcher's plate," said Merry. "He's the cleverest twirler we've encountered this season."

"But he knows he's good," rumbled Browning. "That's what's the matter with him. He keeps boring it into the opposing players."

"For the purpose of rattling them. That's a part of his game. A man as clever as he is don't need to resort to that trick; but Wolfers does it. He learned it in the small leagues and independent teams. He'll get over it if he gets into fast company."

"We ought to haf peen fast enough vor him," said Hans. "Didn't

191

dot pall hit me righdt indo der handts uf Dinker? I hat id lapeled four pases vor. Id peen roppery for der pall der catch him dot vay."

Again Hans seemed on the verge of shedding tears.

"Does this end it, Merry?" asked Rattleton. "Can't we get another game with these fellows?"

"Do you want to play them again?"

"Do I? Ask me!"

"How about the others?"

Every man was on his feet, clamoring for another game.

"We'll beat them or die trying!" cried Ready. "Do get another game with them, Frank!"

"Do!" echoed all the others.

"But make it far enough off so you can pitch yourself," said Starbright.

"Oh, I know I didn't make good, Dick!" snapped Morgan. "No need to rub it in!"

"But you did make good until you pitched your arm off," said the big, blond chap quickly. "I didn't mean to cast any stones your way."

"All right," said Dade. "I know when I'm outclassed, and Wolfers was too good for me. I had to pitch my arm off after he went into the box."

"Cutts was something of a cinch!" snickered Badger. "Why didn't they keep him in? We'd rolled up fifty runs. That's whatever!"

"Oh, great and mighty chieftain!" cried Ready, his flippant air returning; "we beseech thee to arrange another game with the frisky Elks of Elkton. We wish to wipe out the stain. Give us a chance and see us do a bit of fancy wiping."

"I'll do my best, fellows," promised Frank. "But you know I'll not be able to pitch for at least three or four more days. I don't know whether I hurt my ankle much to-day or not. Once or twice I gave it a twist. If I'd put some one else in and let him throw the ball over the pan, it would have been better. But I thought I might save the game. This game may be a bad thing for the Elks. It may frighten the other teams in the league."

"Go after another game right away, Frank," urged Bart. "Put it far enough off so your ankle will get strong. We must redeem ourselves."

The others were just as anxious. Frank found every man on the team was yearning to wipe out the disgrace of defeat, so he agreed to see Jack Lawrence, the manager of the Elks, and try to arrange another game.

CHAPTER XXXI

NO CHANCE FOR REVENGE.

Ben Raybold, representative of the Northern Securities Company, was lighting a cigar at the stand in the office of the Antlers Hotel when he heard about the game of baseball that had been played in Elkton that afternoon.

"The Merries?" said he, addressing the cigar clerk. "Do you mean Frank Merriwell's team?"

"Yes; our boys trimmed those fellows to-day."

Raybold lifted his eyebrows.

"Do you mean to tell me that a local team defeated Merriwell's team?"

"Sure thing. I tell you, we've got the hottest team in Ohio right here in Elkton."

"You must have a hot team to beat those fellows. I've seen them play. They got away with the Chicagos two out of three games in Los Angeles."

"Well, I rather think our boys might do better than that," said the clerk, throwing out his chest.

Raybold smiled a bit.

"Many queer things happen in baseball," he said. "Your team is not a straight local nine?"

"Oh, no," was the proud answer. "We've got a salaried team. That is," he hastily added, "three men are on salary. The others are employed in town. One of them is a bell boy here in this hotel."

The Northern Securities man shook his head in a puzzled manner.

"And such a team got away with Frank Merriwell's nine?" he said. "I don't understand it."

The cigar clerk was touched.

"You don't seem to understand," he said. "Elkton has a team that can make any of 'em hustle. You ought to see our pitcher.

He's from Wisconsin. His name is Wolfers. Mark what I'm telling you, he'll be in one of the big leagues within two years. I think he's a better man than Cy Young or Chesbro, or any of them fellows. He uses the spit ball, and he can put it just where he wants to, which is better than some of the pitchers can do."

At this moment Bob Wolfers, accompanied by Jack Lawrence and Seymour Whittaker, a local baseball enthusiast and a man of wealth, entered the hotel.

"Oh, your pitcher may be a good man," said Raybold, taking his cigar from his mouth and examining it critically: "but you ought to know that Frank Merriwell is, beyond doubt, the cleverest slab artist not gobbled up by one of the two big leagues. The Boston Americans and the New York Nationals both want him."

"Is that straight, mister?" asked Wolfers, butting in and winking at the cigar clerk.

"Yes, that's straight."

"I suppose you know it for a fact?"

"I suppose I do."

"Well, that fellow wouldn't last twenty seconds on either the Bostons or the New Yorks. He's the greatest shine for a pitcher that I ever saw."

Raybold flushed a bit and chewed at the end of his cigar, while he surveyed Wolfers from head to foot.

"I presume you're competent to judge?" he said.

"I presume I am."

"It's a fine thing for a man to have a high estimation of his ability as a judge. Who are you?"

"My name is Wolfers."

"Oh-ho! I see! Professional jealousy. A case of sour grapes."

Wolfers laughed derisively.

"Why should it be a case of sour grapes? Merriwell got his medicine all right to-day."

"Did you ever get bumped?"

"What has that got to do with it? All pitchers get hit occasionally."

"That's right; and, therefore, I claim that you can't judge Merriwell's ability by one game. Probably it will be different in the next game."

"There will be no next game," said the manager.

"How is that?"

"One game wound us up with those chaps."

"Don't you dare play them another?"

"Dare? Ha! ha! ha! That's a joke! Look here, my friend, there's

194

nothing we're afraid to hitch up with."

"Then why don't you give them another chance at you?"

"Because we have games arranged for the rest of this week, and we expect to be playing in the league again by the first of next week. We can't bother with small fry. We play out of town to-morrow and next day, and the Cuban Giants meet us here Saturday."

"I like the way you talk about small fry!" exclaimed Raybold, the tone of his voice indicating that he did not like it.

"Besides," said Lawrence, "I don't fancy Merriwell or any of his crowd want to tackle us again."

"That's where you make a mistake," said a quiet voice, as Frank entered the office, limping the least bit. "We're very anxious to get another game with you, Mr. Lawrence. We think we might reverse the result of to-day."

Raybold's eyes twinkled. He recognized Frank at once, but, having never met him, he did not speak. Lawrence shrugged his shoulders.

"It seems to me you ought to be satisfied, Merriwell," he said. "You got your bumps to-day, didn't you?"

"You certainly hit me enough," confessed Frank.

"Still you are anxious for more. Some people never know when they've got enough."

This kind of talk was most annoying, but Merriwell had perfect self-control.

"That's right," he acknowledged. "Perhaps I'm one of that kind."

"Well, out of pity for you, we shouldn't think of making another game with you, even if we had the opportunity."

"Look here," chipped in Raybold, a trifle warmly, "I believe you're troubled with cold feet. That's what's the matter! You're so pleased over this victory that you want to boast about it."

This angered Lawrence, who declared that it was nothing to boast about and made a great deal of talk to that effect. When he had finished, Raybold said:

"I'll wager a hundred dollars even with any man that you can't defeat Merriwell's team in another game."

Seymour Whittaker pricked up his ears.

"What's that?" he asked. "Your money would feel good in my pocket."

"Do you take my bet?"

Lawrence turned quickly to Whittaker.

"No use to bet," he said. "We can't give them another game. They'll have to swallow their defeat and make the best of it."

"The best of it, or the worst of it," laughed Wolfers. "Too bad they feel so sore. They were outclassed, that's all."

"I'm sorry I can't win that hundred off you, sir," said Whittaker to Raybold. "It would be easy money for me."

Lawrence then inquired if Sprowl was in his room at the hotel, and, being told at the desk that he was, he proceeded upstairs, followed by Wolfers and Whittaker.

"It's unfortunate that these fellows will give you no chance to get even, Mr. Merriwell," said Raybold. "They must be afraid of you."

"I hardly think that," said Merry. "The game to-day could not have frightened them, although it was close until the finish of the ninth inning. They have perfect confidence in themselves. As you are a stranger, it was a surprise to me when you offered to back us in that manner."

"Oh, we've never met, but I've seen you pitch. I was out West a short time ago. Have you the same team you had in California and Colorado?"

"Just the same, except that we're one substitute short. Stretcher has gone home."

"How did you happen to lose to-day? Was it bad fielding behind you?"

"No, sir. In the ninth I failed to make a hit, with two men on the bags. On the other hand, when their turn came, they did get the hit needed, likewise having two men on the sacks. That's about how it happened."

In this manner Frank shouldered the burden. He made no reference to his lame ankle, nor did he explain that he had entered the box after Morgan's arm gave out.

"That was hard luck!" exclaimed Raybold. "Could you beat them to-morrow?"

"No man can predict what will happen in baseball. Look at the poor showing the Boston Americans made at the opening of the season, just when every one expected great things of them. There are no sure things in baseball that is worth being called baseball."

"Of course we all realize that. Evidently you are not satisfied to leave Elkton without another try at the team here."

"Hardly satisfied. Quite the contrary."

"Well, can't you drive them into giving you a game?"

"I don't know how. You've just heard their manager refuse."

"Yes, but men frequently change their minds. Keep at him. Give me permission to see what I can do. Will you?"

"Well——"

"Of course I mean on my own responsibility. I'll not represent you."

"I couldn't think of permitting that, in case you tried to get a game through a wager. I can't prevent you from betting as much as you choose on your own responsibility."

"I understand your position. I believe I heard once that betting was against your principles. You seem to have taken a decided stand on that matter. It's rather peculiar for a young fellow in your position, but I admire you for it. Stick by your principles, say I. I have a theory that it is wrong for a man to do anything he believes to be wrong. Another man may not consider it wrong, and, therefore, for him it may be all right."

"That's a dangerous doctrine to preach, as it's likely to be mis-understood. I have no doubt but there are men who do not con-sider it wrong to lie or cheat; but——"

"Oh, beyond a certain limit my theory does not apply. It applies to some mooted questions. Lying and cheating are things no man can make right by thinking or pretending to think they are right. But you know some strait-laced persons believe attending the theatre on Sunday is wrong. For them it is wrong. I see no harm in it. I feel that it frequently does me good. For me it is all right."

"How about playing cards on Sunday?"

"I see no harm in it. Do you?"

"Yes," answered Frank honestly. "Even if I did not think it harmed me, I would not do it on account of the example I might be placing before others. A man has to consider that."

"If he considers everything of that sort, he'll find himself robbed of much of the pleasure in this life."

"A man can have plenty of pleasure without resorting to license. This life can be enjoyed in a good, healthy way, and the person who takes care not to set a bad example for others enjoys it more than one who is careless and indifferent. I do not believe any young man of my years ever enjoyed life more than I; yet I have been conscientious in many things on account of the example I might be setting before others. It is possible I might drink with-out harming myself, but I know there are fellows on my baseball team who could not drink without doing themselves serious in-jury. If I drank, several of them might drink. Could I be contented and undisturbed if I saw them forming the habit through follow-ing in my footsteps?"

"Well, you put up a great argument, and you've given me some-thing new to think about. Just the same, if I can drive Elkton into playing another game with you through betting that you'll defeat them, I am going to do it. The sandy gentleman was inclined to snap up the hundred I offered. He must have some influence in baseball circles. I propose to keep after him. Leave it to me. On what terms did you play to-day?"

"Two-thirds of the net gate money went to the winners."

"Good crowd?"

"Fine."

"Your share will pay your bills?"

"It ought to."

"Well, if you can get two-thirds in the next game, even if you have to wait several days before you play, you may not lose anything."

"I'm willing to wait and lose money if I can get the game."

Raybold found another opportunity that evening to make some betting talk to Seymour Whittaker.

Whittaker professed a strong desire to wager money on the Elks, but said he could not, as Lawrence would not consider making another game with the Merries.

"Are you one of the directors of the team?" asked Raybold.

"Yes, sir."

"It seems that you might have some influence with him."

"Not enough to cause him to change his mind. He's very set. It's a good thing for you. I'd feel like a robber after taking your money."

"Would you, indeed?" laughed Raybold. "Well, see here, my dear man, I'll give you a perfect snap. I'll wager two hundred to one hundred that you cannot defeat the Merries again, the game to be played here any time next week, with a fair and impartial umpire."

"Why don't you give me your money!" cried Whittaker. "You might as well."

"What do you say? Two hundred to one hundred."

"No use. It can't be done, and you're in luck."

"When does your local paper appear?"

"Thursday."

"I'm going to insert a notice in the paper to the effect that the Elkton team does not dare give Merriwell another chance."

"Don't be so foolish!"

"Look the paper over when it comes out," said Raybold. "You'll find the notice."

Raybold was in earnest. He really did insert a notice in the local paper, paying advertising rates for the privilege. This notice was sarcastically worded and reflected on the courage of the local team in refusing to give the Merries another game. It called attention to the fact that the Merries had on their tour defeated far better known and much stronger teams than the Elks, while it further stated that no team could draw such a crowd, all of Elkton being desirous of witnessing another "go" with the visitors who had given the locals such a tussle the first time.

There was something about this notice that aroused the pride and indignation of the Elktonites. The village hummed over it. The citizens began to tell one another that the Elks must give Frank Merriwell's team another chance.

The Elks were playing in another town, but Lawrence was called up on the phone by two or three persons who asked him why he did not play the Merries again.

Frank had not known Raybold intended to insert the notice. After the notice appeared Merry kept still and awaited results.

He had lingered in Elkton with his team, hoping another game could be secured.

Seymour Whittaker was indignant. He looked around for Raybold and demanded to know why the people of Elkton had been insulted. Raybold laughed and said no insult was intended. Whittaker insisted that the newspaper notice plainly insinuated that the Elktonites were afraid their team would be beaten if it met the Merries again.

"It looks that way to me," said Raybold.

"You know we're not afraid."

"Prove it."

"We will!" cried Whittaker. "I'll have the directors of the team get together. They can instruct Lawrence to arrange for the game. Then I presume you'll squeal on that betting talk you've made."

"Hardly."

"Put your money up now, then."

"All right."

"Two hundred to one."

"That's what I offered. If the game is not played, the bet is off."

They went out and found a stakeholder. The money was put up.

On Saturday the Elks returned home and the famous Cuban Giants appeared to play them.

The Cuban Giants is one of the strongest colored teams in the country, and the people of Elkton believed the real test of the locals would come in the game with the Giants.

Merry knew the directors of the team had held a meeting for the purpose of considering the advisability of playing again with his team, but he could learn nothing as to the result of that meeting.

Somehow, after returning to Elkton, Lawrence kept away from

Frank, who saw him for the first time Saturday on the baseball field just before the beginning of the game with the Giants.

In the presence of the assembled spectators, Frank walked out to the bench and spoke to the Elkton manager, asking if he had decided to give him another game.

"Merriwell," said Lawrence disagreeably, "I never saw a fellow so persistent in seeking a second drubbing. We'll play you Monday, on one condition."

"Name it."

"The winning team shall take all the gate money."

"Agreed!" said Frank, with a promptness that surprised Lawrence. "It's settled!"

"You won't get a dollar."

"Don't worry about me. Will you announce the game here today? It will be the best sort of an advertisement."

"Yes, I'll announce it."

As Frank walked away, Lawrence turned to Wolfers, chuckling:

"Didn't I work that cleverly? The directors instructed me to give him another game. I'd had to have done so on an even break, fifty per cent. to each team, if he had insisted; but I kept away from him and made him so eager he was willing to take terms of any sort. We'll get all the boodle."

Cutts went in to pitch the game, and for five innings he had the heavy-hitting colored boys at his mercy. In the sixth inning he went to pieces and gave the Giants five base bits, which netted three runs.

At that time the Elks had five scores.

Wolfers warmed up at once.

He was greeted with tumultuous cheers when he walked out to pitch at the beginning of the sixth.

The colored boys were stayers. They laughed heartily over the applause given Wolfers.

"We'll put him into the stable quicker than we did the other fellow," said the captain of the Giants. "Get right after him, boys. Knock his eye out. He's a man with a swelled head. You can see it in the way he walks."

But when Wolfers struck out the first three batters to face him, pitching only eleven balls, they began to realize that they were up against a wizard.

The joy of the spectators was boundless. The man from Wisconsin was cheered madly as he struck out the third man.

"That's all right," declared one of the Giants. "We'll fall on his neck next inning."

"Oh, yes you will!" derisively roared a big man. "You'll fall on his neck—I don't think!"

Lawrence seized the opportunity as a favorable one to make an announcement. Walking out to the home plate, he held up his hand for silence.

"Ladies and gentlemen," he called, "I wish to inform you that there will be another game here in Elkton Monday afternoon at the usual hour."

"Hooray!" bellowed the big man. "I'll quit work to come! You can't give us too much of this kind of baseball!"

"It seems," said the manager of the Elks, smiling, "that some baseball players are greedy to be trimmed. They don't know when they have enough. Our first game with Frank Merriwell's Athletic Team resulted in a victory for us. The Merries were not satisfied. Mr. Merriwell has boned us into giving him another game. We intend to give him all he wants. I understand that Merriwell himself will pitch for his team. Bob Wolfers will do the pitching for us, and——"

What a yell went up!

"Oh, that's a shame!" howled the big man, as the uproar subsided somewhat. "Why don't you give them a chance? It isn't fair!"

"We propose to show you just what kind of a game we can put up with Wolfers in the box," said Lawrence. "We promise you your money's worth. Don't miss it."

"We won't!" they cried.

CHAPTER XXXII

PERFECT CONTROL.

Following was the batting order when the Merries again faced the Elks:

MERRIES.	ELKS.
Ready, 3d b.	Kitson, rf.
Morgan, ss.	Cronin, 3d b.
Badger, lf.	Sparks, cf.
Merriwell, p.	Rush, ss.
Hodge, c.	Glade, rf.
Gamp, cf.	Tinker, 2d b.
Browning, 1st b.	Cross, 1st b.
Rattleton, 2d b.	Sprowl, c.
Dunnerwurst, rf.	Wolfers, p.

The Elks fancied they would have an easy thing with Wolfers in the box. Still they were anxious to get a safe lead early in the game, and Lawrence urged them to "jump on" Merriwell without delay.

Of course the Merries were sent to bat first, as this gave the locals their last opportunity.

Wolfers was chewing gum and grinning when he went into the box. He looked more than ever like a wolf, yet he seemed to be very good-natured. The crowd cheered him and he touched his cap in acknowledgment.

"Good old Bobby!" howled the same big man who had made himself heard so often at the game with the Cuban Giants. "You're the boy! This will be a picnic for you."

The usual gathering of small boys was to be seen. Spud Bailey was on hand, and he seemed to be an object of much ridicule.

"Oh, you know er lot erbout baseball!" sneered Freckles, while all the others laughed. "Mebbe you've got it inter dat nut of yourn that them Merriwell fellers will win dis game?"

"I has," acknowledged Spud defiantly.

They jeered him.

"You don't know ernough ter come in w'en it rains," said Freckles.

"You'll know more arter ther game. Frank Merriwell is goin' ter pitch ther whole of this one."

"Dey'll pound him outer der box inside of t'ree innin's."

"I know a man dat's bet two hundrud dollars ter one hundred dat the Merriwells will win."

"He's a bigger fool dan you are! W'y didn't he go burn his money. He'd had more fun wid it."

But Spud was unmoved.

"You wait," he muttered. "You'll see."

Never in their careers had the members of Merriwell's team been more determined to win, if possible. All levity was cut out of the early part of the game. They went at it seriously, earnestly, with heart and soul.

Ready cast aside his flippancy and did his level best to start things off with a hit. The best he could do was to drive a grounder into the hands of Cronin, who whistled it across to Cross for an easy out.

Wolfers continued to grin, although he had anticipated, beginning by showing his ability to strike a man out when he desired.

Morgan fouled several times, finally striking out on a "spit ball," which took a wonderfully sharp jump to one side as he swung, nearly getting away from Sprowl.

"That's the kind, Bob, old socks!" cried the catcher. "They never can hit those."

Badger popped a little one into the air, and the first three batters to face the wonder from Wisconsin were his victims.

"Now get right after Merriwell, boys," urged Lawrence, as his players reached the bench. "Clinch the game at the start, and then take it easy. Put us into it, Kit."

Merriwell did not limp as he walked out. His ankle was tightly supported with a broad leather band. In warming up he had found that his control was perfect. He could put the ball exactly where he pleased, and he felt that on this day he would be in his best form. He also felt that he would need all his skill.

Kitson laughed.

"Just put one over and see me bump it," he urged.

Frank looked round to make sure every man was in position.

"We're all behind you, Merry," assured Rattleton. "Let him

mump it a bile—I mean bump it a mile!"

The first ball pitched looked good to Kitson. It was speedy and quite high.

Just as the batter slashed at it the ball took a sharp rise, or jump, and the bat encountered nothing but empty air.

"Stir-r-r-rike—kah one!" came from the umpire.

Spud Bailey seized the first opportunity to rejoice.

"Why didn't he hit dat?" he cried.

"Oh, wait, wait!" advised Freckles. "Dere's plenty of time. He'll hit der next one he goes after."

But Freckles was mistaken. The next ball was a wide outdrop, which Kitson let pass. Then came a high ball that changed into a drop and shot down past the batter's shoulders. He had anticipated a drop, and he tried to hit it, but did not judge it correctly.

"Stir-r-r-rike—kah two!"

Spud didn't miss his chance to turn on Freckles.

"Shut up!" snapped Freckles. "He's goin' ter git a hit!"

Kitson thought so himself. He picked out another that looked good. It was an inshoot, and it spanked into Bart's big mitt.

"You're out!" came from the umpire.

Spud Bailey stood on his head, but Freckles viciously kicked him over.

Kitson shook his head as he walked to the bench.

"He fooled me," he acknowledged. "Still I should have hit 'em."

"Never mind," said Cronin. "I'll start something."

Ben Raybold was sitting on the bleachers. He smiled the least bit as he saw Merry easily dispose of Kitson.

"He seems to be in his best form," thought the backer of the visitors. "If so, I've won a hundred. I wish I'd made it more."

The eyes of Bart Hodge were gleaming. He hammered a hole into his big mitt with his fist.

"Drop 'em into that pocket, Merry, old boy," he cried. "You know how to do it."

"You bet my life he knows how!" cried Dunnerwurst.

"They're all swelled up over striking you out, Kit," said Rush.

"It won't be so easy next time," declared Kitson. "I'm onto his tricks."

"Plenty of speed."

"Oh, yes; but we like speed."

"Sure. We eat speed. If he keeps burnin' 'em over, we'll fall on him pretty soon and pound him to the four winds."

Merry remembered Cronin's weakness. He kept the ball close to the fellow, and, having both control and speed, found it just as easy to strike him out.

"Well! well!" cried the big man with the stentorian voice. "What's the matter, boys?"

"Get a hit, Sparksie," urged Rush. "I think I can boost you along."

"Let him give me some of those swift inshoots," muttered Sparks.

This, however, Merry declined to do. He kept the ball away from Sparks, although starting it straight at him at least twice. His out-curve was wonderfully wide, and it quite bewildered the batter.

Wolfers had ceased to grin. He realized that Merriwell was "showing him up" in the first inning.

"Oh, well," he muttered, "a strike-out pitcher isn't the whole cheese."

Still he was nettled.

Merry was testing himself. Kitson, Cronin, and Sparks were all batters of different styles. To mow them down in succession would be a severe test for any pitcher.

This, however, was what Frank did. Sparks finally succumbed, declining at the finish to strike at a high straight one, and growling because the umpire called it a strike, although it was not above his shoulder.

Spud Bailey was overjoyed.

"Now, now, now!" he cried. "I guess you fellers begin ter see I ain't such a fool!"

"Oh, he can't keep dat up," sneered Freckles. "He'll go all ter pieces arter one or two innin's."

"Bet you anyt'ing he won't!" flung back Spud. "You ain't posted about him. He's der greates' pitcher in der business. I tole yer so, but you didn't take no stock in it."

"I don't take no stock in it now."

"You will."

"Git out!"

"You will," persisted Spud.

The crowd had been surprised, but it was far from displeased. Having perfect confidence in Wolfers, it rejoiced because the game promised to be close and exciting.

"Frank, you have the goods!" said Hodge, as Merry came to the bench. "Why, I believe you could shoot the ball through a knot hole to-day!"

"My control is pretty good," nodded Merry.

"Pretty good! It's marvelous! Can you keep it up?"

"Somehow I think so. I have a feeling that I'll be able to do just about what I like with the ball through this game."

"Then the game is ours," said Hodge.

Merriwell was the first batter in the second inning.

"Let's see if I can't give him a little of the medicine he's been handing out," Wolfers muttered to himself.

He tried his best to fool Merry, but Frank let the first pitch go for a ball and caught the second one fairly on his bat, lining it out for two bags.

Wolfers turned green.

To himself he swore savagely.

"I'll know better than to give him another one like that," he thought.

Hodge was eager to follow Frank's example. He forced Wolfers to cut a corner, and then he hit the ball fair and hard.

It went like a bullet.

Straight into the hands of Rush.

Like a flash Rush snapped it to Tinker, who covered second.

Frank was caught off the bag, not having time to get back, and the Elks had made a handsome double play.

"Hooray!" bellowed the big man. "That's the kind of work, boys!"

The crowd cheered, and the play deserved it.

Hodge felt sore.

"That was hard luck!" he exclaimed. "I tried to place that hit, but I didn't judge the curve just right."

Naturally Merry felt somewhat disappointed, but he accepted the result philosophically, knowing such things were the penalty of fate in baseball.

Gamp came out not a whit the less resolute and determined. He felt that it was up to him to do something, and he tried hard, but Wolfers was on his mettle at last, and he struck Joe out.

"That's the stuff!" roared the big man. "Now you're getting into gear, Robert!"

Then he urged the local players to go in and hammer Frank all over the lot. Rush was eager to follow this advice. He was too eager, for Merry led him into putting up a pop fly, which fell into the hands of Rattleton.

Glade followed and tried a waiting game. Seeing what he was doing, Merry put two swift ones over the inside corner, and two strikes were called.

Then Glade hit a pretty grounder to Morgan, who made a mess of it, permitting the Elkton man to reach first.

It was recorded as an error for Dade. Morgan was angry, but

Merry soothed him with a word or two.

"Those things will happen occasionally," said Frank. "You'll get the next one, my boy."

"You bet I will!" Dade muttered to himself.

Frank took a chance with Glade, making a long swing before delivering the ball, and then sending it in with great speed.

Glade fancied he saw his opportunity to steal on that swing, and he tried it.

Few who saw the Elkton man go down from first fancied it would be possible for Bart to catch him at second.

The ball had been delivered so that it came into the hands of Bart just right for a quick throw. He waited not a second in making a long swing, but snapped it with a short-arm movement.

As true as a bullet from a rifle it flew into the hands of Rattles at second. And it came just right for Harry to put it onto the runner.

Glade saw his danger and tried to slide under, but Rattleton pinned him fast to the ground.

Once more Spud Bailey stood on his head, and once more Freckles kicked him over.

The spectators were generous with their applause, for they recognized the fact that Bart had made a wonderful throw.

"That's a good whip you have, young fellow," said the big man.

"Pretty work, Hodge!" smiled Frank. "I thought he would try it. Can't fool many of them that way if you keep up that throwing."

"Oh, they'll work for this game if they get it!" said Hodge.

"Haw! haw!" laughed Tinker mockingly. "Don't pat yourself on the back so soon. The game is young."

He walked out to hit.

All the Elks were inclined to be sarcastic and mocking, but they were beginning to realize that it would be no easy thing to run up a safe score early in the game. The Merries were out to win if such a thing could be done.

Frank knew Tinker was inclined to bat the ball into the air, and he pitched with the idea of compelling the fellow to do this. In the end he succeeded, for the batter put up a slow and easy one to Badger, who smothered it.

The second inning was over, and neither side had made a run.

"He won't last," declared Wolfers. "He'll take a balloon trip, same as the other chap did."

"They never can score off you, Bob," declared Sprowl.

"Not in a thousand years," grinned the Elkton pitcher. "It would be a disgrace."

Then he went into the box and handed Browning one on which

Bruce made a clean single.

"Stay there, you big duffer!" muttered Wolfers. "You'll never reach second."

He was mistaken, for, although he kept the ball high, Rattleton managed to bunt, making a beautiful sacrifice.

The wonder from Wisconsin saw that the Merries knew something about scientific stick work. He braced up and did his prettiest with Dunnerwurst.

"A hit must get me!" murmured the Dutchman, as he missed the first one struck at. "Der opportunity vas all mine. Yah!"

But Wolfers led him into batting a weak one to Cronin, who snapped it across the diamond.

Dunnerwurst was out.

Cross returned the ball to Cronin, for Browning had dashed toward third.

Browning got a handsome start and he ran like a deer. He slid for the bag.

Cross tried to block him, but Bruce went round the fellow's feet and grabbed a corner of the bag, lying flat on his stomach just out of reach when the third baseman tried to touch him quickly.

Never could any person unacquainted with the big chap fancy it possible for him to purloin a bag so handsomely. Cronin was sore with himself for giving Bruce the opportunity. He had fancied it would be an easy thing for Cross to return the ball in time to catch the runner, in case the latter attempted to take third.

Merry was on the coaching line back of third.

"Pretty work, Bruce!" he laughed. "You fooled them. They thought they had you."

Ready came out to bat once more.

A signal passed between Wolfers and Sprowl. The latter crouched close under the bat.

Wolfers put the first ball straight over.

It was a beauty.

Ready swung at it.

Just as he did so something touched his bat lightly, deflecting it the least bit, and he missed.

Jack turned quickly on Sprowl.

"What are you trying to do?" he demanded, frowning, no trace of levity in his manner.

"Excuse me," said the catcher sweetly. "I was a bit too close."

"Better get back a little."

Again Wolfers put the ball over the very heart of the pan.

Again Jack's bat was tapped lightly and deflected.

Ready dropped the end of his bat to the ground and stepped onto the plate to prevent Wolfers from pitching.

"Mr. Umpire," he called, "I wish you would watch this catcher. He is rather careless with his hands."

"Oh, come off!" cried Sprowl. "Don't cry baby if you can't hit a straight ball. It's your own fault. Give him another, Bob. He never made a hit in his life."

Hodge had seen Wolfers deflect Ready's bat.

"Play ball!" commanded the umpire.

"Get off that plate, or I'll put the ball through you!" snarled Wolfers.

"Get off, Jack," called Hodge. "I'll watch him. If he does the trick again, I'll talk to him a bit."

Sprowl looked at Bart and laughed.

"You wouldn't frighten any one," he said. "Why don't you fellows play ball? Are you going to cry baby so early in the game?"

"That's the talk!" roared the big man. "Make 'em play ball! Of course he can't hit Wolfers, and he wants to work his way down to first somehow."

Few among the spectators had seen Sprowl touch Jack's bat, and therefore the crowd was opposed to him. Jeers and catcalls came from every side.

Ready was angry. For once in his life, he had quite lost control of his temper.

"If you keep it up," he growled to Sprowl, "something will happen to you."

Then he stepped off the plate and Wolfers snapped the ball over like a flash.

"Str-r-r-rike—kah three!" cried the umpire. "You're out!"

How the crowd did laugh and jeer at Jack.

"That's what you get for crying baby!" yelled a shrill voice.

"It will be Mr. Sprowl's turn to bat in a moment!" said Hodge, as he picked up the body protector.

Frank heard these words.

"None of that kind of business, Bart," he said grimly. "It won't do. We're not playing that sort of a game."

"But are we going to stand for this?"

"We can call the attention of the umpire to it. He'll have to stop it."

"He doesn't seem inclined."

"We'll have to make him inclined, then. I think he's pretty near square, although it's likely he sympathized with the locals."

"Of course he does! We've got to fight for our rights, if we get them."

"That's true; but we'll fight on the level. No crookedness. No trickery."

So Bart went under the bat feeling rather sore and very anxious to get even with Sprowl.

CHAPTER XXXIII

A BATTLE ROYAL.

Cross hit to Frank, who tossed the ball to Browning for an easy out.

Then it was Sprowl's turn.

As Bart crouched under the bat of the tricky catcher, he muttered:

"I want to give you a warning, Mr. Man."

"Oh, do you?"

"Yes."

"Go ahead."

"If you hit my bat with your mitt when I'm striking you'll be sorry. I won't stand for it."

"Why, what will you do?"

"You'll find out!"

Sprowl laughed sneeringly. Then he batted a grounder to Ready, who made a poor throw to Browning, and Sprowl reached first.

"Don't talk to me!" he cried. "Don't warn me! I always get a hit when somebody threatens me."

"Dot hid dit not get you!" cried Dunnerwurst. "Id peen not a hit. Off Vrankie Merrivell you got yet no hits ad all, and maype you vill nod dood id efer so long as I live."

"Why don't you learn to talk United States?" cried Rush, who was coaching.

"He can talk better than he can play ball," said Sprowl, in his nasty way.

Wolfers strode out with his bat.

"Got a hit off me, did you, Merriwell!" he thought. "Well, here is where I even up."

Then Frank fooled him handsomely with a swift rise, a drop and a "dope ball." Wolfers struck at them all. He fancied the dope was coming straight over, but the ball seemed to pause and hang in the air, as if something pulled it back. This caused the batter to strike too soon.

"Str-r-r-rike—kah three! You're out!"

The man from Wisconsin turned crimson with anger and mortification.

"Oh, I presume you think you're a great gun!" he snapped at Frank.

"Not at all," retorted Merry. "It's no trick to strike you out."

This infuriated Wolfers.

"I don't think it's much of a trick to strike you out," he flung back.

"It's dead easy for a good pitcher to do it," laughed Merriwell.

"Oh, you fresh duck!" muttered Wolfers, as he walked to the bench. "Just you wait! I'll give you your medicine."

His appearance of good nature had vanished like fog before a hot sun. He was now consumed with rage and a desire to outdo Frank in some manner.

"Lace 'em out, Kit!" implored Sprowl, as Kitson advanced to the plate. "He's easy."

Never in his life had Merry pitched with greater ease. He used curves, speed and a change of pace, having perfect control. Although he could handle the "spit ball," he did not attempt to use it. He did not believe it necessary.

Kitson was anxious to hit. Merry seemed to give him pretty ones, but the ball took queer curves and shoots, and soon the right fielder of the Elks struck out.

The third inning was over, and neither side had scored. It was a battle royal between Wolfers and Merriwell.

Up to this point two clean hits, one a two-bagger, had been made off Wolfers.

Merriwell had not permitted a hit.

Morgan opened the fourth by smashing a hot one along the ground to Rush, who stopped it but chased it round his feet long enough for Dade to canter down to first.

"Here we go!" roared Browning.

"You won't go very far!" sneered Wolfers.

Badger tried to sacrifice, but his bunt lifted a little pop fly to Wolfers, and he was out.

Then came Merriwell again.

"Don't let this chap get another hit off you, Bob," implored Cronin.

"No danger of it," said the pitcher.

But on the second ball delivered Frank reached far over the outside corner of the plate and connected with the ball, cracking out a hot single that permitted Badger to speed round to third.

Merry took second on the throw to catch Badger at third.

The look on the face of Bob Wolfers was murderous. He stood and glared at Frank, who smiled sweetly in return.

"You're the luckiest fellow alive!" said the Elkton twirler. "I saw you shut your eyes when you struck at that ball."

"You're so easy that I can hit your pitching with my eyes closed," retorted Merriwell.

Imagine the feelings of Spud Bailey. He was strutting now in the midst of the village boys, not a whit intimidated by threats of a "walloping" after the game.

"I told you fellers how it would be before der game began," he said, throwing out his chest, with his thumbs in the armholes of his vest. "It couldn't help bein' dat way. Dey're bangin' der eye outer Wolfers, but I don't see 'em hitting Frank Merriwell any."

"Wot sorter feller are you ter go back on yer own town, hey?" savagely snarled Freckles. "We'll all t'ump yo' as soon as we git ye off der groun's!"

"I ain't goin' back on me own town!"

"You are!"

"I ain't goin' back on me own town!" asserted Spud. "How many Elkton fellers is dere on dat team? They've dropped all our players an' brung fellers in from ev'rywhere. If Frank Merriwell's team was playin' fer us, all you fellers would be yellin' fer them."

This sort of logic did not go with the other boys, nevertheless, and Spud was very unpopular.

Once again it was the turn of Bart Hodge to bat. He gave Sprowl a look as he came out.

Sprowl snickered.

"You scare me dreadfully," he said.

"Keep your paws off my bat when I'm striking," warned Bart.

Wolfers started with a drop.

Bart missed it.

He longed to get a clean, safe hit to right field, being satisfied that Merry would score on it if obtained, following Morgan in.

The suspense was great, for every one realized that a hit meant one run—possibly two.

Then Bart began to make fouls.

Once Sprowl touched his bat, but he fouled the ball. He felt that he must have made a safe hit only for that light deflection of the bat just as he swung.

"Did you see that, Mr. Umpire?" he cried.

The umpire had seen nothing.

Like Ready, Bart stepped onto the plate and turned to Sprowl.

"I want to tell you something," he said, in a cold, hard tone. "This is it: If you touch my bat again I'll turn round and punch your face for you! Is that plain enough?"

"I'd enjoy having you try it!" flung back Sprowl.

"You're quite certain to have the enjoyment."

"I haven't touched your bat. You dreamed it."

"You hear what I said and take heed."

Then Hodge stepped off, but he was ready to hit, so that Wolfers could not catch him napping, as Ready had been caught.

Wolfers took plenty of time and sent one straight over the outside corner.

Sprowl again touched the bat with his mitt just as Bart started to strike. True to his threat, Hodge flung the bat aside and sailed into the tricky catcher with both fists.

Sprowl seemed to expect it, for he snapped off his mask and met Hodge halfway.

He did not last long, for Bart smashed down the fellow's guard and struck him a blow that sent him down in a heap.

What an uproar followed!

Several of Bart's companions rushed from the bench and seized him, while players of the other team hurried to get between the two.

"Time!" yelled the umpire.

Ladies in the stand screamed and one fainted.

Men rose up and shouted incoherently, while the crowd from the bleachers poured onto the field.

It seemed that the game would end in a free fight.

In the midst of the excitement Seymour Whittaker forced his way into the midst of the struggling, wrangling mass of men.

"Gentlemen!" he cried; "be reasonable! I've been watching this thing. I played ball myself once. I saw our catcher touch the batter's stick! He did it twice and did it deliberately. The umpire may not have seen it. The batter warned our catcher. He had a right to be mad. Don't break this game up in a free fight! You know I have wagered money on our boys. I believe they can win, but I want them to win honorably. Wolfers doesn't need a catcher to help him by such tricks. He can pitch well enough to win without such aid. Let's be square. Let those fellows settle their trouble after the game is over. We're not rowdies here in Elkton. We want to see square baseball. This business will hurt the game. Go back and sit down, all of you."

These words were enough, although other men now declared that they had seen Sprowl touch Bart's bat. The crowd was quieted, and began to walk off to the bleachers.

Sprowl had been struck on the cheek, and Bart's fist left a bad bruise there.

He swore he would get even with Hodge. His companions induced him to agree not to press the matter until after the game was finished.

Finally things quieted down and playing was resumed.

Hodge asked the umpire to give him a pass to first on the interference of Sprowl; but the umpire had not seen it, Sprowl denied it, and Bart was declared out on the third strike.

This made two men out, with Morgan and Merriwell on third and second.

Gamp was the batter, and everything seemed to depend on him.

Wolfers was on his mettle. His pitching against Joe was superb, for the tall chap did not touch the ball.

The Merries had been prevented from securing a run. They felt that they had been defrauded, for to all it seemed likely that Bart might have made a hit only for the interference of Sprowl.

As a pitchers' battle the game was a great exhibition. Although seven hits were obtained off Wolfers in seven innings, the visitors could not score.

On the other hand, being in the most perfect form, Frank did not permit a hit in seven innings.

The eighth opened with Badger at bat.

Buck managed to roll a slow one into the diamond.

Both Cronin and Wolfers went after it, bothering each other, and Buck reached first by tall hustling.

Then came the hit of the day.

Merriwell was the man. Each time he had faced Wolfers there was "something doing." This time Wolfers tried harder than ever to strike him out; but Frank slammed the ball against the centre-field fence for three bags, sending Badger home with the first run of the game.

Spud Bailey nearly died of delight.

"I knowed it!" he whooped. "Wot d'yer t'ink of him now, Freck?"

"He's a lucky hitter," said Freckles.

But the sympathy of several small boys had turned to the visitors. They admired Bart Hodge for standing up for his rights.

"G'wan, Freck!" they cried. "He's a corkin' player, an' you know it."

"I hope them fellers win," said a tall, thin boy. "Dey're all right."

"They'll win; don't worry about that," assured Spud.

Ben Raybold and Seymour Whittaker had found seats together after the excitement caused when Hodge hit Sprowl.

Raybold had complimented Whittaker on his manliness and sporting blood in taking the stand he did.

"It may cost you a hundred dollars, Mr. Whittaker," said Raybold.

"I don't care a rap!" retorted the Elktonite. "I want to see a square game, win or lose."

After Frank's hit, Raybold asked Whittaker what he thought of Merry.

"He's the greatest ball player I ever saw!" exclaimed Whittaker. "We must have him on our team."

"You haven't money enough in the State of Ohio to get him on salary," said Raybold.

That run obtained by Badger was the only one secured in the eighth. The Elks tried hard, but they could not fathom Merry's curves.

In the first of the ninth the visitors did nothing, Wolfers striking out three men, one after another, as fast as they faced him.

Although the Elkton pitcher was sore, he kept up his good work. He was not a quitter. He played ball right along, never failing to do his best.

When the Elks came to bat in their half of the ninth Jack Lawrence implored them to get a run somehow.

"Don't let them shut us out!" he entreated. "It will be a disgrace!"

"I thought so a while ago," said Wolfers, in a low tone; "but it will be no disgrace to be whitewashed while batting against a fellow like that Merriwell. I didn't think he could pitch at all. He's the best man I ever saw toe the rubber! I'm going to tell him so after the game. Why, Lawrence, we've got a team of hitters. Every man is a sticker. Do you realize that we haven't secured a single safe hit to-day?"

"I realize it!" groaned Lawrence.

Nor did they secure one. For Merry it was a "no-hit, no-run" game. Although he struck out but one man in the ninth, the other two batted easy bounders into the diamond and were thrown out at first.

The game ended one to nothing in favor of the Merries.

Bob Wolfers was the first to reach Frank and grasp his hand.

"Boy, you're all right!" he cried. "If I've said anything unpleasant, I apologize. You're a gentleman, too! As a pitcher, you've got any youngster living skinned a mile!"

The Elks remembered what had followed the first game, when the Merries were defeated, and they did not fail to cheer for the winners.

"Sa-a-ay, Mr. Merriwell—sa-a-a-ay!"

Frank looked round.

Spud Bailey and a dozen other youngsters had managed to crowd as near him as possible. Freckles was with them, hanging back a little.

"Dese are me frien's," said Spud, with a wave of his hand. "I tole 'em wot you could do, an' now dey know it. Dey t'ink you're de goods. Permit me ter introduce 'em."

"With pleasure," smiled Frank.

And he made every one of them—even Freckles—as proud as a peacock by shaking hands as they were presented by Spud. In after years they would boast of the day when they shook hands with Frank Merriwell, the greatest pitcher "wot ever was."

THE END